Praise of The Second Highest World War:

"Professor Anoop Chandola's *The Second Highest World War* is a fine work of fiction about one of India's least well-known regions, the author's 'native' Garhwal Himalaya region of the remote Northern Indian mountains. Anoop is a brilliant writer and understands India as few others do. His compelling work is at once deeply true yet wonderfully imaginative raising his story to the highest level of fictive art."

—Dr. Stanley Wolpert, *Professor of History at the University of California, Los Angeles, and author of the Hollywood movie novel "Nine Hours to Rama."*

"The long fiery action of WWII, which prompted my own military career, engulfed countries as distant as India. Could the Allies have won WWII without India? The mind-blowing story of this novel clears up a lot of smoke to reveal how the heroism of unheralded soldiers from a remote Himalayan region turned the war around in favor of the Allies. Professor Chandola removes the curtain to expose the reader to a long hidden view of the role played by India as told through the dramatic memoirs of the young son of a WWII front-line officer from the Indian Himalayas."

—*(Ret.) Lt. General K.S. Garewal, PVSM (India).*

The Second Highest World War

For:

Windows Live Books Publisher Program

Publisher ID: 2000685

Anoop Chandola

6041 N. calle de la Culebra
Tucson, AZ 85718

E-mail: chandola@email.arizona.edu
Phone: (520) 742-4059

The Second Highest World War

The Rama Theater

Anoop Chandola

Authors Choice Press
San Jose New York Lincoln Shanghai

The Second Highest World War
The Rama Theater

All Rights Reserved © 2002 by Anoop Chandola

No part of this book may be reproduced or transmitted in any form or by any means, graphic, electronic, or mechanical, including photocopying, recording, taping, or by any information storage retrieval system, without the permission in writing from the publisher.

Authors Choice Press
an imprint of iUniverse, Inc.

For information address:
iUniverse, Inc.
5220 S. 16th St., Suite 200
Lincoln, NE 68512
www.iuniverse.com

This book is fiction. All characters, names, and events, except the obvious historical and political ones, are author's creations and any resemblance to actual persons, living or dead, places or events is purely coincidental.

ISBN: 0-595-22229-3

Printed in the United States of America

In memory of the innocent victims of World War II.

"Death ends enmities."

—From the *Ramayana*.

Contents

PART I: GOING UP

Chapter 1:   Author's Lament: The Background 3
Chapter 2:   The Enchanting Eve 19
Chapter 3:   The Rude Awakening 35

PART II: THE RAMA DRAMA

PART III: THE FALL YEARS

Chapter 4:   1943–44 135
Chapter 5:   1944–45 157
Chapter 6:   1945–46 179
Chapter 7:   1946–47 197
Chapter 8:   1947–48 219

Acknowledgments

My father, a Second World War soldier, has always encouraged me to write about WW II. Sudha kept reminding me since our marriage to write my wartime experiences of the *Rama Lila* or the enacting of the *Ramayana,* the third longest epic story of the world. In producing the first translation of the Rama Lila as "The Rama Drama" (Part II), I have to share credit with many individuals. Mr. Ratan Lal Jain, the Chairman of the Rama Lila Committee of Srinagar, whole-heartedly permitted me to video and use the entire Rama Lila of September-October 2000 for any purpose. My brothers, Bipin and Krishna, provided me the Rama Lila texts of Tehri and Pauri. Rekha, my sister-in-law, and Apurva, my nephew, facilitated my participation in the Srinagar's Rama Lila. R. D. Juyal kindly gave us his copy of Pauri's Rama Lila text. These videos and hand-written texts varied among themselves and were considerably different from what I knew as a young spectator. Any way, I never expected a constant or consistent version of this dynamic folk tradition. While keeping the core story intact, I have presented here an integrated translation, including a few additions from Valmiki and Tulsidas. In the process of integration, I filled several gaps with the oral recollections of some WWII-period spectators to whom I am grateful. *The Rama Drama,* though not necessary for reading the novel, is relevant to understand the social-cultural paradox. I have benefited from the historical accounts of Agra and Tehri given by the late Shriram Sharma and the late Dr. Shiv Prasad Dabral. Nicloc R. Stern made many appropriate changes in the original draft and Prof. Paul Turner added a few more later. Lt. Gen. Kehar

Singh Garewal, a WWII veteran and recipient of India's distinguished military award of PVSM, was the chief consultant for its war aspects. Dr. Stanley Wolpert, a veteran professor of South Asian History at the University of California (Los Angeles) and author of the Hollywood movie "Nine Hours to Rama," graciously endorsed the novel. Shakuntla Singh selflessly prepared a picture ("Rama and Hitler in Fight") for the cover according to my specifications. Baljit Singh Sull gave me his generous technical support. Varn, my son, and Neha, my daughter-in-law, offered several suggestions and corrections. Dr. Suresh Raval, a professor and colleague in the department of English literature of my university, offered a useful critique. I express my sincere appreciation and thanks to all of them. I also gratefully acknowledge the translation of the song "*Shri Rama Chandra kripalu bhaja mana*" from F. R. Allchin's translation of Tulsidas' *Vinaya Patrika* (*The Petition to Ram*, George Allen & Unwin, London, 1966). All other translations are mine. Finally and most importantly, the publishing team of iUniverse and Barnes & Noble deserves my sincere gratitude.

Part I

Going Up

Chapter 1

Author's Lament: The Background

As is customary, first about the manuscript of this wartime story. I remember my history teacher's dilemma, which I thought must be resolved. He is very old now and recently reminded me of it again.

Why is it that the face of World War II has appeared in print or film so often, but very seldom the back? The face is easy to recognize and it's the topmost part of the body. But the back, though the second highest part, covers far more area than the face. Why do we always maintain that to be stabbed in the back is worse than in the face?

One partial way to answer these questions was to prepare a manuscript with a real, behind-the-scene war story.

But that would not be as easy as writing the real experiences of real soldiers in the real battles. I have more interest in such real, untold stories. Even though I have lived in the U.S.A. since I was 22, my tender memories of the period during World War II keep haunting me. My father fought at the Burmese front. Several others from my native Garhwal Himalayas also fought at different theaters in Africa, Europe, the Middle East, and South-East Asia during this period of unprecedented human crimes. The best time for us to tell war stories was Dashhara in the month of October. I decided to collect and recollect those stories during my visit to India in 1998. But the task remained unfinished and frustrating.

Then in the year 2000, I got another opportunity while I was working on the folk Rama Theater or Rama Lila of the *Ramayana* epic in India. I was visiting my father at Allahabad. He, being a very religious priest, wanted to see the preparation of the forthcoming Kumbh Parv or the Pitcher Festival. This time it was the Maha Kumbh Mela or the Mega Pitcher Meeting, which takes place every twelve years. It was inevitable that the Mela would break its own past records as the biggest meeting of humanity. Even some Hollywood celebrities had already made reservations to stay at Allahabad, known as God's city. The most godly place here is where the two holiest rivers meet: the Ganga or Ganges and the Yamuna. This place is called Sangam (Sanskrit *samgama*). It means 'meeting or mating.' Its mythology includes an interesting story.

When created by Vishnu, Brahma the Creator did not know how to be a creator. But he meditated and found out how to create. It was asexual creation, for he was the only Being in the beginning. He reproduced lots of boys out of his brain. And then he reproduced an extremely beautiful girl, who was called Sarasvati. Now sexual awareness. Physical attraction. He married her. Eventually he begat all sorts of beings, including the gods and the demons, who started fighting stupidly and very violently. As a good parent, Brahma counseled them to live by cooperation instead of confrontation. Following his advice, they churned the ocean together in search of common prosperity and immortality. Finally, a pitcher full of immortalizing elixir or *amrita* 'ambrosia' came out of the churning. The gods never wanted the demons to be immortal. So they ran away with the pitcher. On the way, a few drops spilled from the container or *kumbha* at the Sangam! At that time there were three rivers meeting here, hence the Sangam was also called Triveni, the Tri-Braided venue. The third river was named after Sarasvati, the daughter of Brahma. The meeting of these three holy rivers makes an outstanding confluence. Therefore this confluence is called Prayag Raj or the king of the confluences, even though the Sarasvati has never been seen.

Even today, devout humans can feel the difference between life and death and immortality when they take a dip at the Sangam or Prayag in its chilly Himalayan waters in January, the coldest winter month. The ancient Sanskrit name of Allahabad is *Prayaga*, which means "Confluence."

My father has another reason to visit this place. These two rivers originate from his native region in the Himalayas. His birthplace, the town of Tehri, is only a few miles down from Gomukh, the source of the Ganges or Ganga. He firmly believes in the Ramayana story that King Bhagiratha brought the Ganges from the Himalayas down to the Indian plains all the way to the Bay of Bengal, to wash away the sins of some of his brave but arrogant ancestors.

So the Ganges is also called the Bhagirathi, the river of Bhagiratha, and the glacier from which the river gets its waters is called Bhagirath Shikhar "the Bhagiratha Apex." But, the mythology shows even a higher origin of the Ganges. Bhagiratha was the ancestor of King Rama, the hero of the *Ramayana*. He performed austerities to propitiate Vishnu and Shiva. With the favor of these two gods, the Ganges descended from the heavens upon the Himalayas. Then Bhagiratha requested her to flow all the way to the Bay of Bengal. A person of high origin must come down to lift the downtrodden. Mother Ganga's Himalayan message is as forceful as her flow.

The mayor of Allahabad at this time was Rita Joshi, whose ancestors also came from the Garhwal Himalayas. She, thus, had one more reason to make this year's Mela the greatest meeting of humanity. As a matter of fact, the Maha Kumbh fair breaks its own record of the highest human assembly every time it takes place. The waters make no distinction to anyone present in this assembly. That's what everyone sees here. The mayor has struggled to keep that fair view of the Ganges open to all.

As my father and I were almost at the Sangam around 9 a.m., I heard a man calling, "Hello, Pandit ji, hello Pandit ji!" My father turned his face around and found that it was his old friend Col. Fateh Singh. They hugged each other and then Father introduced me to him. I touched his feet as my father addressed him as "bhai ji" or big brother. When I explained the purpose of my visit, he became silent for a minute or so. He looked stout and alert and must have been more than 86 years old as my father addressed him as "bhai ji." Moreover, he was a lieutenant in World War II, unlike my father, a plain sipahi (sepoy) or soldier. His *rajput* name Fateh is "Victory" (in Arabic) and Singh is "Lion" (Sanskrit *simha*).

He broke his short silence, "Could you be interested in my story?" No one before him was willing to offer his stories without my personal request, repeated several times. I guess, my father's relationship with him earned this favor.

"Yes, Tau ji." I addressed him as my senior uncle or Tau ji. "That would be very kind of you. I need an appointment at your convenience. Then I can record your war experiences on my tape recorder."

"No, you do not need to record anything. I have a manuscript."

He gave me an appointment for the following Saturday evening at his nephew's house where he was staying.

I went to see him. His nephew, Vijay, told me that his Tau ji (older uncle) had to leave for Garhwal because of his wife's unexpected sickness. But he had left a manuscript for me. Vijay gave me the manuscript while his wife, Urmila, served tea and snacks. He said, "Tau ji wants you to publish this manuscript." As I looked at his face, I saw tears in his eyes. I thought the manuscript must have contained the colonel's very painful war experiences.

So I asked, "Which theaters do these experiences come from?"

"That you will find out, anyway, when you read the manuscript. But why don't you go over the preface with the tea!"

"I will. But tell me why he thinks that I should publish this manuscript." He agreed to tell me.

The colonel had a son whom Vijay called Chander in his conversation. Otherwise his full name was Ram Chander Singh, named after Rama Chandra, the hero of the *Ramayana*. When the colonel was back home after the war (promoted to captain from lieutenant), Chander moved to New Delhi with him and his mother and eventually went to America to study journalism. There he met Kristi Mueller in his class. They were married there. The colonel had left with the manuscript a black and white photograph of the couple's wedding. Kristi looked so beautiful! She, like her many European ancestors, was deeply interested in India's culture. This was another reason, according to the colonel, for her interest in Chander

The couple came to India and settled in Garhwal. There Kristi became very much interested in the Rama Lila or Rama Theater as well as local life. Rama is Vishnu's incarnation. The highest temple of Vishnu is in Badrinath Puri (Vishnu' city), over 10,000 feet high in the Garhwal Himalayas. Approximately from mid April to early October this little town is open to visitors, who come in hundreds of thousands. Those who are believers sit inside the temple and listen to the stories of Lord Vishnu's incarnations, such as Rama in the *Ramayana*. Due to snowfall starting in October, the story of Rama or Rama Lila during Dashhara cannot be staged here. Otherwise, it would have been the highest place for the Rama Lila.

The second highest town in this area where the Rama story is performed in the open-air theater is Puri, meaning "Polis." But its real Sanskrit name would be Prakotika "rampart, fort" and it is no wonder that the British government chose it to be the district headquarters. The town is surrounded by Shiva's peak, Kim Kala, in the west and Rama's peak, Rama Raja, in the east, at an altitude between 6,000 to 7,000 feet. The Adhwani and Kandolya forests, with their easily accessible peaks in the south, offer a variety of hikes and campgrounds. Across to the north is the snow-covered roof of the world if the average height of the daunting peaks is considered: Bandar Poonchh, Trishul, Chaukhamba, Nanda Devi, Nara, Narayana and several other peaks stand between 22,000 and 26,000 feet high behind which hide Mount Kailasa and the lake of Manasa or Manas (*Manasa-sarovara* 'Mansarovar') in Tibet.

Some world tourists claim that only from Puri can you view the widest opening of the highest mountain range of the world. And below the snow line lie the dense forests of the majestic deodars and other alpine trees including oaks. It's not easy to count the big and small rivers and streams that replenish the waters of the Ganges and the Yamuna. By and large, Puri offers the highest panorama.

Kristi with her interest (and I guess, with her charming beauty) became the honorary chairwoman of the Rama Lila Committee. For the sake of his American wife, Chander prepared this manuscript, as Vijay explained. The manuscript, I thought, started with an epilogue, which Vijay wanted me to read right then. I did read it right then since Urmila insisted that I had to have dinner with them. The epilogue was a dialogue between Chander and Kristi. It served as an introduction or preface to the story that followed it. The epilogue went like this:

*　　*　　*　　*

"Rama-Rama, Rama-Rama, Rama-Rama…" I was shouting in the middle of the night in my bed, almost crying. My wife was startled by my panting.

"What is this Rama-Rama?" She asked while trying to calm me down. "Let's wrap ourselves properly and sit out in the verandah. You need fresh air."

"That's a good idea. Just cover yourself up with a shawl. I don't want June's Himalayan breeze to penetrate your body. So tender, so beautiful!"

We sat out on the two bamboo chairs, watching the "four-pillared" Chowkhamba range, with its never-melting snows on the top. The range continuously releases these snows as water into several rivers in its lower regions. And the stars all over, with the Milky Way, matching the brightness of the snows.

"So what was your Rama-Rama, some sort of panorama—?"

"No, no, Honey!" I interrupted her, "it is Rama, Lord Rama, the hero of the *Ramayana*. I saw a sage, looking like Tulsidas. He said to me, 'Write my Rama's Drama in the Himalayan way.'"

"But you are a devout atheist. Why would any sane person, let alone a sage, ask you so?" Kristi asked me with a clear picture of disbelief in her eyes.

"Honey! This is just a dream. It obviously is influenced by the story of Valmiki."

"What story?"

"Long ago. There was a sage, some time after the Vedas and before the Buddha. That is the sage Valmiki I am talking about. One early morning he got up, went out from his forest hermitage, for toilet and bath. It was still dark. Suddenly, he saw a *krauncha* bird crying. Its beloved mate was shot by a hunter. The sage saw a hunter doing it. So he, too, cried. And cursed the hunter: Hunter! May you never achieve honor, for you killed a mating bird."

I recited to her the famous curse-verse of Valmiki in Sanskrit as I continued, "His compassion moved the Creator. The Creator appeared to him. He asked the sage to tell in his own words the story of Rama. Why Rama's story? Because Rama was an ideal son, an ideal brother, an ideal husband, an ideal friend, an ideal king. Only God could be so ideal a human. The Creator convinced Valmiki of the appeal of the story, 'Your story would move everywhere as long as the rivers flow from the Himalayas.'" I looked into her big beautiful teary eyes.

"Honey! Are you crying?"

"What if someone killed you or me when we were in bed?"

"Yes, we two lovebirds!" I was just trying to laugh it off.

"I want to have your child. It is now our fifth year of marriage. Ravana deprived Rama and Sita of their love for so many years. Poor

Sita! She had to prove her love for Rama through the fire ordeal. Then finally she bore Rama's son, Lava. That's what I have heard."

"So my dream is inspirational."

"How is it inspirational? I don't see any good in it—"

"I told you, the Tulsidas-looking sage wants me to write our Himalayan version."

"You mean the Himalayan Ramayana? Why the Himalayan?"

"Two reasons.... First, Tulsidas believes that Lord Shiva created the Rama story in his own Manas. He meant the lake Manasarovar in Tibet, even though Manas means 'mind.' The lake Manasa is at the foot of Mt. Kailasa. And Shiva's wife Parvati means 'the mountain born.' She is from the Himalayan mountains. He narrates here to his wife the story of Rama, the Ramayana story. That is the story Tulsidas believes is his epic *Ramacharitamanasa*. He wrote that epic in the Avadhi language for his own pleasure. He was an Avadhi speaker, easy for him. His was the linguistic region Avadh. That is Ayodhya, Rama's capital—"

"What is the second reason in your *Manas*?" Kristi put her hands over her head.

"Not in my head. It was in the heads of the two attendants of Lord Shiva. They exploited the sex scandal of a sage. The sage was Narada. He was one of Brahma's children evolved directly from his brain cells. The first progeny—"

"Sex scandal! Of a sage! Ha, ha?"

"Actually the author of the Sex Science or *Kama Shastra* is also a sage. Vatsyayana is his name. Never ridicule sages for their interest in this matter. Once in a while, they, too—"

"O.K., what's the scandal?"

"Sage Narada cursed the two attendants for ridiculing him. They became Ravana and Kumbhakarna in their next lives."

"You mean these two demon brothers were Shiva's local attendants!"

"You have seen how some local Garhwali men behave! This particular scandal is shown on the first night of the Rama Lila. Then the rest of the nine nights' story, all stemming from that scandal. By the way, all the demons speak Garhwali in the local Rama Lila."

"What other languages are spoken there? And by whom?"

"Humans and animals speak in Hindi."

"Did you say animals?"

"The Ramayana story makes it clear. Hanuman is a monkey. Jambavan is a bear. Rama and Lakshmana are humans. In the old story, all these characters communicate in Sanskrit. And they do many amazing things for each other."

"What kind of a linguistic philosophy is that?"

"Actually, it is more than a linguistic philosophy. You know that the ancient Sanskrit grammarians started linguistics: the science of language. Eventually they came with eight simple elements. Call them eight questions—for easy understanding. These questions are answered. That answering is thinking. It can come out as a sentence or action. Humans and animals share the same questions of conscious behavior. That's what the Ramayana suggests."

"Oh, come on Chander! The Ramayana is a story, not a behavioral science book."

"This is the problem with you Westerners. You don't want to see animals like humans. Only humans have souls. Plain nonsense. Whether or not humans or animals have souls, all of them have brains. Let me give you here a simple but real behavioral understanding of your pets. You will have more love and respect for your pets after this. Just believe me, there is a common brain code which humans and animals share. Did you ever have a pet?"

"Yes, my parents had two dogs."

"Did you or your parents interact with those dogs? Or did those dogs interact among themselves?"

"All the time, of course."

"How about you and your parents with each other?"

"Don't be silly, Chander. Even if I am alone, I think and do things with or without speaking."

"Any doing or speaking you act out is because you think in those eight questions before you act."

"So what are those eight questions?"

"What is the activity? Who is its doer? What is the instrument for it? What is its goal? Who is its recipient? What is its origin? What is its base in terms of time and place? What are other specifics? The specifics are for these seven questions."

"What you are trying to say is that the Ramayana is the story of the unity of all beings. And I'm going to understand the Ramayana monkeys and bears, and even Rama. All because of these questions or their answers. How?"

"For example, Hanuman or Rama is in action. Just ask then these questions—one by one. You will see that he is doing some activity. He is the doer of it. He may be doing it with some means. Somebody may be receiving that activity. The activity may start from some point. There is always a time or a place of that activity. Then the elements in those questions could be good, bad, long, short. Virtually countless specifications. Including the past, present, future, or the manner of the activity—you want to specify whether it happened yesterday, today or quickly, slowly, whatever."

"But that is all our human imagination."

"Did you ever give your dog a ball to play with?"

"Many times. He himself would pick up the ball, give it to me. Then I'd throw it back to him." "So you and your dog did many things, together. Was your dog so dumb that he did not understand your activity of throwing?

"No, of course, he knew what I was doing."

"Okay, he understood that activity. He knew that you were the doer or thrower. Your hands were the instruments of throwing. The goal was the ball. The dog was the recipient of what was being thrown. This activity might have started from your porch, at noon. Or in your front yard. These were the time and the place of the activity. Now you can count how many questions we have seen in this act. You threw the ball to him, because first you planned so, in your head. The planning takes place in a fraction of a second."

"Oh yes. I call it 'thought.'"

"You may use any popular term for your convenience. Thought, mind, whatever. But such terms do not explain what elements or questions that plan is made of. Or how those questions are answered into our actions. That is, actions of speaking or doing—"

"Give me an illustration!"

"Suppose you spoke a big sentence like this: 'I quickly threw a small ball to my dog from my porch in the front yard at noon.' In this sentence, you see the same elements. Why? Because they first occur in the plan. In grammar, the elements or their answers may be called differently. So you call 'throw' a verb instead of an activity. Call 'I' a subject instead of a doer. Call the 'ball' an 'object' instead of a goal, etc. Or you can call 'small' as a specific or adjective of 'ball.' Or 'quickly' as a specific or adverb of 'throw.' Another specific of 'throw' is its past tense. Animals and humans do not really act with such grammatical concepts. They work with a common code. The code consists of these eight basic questions or answers—"

"But I have a suggestion—"

"The main thing you have to remember is this: There is no basic difference in human and animal consciousness. Proof? Humans and animals are able to interact. This is because they work with the same simple code of consciousness. I explained it here so you could have more fun. That is, with the Ramayana characters. Actually you can have now an analytic understanding of your working self. Me, too. Of any animal…Yes, after you finish laughing, let me know what is your suggestion?"

"I am laughing not because I doubt your pet theory, but because you are simply talking and talking. Say something. Why don't you connect the local Rama Lila and life with the Great World War? Let the world know the untold story."

"Fine, I will do so. The Himalayan theater of Puri and World War II. Tulsidas wrote for his own pleasure. I will write for your pleasure. How does that sound to you?"

"Good. Did Tulsidas really write for his pleasure?"

"No. It's for everybody's pleasure. But remember, I am a journalist. Language is my medium. If no language, then no possibility of human culture and civilization. Language is the difference between human and animal ways of expression. Among Brahma's first brainchildren, one had to be a journalist. Narada is the first journalist."

"No wonder why you gave me a brainy theory of communication! So your profession is among the oldest ones! That's a mythical claim."

"After language, journalism became the first real linguistic profession. How could language speakers live without news and stories? Just impossible."

"But your story must make sense."

"I write what I see in people's life, *bios, vivus*."

"That's Greek and Latin for 'life.'"

"And *Jivas* in Sanskrit…Human life is a story of mythical meaning and existential reasoning. But remember, my child and adult may commingle. I tell you now about what I saw then."

"What do you mean by that?"

"Mixture of past and present tense."

"Look, forget the grammatical niceties. Forget the common code of understanding, and of the verbal and nonverbal action. Don't make things complex. Write every thing in plain English. Forget literary conventions, artistic descriptions, fantasies. As you said, write about life."

"I will. Just consider all the characters as humans. And I promise that they will talk in English. Even when their English is like a Himalayan trail—some times plain, some times zigzag. But you will be able to walk on it, able to enjoy the difference! Just say 'I will walk.'"

"I will! By the way, every life is a trial, I mean a trail."

"Both."

* * * *

I finished the dialogue as well as the tea.

"The real manuscript begins after this dialogue. But that intellectual discussion in the beginning fits. Here you have two intelligent persons, talking about a great story," said Vijay.

"Yes, it's clear. Where are they now?" I asked.

"You mean Chander and Kristi?"

"Yes!"

"They are gone," Vijay paused and went inside.

Then Urmila intervened, releasing a long sigh, "They were killed in a car accident in Delhi, just one day before their eleventh wedding anniversary. A big truck hit their car. The truck driver was drunk."

"That's terrible. Just terribly sad…Were there any children with them?"

"They didn't have any children."

"Kristi wanted children so much. I noticed that from the dialogue."

"She could have followed Sita's model if they were living today. She cloned her son Kusha after her first son Lava. Our neighbors, the Saksenas did that. You should see their son Rahul. What a handsome active and brilliant boy! He is their test-tube baby."

"Thanks to even more advanced reproductive technology, virtually any couple can have their biological babies now."

Vijay came out with a photograph in his hand and showed me, "Here are the late Chander and Kristi!"

I saw the picture and said, "Urmila told me how they died. That is so sad. What a beautiful couple!" I kept on looking at the photograph.

Then Vijay added, "My uncle considers this manuscript as his grandchild. That's why he wants it to be published."

"Of course, I will try." After I paused a little bit, I continued again, "Vijay, would you mind if I asked you about your uncle's attitude toward Kristi?"

"His acceptance of an American as his daughter-in-law?"

"Exactly!"

"A local friend, too, asked Tau ji long ago. He answered 'Who marries a girl from his own family? Why does it matter if the daughter-in-law is from one house away or half the world away? Once she is my son's wife, isn't she a family member, our family goddess, our Lakshmi?'"

"The Indian ideal, indeed."

"Well, she was accepted by the Puri people. They made her the head of the Rama Lila Committee. That position avenged the sporadic insults here and there."

"What insults?"

"For example, the pujari priest of the Rama temple wouldn't let her come in. He told her that she was like an untouchable."

"Didn't Chander protest?"

"He did. In many ways," said Vijay. Then with a momentary pause he continued his professorial lecture, "He told the priest that he couldn't be a temple priest. A meat eater and a priest! A fake priest. And Kristi was a vegetarian. And there were no temples in our Vedic religion. In any case, this temple was made by the untouchables. The priest also retaliated that Vedic Brahmins ate meat, Rama's priest teacher Vasishtha ate meat, and Rama himself ate meat. Chander believed that religion must be out if we have to achieve social salvation. What good is a religion if it discriminates against women and low castes! Religion has blocked the majority population's social mobility. And then we complained against the British signs that said 'Dogs and Indians are not allowed here.' We have been doing that for thousands of years with our own people. And on and on he said so many things, very realistically. After all he was a journalist. Report as you see. And report in plain and simple language. Everybody should be able to understand what is being said."

"Yes, I can see that in his dialogue. There, the most impressive thing is his emphasis on writing about life, with no motive of literary or creative art. I agree, nothing is more important than life and its knowledge, even through stories."

"Another surprising thing, no matter what humiliations, Kristi loved Indians and Indian stories. And Chander loved her. Their love life itself is an international story. Now you have to find a publisher in America for Kristi's sake."

"Well, let me go through the whole story first. I am hoping that it is not loaded with intellectual stuff. Publishers want salable stuff."

"You and I know very well that in the West love for intellectual stuff is unbound. We accept Western education because of its intellectual value. The intellectual things of Chander are in journalistic style. That makes every thing easy to understand, and intriguing. Moreover, this manuscript is all story, an exciting life story."

It's not that I didn't value Vijay's opinion. He was teaching here at the university as a professor of art history. But one must judge on his or her own. The next thing I will do is read the manuscript myself.

Chapter 2

▼

The Enchanting Eve

"Jay Badri Bisal! Jay Gabar Singh! Jay Darban."

Years later I understood the meaning of the war years of my life. For example, this song line is partly about World War I. But I didn't know then. I am reflecting now. This was the benedictive opening of Bisram Singh's song I heard the night before the first day of Dashhara in October, 1942. His voice was a loud tenor, easily audible from across two creeks that divided his village, Kandy, and my village, Rajkhet.

The two villages were only about one and a half miles below Puri, the polis of the Garhwal Himalayas. The total population including the adjacent villages must have been less than four thousand. Its ancient name Prakotika was more suitable for its strategic location. Interestingly, it had no military cantonment. Nevertheless, Pahari or Hilly soldiers had been recruited here in huge numbers since it became the district's administrative headquarters. The nearest cantonment from here is Lansdowne, without the snow problems of Puri since it is more than thirty miles south on a lower mountain. The three Pahari regiments (formerly rifles), namely the Garhwal Regiment, the Gurkha Regiment, and the Kumaon Regiment have established their reputation for bravery.

Gabar Singh Negi and Darwan Singh Negi (Darban), the two Garhwali heros in Bisram's song were next to Badri Bisal (Sanskrit *Badari*

Vishala 'God the Great'). Victory or 'Jay' (Sanskrit *jaya*) to them. The Victoria Cross, the highest honor for bravery, was given to Gabar Singh (posthumously) and Darban Singh in World War I.

The British treated the Hilly or Pahari soldiers almost like their own Scottish soldiers, even though the Pahari men looked clearly different from the Scotsmen. (Actually because of their partial Tibetan features, the Paharis looked different even from the plains Indians, the *desis*).

The Scottish influence and treatment is visible and audible even today.

For example, old Garhwali soldiers prefer Scotch whisky to any other brands (a few such as XXX Rosa Rum would be exceptions!). Scotland's bagpipes, not India's shahnai (an oboe-type reed instrument), are the auspicious instruments here. The big dhol-damau drums with the bagpipes can be heard miles away. If gunshots are heard with the bagpipes then it is definitely a marriage celebration. At this time men are happier if they can get hold of some whisky. Otherwise, the local *Koda ki daru* or Koda's liquor is good enough. Koda or Kodu is easily grown here for flour and alcohol. Bootlegging could be considered no problem here. Any type of alcohol and meat (except beef) are important in the Himalayan diet.

But Scotch soldiers are not responsible for such a diet. Paharis follow the tradition of the ancient Hindus (who never called themselves 'Hindu', a name given to them by foreigners much later) and relate this dietary culture to Vedic practices. If the plains Hindus consider meat eating bad, it's because their hot climate is not good for it; in the cold Himalayan climate, heat-generating foods such as meat (except beef) are necessary. This is what the hill people often tell the vegetarian people from the plains! Hemp or *bhang* is found wild here almost everywhere and it is also heat-generating food!

This diet theory applies to men mostly. Very rarely would women be observed using bhang. And brhamin widows usually give up eating meat. If it were not for the Himalayan women, the plains Indians (the *desi log* 'country people') could have considered the Himalayas total wilderness.

Bisram's daily diet was deeply influenced by this theory. His midnight songs, as my mother told me, were caused by his drinking and use of bhang. His Sanskrit name Vishrama, pronounced Bisram in the Garhwali language, means 'rest.' But his wife, Chakti, would tell everybody including my mother that Bisram was a restless man. She, even though an energetic rajput woman, had no control over his musical marathons. He would leave his house, singing, passing through several streams, villages, and hills overnight. No Himalayan tigers and bears ever attacked him. Fearless he was, as a brave rajput was expected to be. Always dressed up in military clothes, he sang songs of heroes, their bravery and love. His frequent song had a woman whose name was Kiri:

> Slip out Kiri, you widow's daughter!
> Redder are my berries than your apricots.
> Slip out Kiri, you widow's daughter!
> Sweeter are my berries than your apricots.

I asked my mother, "Ma, who is this Kiri?"

"Some young girl is lost or he thinks that she may hear him out. So he is looking for her," she laughed.

"But that is so sad, Ma. When did she get lost?"

"No girl is lost. That is just a song. He is the one who is lost. Go upstairs and get some sleep."

I understood that there was no real search. No one could have believed, not even his wife, that there would be a Kiri or a 'slender' young woman waiting to be found by him in the middle of the night.

Much later I reflected that such a song would have been more suitable for his grown children. But he had none. Both, he and his wife, were in their forties. When he was married, he was absent at the altar because of his sudden military transfer. So his wife was married to his sword. This was accepted as a legal marriage. The sword represented a rajput's image, the image of bravery. He had a brother, Sohan, almost like his son in age. The parents died early and Bisram took care of Sohan. Chakti, the sister-in-law, was like a mother to Sohan. Otherwise, his older brother's wife (*bhabhi*) and her younger brother-in-law (*dewar*) could joke lightly with each other like equals.

In the 1940 World War, Sohan was killed at the battle of Gallabat in Sudan. A few months before his death, Bisram and Chakti had already found a beautiful girl for him. Some suggested "sword marriage" for her, too. But Bisram and Chakti didn't allow that. The girl was married later to another man.

Bisram began drinking cheap alcohol and smoking bhang after Sohan's death. Before that he didn't even touch tobacco, a very popular thing even among older women, let alone men. Sohan was not the only one who was killed at Gallabat. Several other local soldiers lost their lives there. Many other locals had also died a little later at the 1941 battle of Keren in Ethiopia. The government praised the bravery of the Pahari soldiers.

But the World War histories known through European languages don't record the burden that Bisram's songs echoed in the hills and valleys around Puri, usually during late nights. This burden was the white man's burden carried by the people, unknown to Europeans. Thousands of Indians died to protect Europe's freedom. And millions suffered back home for that freedom.

My father, a lieutenant at that time, was not fighting with Europeans against Europeans. He had just been given orders to be ready for the South East Asian Theater against the Japanese. America had been drawn into the war by the Japanese attack on Pearl Harbor the previous year. And India was sucked into the bloody wars of the Europeans, Japanese, and Americans. It became a "sink or swim" situation for Indian soldiers on their own borders. Mahatma Gandhi had just started his new "Quit India!" movement as an ultimatum to the British rule. But the British wanted more and more Indian soldiers. So almost every Garhwali had one or more relatives fighting. My mother, worried about my father, would hear the news and often repeat the same. How many husbandless wives? How many fatherless children? How many sonless parents? What's the point?

Now Bisram was a brotherless brother. Such were the overtones of his songs.

The next night was the first night of Dashhara. The Rama Lila or Rama's Play at the Rama Theater of Puri during the Dashhara festival was the biggest source of local entertainment. For ten nights plus the eleventh day of the parade, all of it was free. There were no cinema theaters, no TV-Radios, not even railroads or electricity.

I could have gone the previous year to attend the Rama Lila, but Mother wouldn't allow me. I was only a seven-year-old baby then! My first big entertainment month would be in October 1942 when I turned eight. Anyway, I was used to going this far as a third grader, on my way to the Mission High School, not too far from Puri's Rama Lila Theater.

There were two other schools in Puri from where many young actors for the Theater were drawn. The Mission High School was the oldest and the best. The actors for the roles of Rama, Sita, and Lakshmana were often selected from this school, a Christian institution organizationally. The population of the school fluctuated between 350 and 370 including students, faculty, staff, and other workers. The majority were Hindu. All the Christians were local converts. A few local Muslim students were noteworthy as they belonged to Puri's business community that generously contributed money to the Rama Lila. But like other people of Puri, no matter what religion or caste they belonged to, all participated in the Rama Lila not only as part of the audience but also as actors. Merit was the only consideration for the selection of the actors.

My Hindi-Sanskrit teacher explained later that the Rama Lila Theater followed the ancient tradition of Bharata's *Natya Shastra* ("The Science of Drama") that the theater must be open for all, inside as well as outside.

There was only one exception. All roles were played by males, including the female roles. Parents would allow their young daughters to watch the Rama Lila in their own company, but not be part of Rama's company!

Officially the school was part of the town of Puri, but was closer to our village, about one hour's hike one way. A hike meant walking on narrow trails that linked one village to another village or town. The trails, called bridle roads, linked two towns and were wide enough for three horses to walk parallel. Kandy and Thaula—the two villages between our village and Puri—had alternative routes to our village. One was faster and the other was slower. The latter trail was slow because it zigzaged and was slightly wider. Another village—Gwar—was located almost at the base of the hill across from our village hill, with a big noisy creek, called Pan Gadnu, in between the two. Nevertheless, the two villages were at a shouting distance. Folks from Gwar had to pass by our village on their way to Puri. Our village was not as big as Thaula or Kandy. Nevertheless, it had three subdivisions. Between each subdivision were half a dozen terraced fields and orchards.

The lowest subdivision (in altitude) belonged to the Bhatra brahmins, all descendants of one great-grandfather, divided between seven houses. The bigger house had more families than the smaller one. Each house had two stories. The Bhatras owned the best land, mostly around the big creek, good enough to grow the world famous basmati rice. The forest above and across the creek was all theirs.

Although it is true that the Bhatras of our village had one common ancestor, they did not have some other things in common. Occasionally, I saw some Bhatras not speaking to each other even when they were living in the same house. Very soon, after a few years, I understood that their reasons for tension ranged from land to lust. Some had less land, some too much. Some had several wives and also women who were not exactly mistresses or whores. Some had none. And then there were other wild actions and unfair affairs.

The middle subdivision was occupied by one mason, one *baddi*, and two tailor families. One house had two stories and the other two were single-storied. Except the mason's house, all the houses here were in a shape that would not be considered enviable. These were landless low caste people (untouchable or *dom*), but some of them farmed others' land, in addition to providing their services to brahmins and rajputs, the higher castes (*bitth*). The tailors were drummers, too. Their drums were needed in every auspicious ceremony, e.g., weddings. The baddis were dancers, but sold their own handmade baskets and combs. Being entertainers they needed horses to roam around and perform folk dances. So horse trade was also their part-time activity. A few years before (this time), three other families had left the subdivision, as they became Christians.

The upper subdivision, where I lived, had four rajput families—all of them my father's cousins. Some third, some fourth cousins. Each family had separate houses. Two of them lived mostly in nearby Lansdowne and would come once in a while every year to check the houses, which otherwise were looked after by us. We rajputs shared another small forest of the whole village, but each family had a couple of orchards attached to their houses and owned a good number of fields.

The rajput and brahmin women worked at home and on the land whereas the men had several kinds of government and private jobs including farming. Most of our subdivision's fields were farmed by the folks of the middle subdivision according to the rule of 'tihar' in which one third of the crop went to the landowner. The school-age children attended two schools: (1) the Khal Primary School located across our village creek over a saddle and (2) the Mission High School in the middle of a forest and two small creeks; the forest, which overlooked the village of Thaula, separated the School from Puri in the west; between the School and Puri were a Church and a cemetery. Our trail to Puri divided the church up and the cemetery down.

One common element of the three subdivisions was their representation in World War II. Four men from the lowest, one from the middle, and two from the upper were fighting at the various theaters.

For my first night of the Rama Lila, I had been given some preparatory information. Our village party of spectators would consist of young boys and girls of my age as well adult men and women of any age. The Rama Lila grounds, *Ram Lila Maidan*, in Puri was about two and a quarter miles from our village. It would take about one and a half hours to go up to the grounds, but only about one hour to go back down to our village. Going up, there would still be some daylight left half the way. To walk down on a hilly trail like ours was quite a challenge. We had to go through three gradually rising saddles, four small creeks, with mostly thorny bushes and trees everywhere, not to mention natural gravel rocks generously covering the trail.

Some lifesaving advice was given to everyone. Any funny noise from the bushes and there would be commotion. If it were a tiger, you could quickly climb a tree. You would be safe if you could get a climbable tree, at least up to twenty feet high, beyond the reach of the tiger. But a bear would grab you even if you were at the top of the tallest tree. You would cut the risk in half if you started out two hours early.

"Take a dari and a shawl in your school bag." Ma said.

"No Ma, I feel hot when I walk up." I didn't want to sit there on a dari (durrie mat) all wrapped up. What's the fun if I couldn't move around with my buddies!

"You will need them at the Ram Lila grounds. It's chilly up there. The winds from the Chaukhamba will tear your body after midnight. And always stay with your group."

The Ram Lila Party, as the group of spectators from our two villages was called, also expected five to eight boys from our village and four to six boys from Gwar, the village across from ours. As a new member of the group, I had to understand some unwritten instructions:

Eat your dinner early and leave for Puri with at least two or more boys of your age. But while coming back, you would need the company of the elders, especially men. So the walking speed would be slower due to darkness and mixed company. There would be one or two lanterns with the returning party, good enough to see the path and also scare away any attack-ready animals. Shout like crazy occasionally if you are without adults or lanterns. If you have to pee, which would be unavoidable after sitting for four or more hours at the Rama Lila grounds, don't go too far off the trail. There won't be any problems because the womenfolk would walk ahead of the menfolk keeping a few yards distance in between them. And wait if you see women in the bush. Don't begin to shout. A big list of do's and don'ts.

My mother suggested all this because she was not coming with me. Most women, unless sick or too old, would go to watch the Rama Lila, but not necessarily every night. But Mother and two other women of her age would not go at all. My father would have liked both of us to enjoy the Rama Lila together. But he was in the War.

One of the other two women was my aunt, Kanti. Her husband, Nawal Singh, was my father's third cousin, a few years younger than my father. Uncle Nawal was also in the War as a second lieutenant. On top of the war scare, Aunt Kanti had to look after her blind mother-in-law and a four-year old daughter with a disease. The disease was later discovered to be meningitis. Her father-in-law, Granduncle Jagdish, died last year.

His death was due to a simple accident. He slipped down a ravine while trying to reach ripe black raspberries (*kal hinsar*) hanging down from a thorny creeper. He must have been hungry. After remaining several days comatose, he passed away. He could have died in World War I when he fought against the Germans. His war hat with seven bullet holes was still in the family. Death in the war would have given him some honor. Here at home, even his own son was not able to attend his funeral. Four men of our village cremated him immediately. (Women do not attend funerals.) Nevertheless, Aunt Kanti was left alone to take care of the disabled family.

The other woman, Goda, was from the Bhatra's subdivision. She was not allowed by her husband Prem Lal to move around freely like this. She must have been a few years younger than my mother, about 23 or 24. But her husband must have been close to 50. She was perhaps his second wife. There was a rumor that she might have been preceded by a secret mistress. But before her, there was definitely a wife who died leaving one daughter and two sons behind. How did she die? They say that Prem Lal killed her by beating her constantly. Prem Lal was a police officer. No serious investigation was possible. Prem Lal used to beat his children so much that their maternal uncle took over custody. That made Prem Lal free to look for another woman. The other woman was Aunt Goda whom he married just two years ago. She was too young for him, my mother and some others said so very often.

One year after her marriage, I saw Aunt Goda in our house at lunchtime. She seemed to be very happy. I don't remember why she looked so happy. There is a saying in Garhwali: When somebody is very happy he or she will be willing to dance in the nude. Nobody would take this proverb seriously. She said to my mother, "Didi, I am so happy today. I want to dance naked!" She addressed Ma as Didi or older sister, but behaved like an equal. Before Ma would have said any word of advice against vice, she literally dropped her petticoat (underwear) and began to dance while laughing. Ma quickly held her hand and stopped her and wrapped her with a sari. I was standing there and also laughing. "Get out of here, now!" Ma scolded me. I had no choice.

A few months later, she came again around lunch time. She complained of pain in her arms and asked Ma to give her something to eat. Ma gave her a couple of *roti* breads. She began to sob. "He beat me last night," she said.

After eating the rotis, she asked my mother if she had any ointment and bandages. Mother went in the other room. By that time Aunt Goda (who, unlike Aunt Kanti, was not related to me) had taken her clothes off. I was aghast. Her neck and breasts were bruised; her legs had red patches all over them. There were blood spots here and there all over her light Himalayan skin.

In about two minutes, Ma came back with some stuff in her hands and saw both of us. "Chander, why don't you go in the other room. Just study there!" At this time Mother could see my stunned face. I couldn't concentrate in the other room. I was feeling very strange. Even though I was only six, I wondered why such things could happen to such a beautiful body! Until then I didn't know that men and women were so different. And women looked definitely better than men.

Six boys from my village and two from Gwar had already told me that they would join me the following day for the Rama Lila. Having only two boys from Gwar would mean that if one of them decided not to come, then the other might not come. If only one were to come, then he must be accompanied by an adult male or he would have to stay in our village because of the half a mile of uninhabited area between Gwar and our village.

The big creek of Pan Gadnu between our village and Gwar had its own mysteries all the way until it met the gracefully flowing Alakananda river eleven miles later. Tigers and bears visited the creek not only for water, but for food, too. Humans, too, drank its water, even though each village had a small spring for drinking water. It was also used for toilet and bath. In Himalayan villages there were no toilets and water facilities in or near residential areas. Everything was in the outskirts.

The creek had been respected as there were several sacred spots around its banks along its length. A couple of miles further down it became a 'gad' or a small river instead of a 'gadnu' or creek, where other smaller creeks and streams joined it. Further down another 'gad' joined it making a large pool at the confluence. The pool was called 'kund' which meant 'pool.' The confluence was respected; every year on the day of summer solstice a big sacred fair was held there.

That year, I watched that fair for the first time. A man almost died there at the dance. While the man was writhing in pain, many others were laughing and taunting "Eat more sweet balls. Here they are" and then throwing mud balls at him. It was horrible.

The Pandau, as the dance is popularly known in Garhwali, is based on the stories of the Mahabharata, the longest epic of the world. Even though this Sanskrit epic is as old as the Ramayana (or even older), the Garhwali version makes it look so recent and local. For example, the five Pandava brothers are invited to a dance (thus the name Pandau for the dance). Sometimes their common wife Draupadi also accompanies them in the dance. Their adversaries are called the Kaurava brothers, who are their own one hundred cousins, headed by Duryodhana and Duhshasana. They, too, join the dance. The cousins fight among themselves to claim their ancestral kingdom.

Actually, local men perform a circular dance. In the middle or on the side of the circle stand the two drummers, who are shamans. The big bass drum 'dhol' and the timpani size drum 'damau' can hurt your ear drums if you dance too close to them. It becomes worse when the two teams play drums together. That is what happens in this fair, controlled by the two large villages of Barsura and Bidoli nearby. Each village comes down to the kund with its own parade headed by the two drummers of dhol and damau. In order to avoid rivalry between the two villages, their drummers play together intermittently at the dance.

When I reached the fair, the dance was already on: Four drummers were facing the big circle of male dancers. After a few minutes of drumming and singing praises of Bhima, the most robust and glutton Pandava brother, the shamans succeeded in invoking his spirit. Successful possession by his spirit was suggested by the uncontrollable shaking and screaming of the possessed man. But there was a test. The man who was possessed by Bhima's spirit had to prove that he was now Bhima.

So the shamans asked him to eat mud if he was really the hungry Bhima. The man ate some mud. Then there was a big log, which could have been lifted by three or four men together. But the possessed man lifted the log. He proved that he was Bhima and had to be honored by the best food. Two men immediately brought a big plate full of sweets and snacks which the man finished quickly, another evidence of the real Bhima spirit within him.

After this man became his normal self again, the shamans started invoking another spirit. This time Parvati, the Mother Goddess.

Hindu mythology has many stories about Parvati. She is from these Himalayan mountains as her name Parvati means 'born of Mountain.' Being a mountain goddess, also known as Durga, Kali, Gauri etc., she is the most favorite here. She rides a lion when she moves from one place to another. There is no limit to her power because she is the power or Shakti. Sometimes she visits the kund with her husband Shiva. In order to please the Shakti goddess, a sacrifice of animals, such as goat, sheep, or fowl is sometimes offered for her (and her lion, too); the meat is shared by the devotees in the form of sacred food called 'prasad.'

The shamans were singing all these descriptions of Parvati, the Mother Goddess, to invite her. A man began to shake and scream in a female voice. He got close to the drummers who gave him a further test. They praised her lion. The man roared like a lion. He passed the two tests. According to the mythology, in order to marry Shiva, Parvati ate nothing but wild leaves or 'parna.' Even with this sacrifice, Shiva did not show up to propose to her. Then she left eating 'parna' (fern): thus Parvati became known as Aparna, the 'non-parna' goddess.

The same two men who brought a plateful of sweet balls earlier quickly came with a few twigs of kandali, the scorpion plant. One leaf of it in contact with human skin was more than enough to instantly cause big burning blisters and terrible pain. The Mother Goddess is Shakti 'power.' What power these wild poisonous leaves could have to harm her! She ate a lot of them when waiting for Shiva's favor of love.

The shamans asked the possessed man to eat all these twigs. The dumb man grabbed them by his shaking hands and put some in his mouth. He screamed and screamed, not in possession, but in pain. The red blisters were quite visible on his hands and face. The drummers stopped their music and the two men took him out of there. I heard his loud screams, not roars, of writhing pain in male voice, while some onlookers welcomed him by saying "Namaste, Devi!" or 'Salutation to you, Goddess.'

The kund showed its Shakti during monsoon rains, when swift rapids often swept down small buffaloes, cows, goats, sheep, etc. and deposited them into its swollen banks. But the watermills and irrigation channels definitely felt the benign effects of the shakti of the creek.

In 1942, there were three watermills along this creek near the crossing between our village and Gwar. Wheat, barley, kodu, and maze were the main grains that these mills were used for. Their flour, accumulated around the grinding stones, was a great delicacy for cattle. The door of each mill was missing, just a big wood pillar dividing the entrance vertically, allowing only humans to pass through. Whoever had to use these watermills or go at night to Gwar from our village knew one watermill story very well.

One early morning, my late grandfather's farmhand did something that no one should do. He was a strong man in his early forties. In order to avoid competition with the other mill users, he left our house with a heavy gunnysack of wheat. Following a common pattern of hillmen here, he loaded a heavy sack on his back with suspenders allowing him to carry a stick in one hand and a lantern in the other. The extremely narrow trail to the watermill passed through a small but very steep gorge that was called 'bhel.' This trail was an alternate route to Gwar, but was meant primarily for watermill use.

Bhimu descended down on this trail and reached the watermill. The moment he was about to enter the mill, a big bear came out from inside yelling and stood on his hind legs with two arms outstretched to charge at Bhimu. Even though Bhimu means 'robust,' no human body could be immune to the paws and teeth of a big black male Himalayan bear who had already assumed an attack posture like this. To make matters worse, Bhimu had a gunnysack on his back with about 100 kilos of wheat in it and it was still pitch dark. Otherwise he could have run downward in a zigzag pattern, a strategy that sometimes works, against an attacking Himalayan bear. Sometimes a strong man with a strong stick could manage to beat a small bear enough to scare him away.

But everything was against Bhimu. He, heaven knows how, quickly dropped down his stick and lantern, but not the gunnysack. With his hands free, he also stretched them and grabbed the bear's stretched arms around the pillar that stood now between the two. Bhimu used the pillar like a churning rod against which he kept on rubbing the bear's chest with so much pressure that people heard the cries of the bleeding bear.

Bhimu kept on hurting the bear. The more the bear cried the more Bhimu tore his chest by churning it around the pillar, which was neither smooth nor thin. By the time people came to help Bhimu, the poor bear was dead and Bhimu was slowly emptying the wheat sack into the container that contained the grist for the pair of grinding stones below.

In a matter of a few hours I would know how this story would play out with the boys from Gwar.

Then I looked outside my window. Bisram's song was no longer audible. I could hear the noisy creek of Pan Gadnu. Its resident night bird, called *gadkosru* (Creek Curser), had also started uttering its own name every other half-minute, an indication of midnight and more.

Where could Bisram be now? Maybe on the other side of the hill looking for Kiri. How about his wife? Would she be interested in the Rama Lila?

After pondering these questions I must have fallen asleep, but I don't remember when.

Chapter 3

▼

The Rude Awakening

The next day marked the first holiday. By 5 p.m. I had finished my dinner quickly. The fastest way of finishing dinner in Garhwal was to eat a "roti roll" (rolled up vegetables or any thing inside a *roti,* the flat round bread mostly made of wheat flour). When I had already eaten half a dozen of them, Ma scolded me, "Eating food in a roti roll is good for small children. You are a big boy now."

"Ma, the roti roll is the Himalayan answer to the English sandwich."

"Only if you don't have a Himalayan stomach! You are going to eat roti and vegetables the way big boys eat." That meant I would have to tear off a small piece of roti, then pick up one piece of vegetable with it, and then eat it piece by piece. No wonder the English occupied India so fast. They ate big sandwiches, while we ate rotis in small pieces. I decided not to eat roti rolls. Maybe, some day I would try sandwiches.

After my spicy roti roll binge. I waited for the others in front of a big cave called Bagh Duln, or 'Tiger Den.' This place, where tigers have been spotted occasionally, was the meeting point for Rama Lila goers. It was a few hundred yards west of our house. When I reached there, I expected to see the two boys from Gwar—Harit Satti and Dhan Satti.

From our village more boys were expected to accompany me. There were plenty of boys in my age group. Some of them were students at the Mission School, where I would go the next year for third grade. The School held classes from the third to the tenth grade. My father and many other men of our village had been students of this School. I was excited about going there. Not every boy going there was excited. Some had great difficulty in passing their examinations. I was doing well at Khal Primary School and hoped to do well at the Mission High School, too.

But so far only Harit and Dhan, cousins to each other, had promised to show up at Bagh Duln! Dhan was older than Harit by two years. Both were school friends of Gambhir and Bhajnu, my two buddies from my own village. This would be Harit's first trip to the Rama Lila, even though he was one year older than I. They had already told me that they would bring a cucumber and some spicy salt for the road. Instead I found only Gambhir and Bhajnu and a cucumber in between them.

"Great, you brought that little cucumber, Gam." I said. In the village, everybody was considered a relative, even if he or she was not a real one. For example, Gambhir was a chacha, an uncle, to me. Nevertheless, we treated each other as chums, so I called Gambhir "Gam." Later I came to know that such "relative rules" were followed throughout India.

"I have more than this. If you are hungry, just ask me," he said. Bhajnu rolled his glittering eyes.

Then Gambhir showed me a paper bundle. "Arsas," he said.

An *arsa*, a round tennis ball size pastry prepared with fried cream of rice, made me as happy as Bhajnu.

"It's good that Anrit is not coming. No hope for arsa otherwise," Bhajnu said.

I was not happy, however, to hear that news. Anrit was not only robust, but also oldest among us. Ma and others predicted that he would grow taller than his father, who looked to be more than six feet (a very unusual height for males in the hills). "What happened to him?" I asked Bhajnu. He and Anrit were in the same grade.

"Nothing happened to him. He just doesn't want to come," Bhajnu said gleefully.

Then Gambhir interrupted, "His father has disappeared."

"But my mother did not tell me...Is anyone looking for him?" I asked in big surprise.

"No. He told Anrit and his mother not to look for him. He has left his job and home, for ever. He is now a jogi." Gam replied.

Jogi and *jog* are local pronunciations of *yogi* and *yoga*. But in reality, the difference is more than the pronunciation. Jogis or jognis are monks and nuns. They beg and wander (hence 'jog') from one place to another place (homelessness is 'detachment,' a requirement for renunciation or samnyasa, pronounced here as 'sannyas'). A yogi, on the other hand, is he who practices yoga. I understood these interesting differences later.

With the War, the number of soldiers as well as of jogis and jognis began to increase. Poverty, especially shortage of food, was felt not only in Bengal, where the most infamous famine took place, but everywhere in India. The government had already started a system of rationing. Each household had a ration card with which one would buy certain items such as wheat flour, rice, sugar, and kerosene oil, etc.

But sometimes the rationed items were not available. Many untouchables with large families began to beg. The "high" caste people wouldn't beg. They would borrow in cash or commodities. Who couldn't beg or borrow practically starved. Many from high castes became jogis, thanks to the dire poverty that was created by the War.

Uncle Ishan, Anrit's father, did not face these circumstances, and yet he decided to be a jogi.

"Jogis beg. If Uncle is a monk, who will support his children?" I asked with real concern.

"Anrit's mother," Gambhir said as if there was no problem.

Maybe Gambhir knew how to survive in a fatherless family without having to beg. Part of my father's military salary came to my mother by money order every month. This was the rule in this area: Every wage earner working outside the area had to send money home to his family. The family economy was mainly a money order economy.

For a few minutes I kept wondering. Why had Uncle Ishan left his job as Puri's postmaster to become a monk? Why had he left Auntie Jaya and why had he no love for his son Anrit, no love for his two little daughters, Bijji and Soni? Although they were brahmins, the Bhatras were not supposed to behave in a 'detached' way.

I began to imagine how Uncle Ishan might have looked. Ochre robes, long beard and mustache, long hair. Or maybe with a clean shaven head, topknot in the middle, a begging bowl or bag, a water pot, no leather shoes or even barefooted, carrying idols of some gods or goddesses. While begging, he would be saying mantras like "Hari Om" or just "Rama, Rama" or perhaps observing a complete vow of "silence" (*mauna*), or quietly counting the beads of a rosary. Why had he chosen such a way of life? A bum?

"What are you thinking about?" Gam asked me.

"The Gwar boys promised to come and bring cucumbers. But I don't see the Gwar boys anywhere." I just said looking down through the trail.

"Cucumbers? Their cucumbers are something else. One would be enough for the whole party." Bhajnu quipped. But I kept thinking about Uncle Ishan

The hill cucumbers grow as large as long medium size watermelons and they were now in season. Gwar village had big orchards, from where the people of neighboring villages, as well as the grocers of Puri bought their vegetables and fruit. The parents of Harit and Dhan were known for growing high quality potatoes and onions. They sold milk and ghee (clarified butter). The other families, all of them brahmins with the caste name 'Satti', grew and sold the famous *basmati*, 'scented' long grain rice. But their cucumbers and bijora lemons were also famous all around. The bijoras were not only sweet, but as large as medium size melons. Thanks to Mother Nature, these large, melon-like bijoras grew on creepers and stayed on the ground. If they had grown on trees, the region would have had a record number of head injuries!

"Because of Gwar, we never have a shortage of vegetables and fruits." Said Bhajnu breaking my chain of thinking.

The Bhatras from our village grew all these things, but would never think farming their business. Just as a brahmin (*brahmana* 'priest') class person was not a business (*vaishya*) class or merchant caste person, the Bhatras considered selling grains and vegetables beneath their dignity. The rajputs were considered warrior (*kshatriya*) class people, but in practice they did not hesitate to do business. In fact, they conducted most business and trade since there were no people of the vaishya or business castes in this region.

The lowest (*shudra*) castes, whom the higher castes called *dom* (untouchables), could have taken interest in non-traditional businesses, but they did not have the resources and social status the higher castes had. Some of them did grow grains like wheat, rice, kodu (a rye), jhangoru (a rye) and some beans like urad (black beans) and lentils in our fields, and a few vegetables like chhimi (green beans), karela (bitter cucumber), kaddu (pumpkin), lauki (long thick squash), chachinda (long thin squash) , and godri (a grooved squash), enough for their bare subsistence. Sometimes, they had to go along Pan Gadnu and pick up wild lingura (eatable ferns), asparagus, mushrooms, tairu (a wild root), and even kukurdara (a wild creeper) and kandali (a plant).

The last two—kukurdara and kandali—were problematic when touched. The little ripe red berries of kukurdara creepers caused itching. But it was not as horrible as kandali, which caused unbearable pain and blisters on contact. Mushrooms and lingura were clearly recognized as the poisonous and the nonpoisonous types.

Even those who grew plenty of vegetables in their gardens would cook these free gifts of nature as delicacies. Kaphal, hinsar, kingor, melu, khaina, anwala, ghingaru, jamun, figs, etc. were also free fruits growing wild, everywhere in these hills. Pine nuts were available anywhere over 5000 feet. The other free gifts of nature were the wild animals. Fish, deer, swine, quail, fowl, partridge, and even porcupines. Except fish, other animals were hunted with guns. Almost every soldier brought home a gun. Even brahmins hunted. Uncle Prem Lal and his brothers Keshab and Sundar were very well-known hunters.

Outside the Hindu caste system were a few Christian and Muslim families in Puri. Muslims were the real business community here and had business connections with the adjacent plains from where their forefathers migrated. However, some brahmin communities, like the rajputs, did engage in various commercial ventures. The Sattis were a good example.

There was an exception, a woman whom we called Lathi dadi or Grandma Lathi. Her real name was Lata (meaning 'creeper'), but she looked and behaved more like a *lathi* (meaning 'stick'). Her polygynous Bhatra husband, Sirdhar, left very little for her and her children. Just a house, which luckily was surrounded by a few orchards and was a common property of the three widows and children of Sirdhar. The fields Sirdhar owned were now under the control of his big brother, Gobind. Sirdhar failed to pay the loan he took from Gobind. So Lathi followed the Gwar model of selling milk and ghee.

Gambhir was Lathi Dadi's son. He had two stepmothers, both seniors to his mother. The first one, Mira, had one son and two daughters, all married. The second one, Guna, had one daughter, who was close to marriageable age in local standards, sixteen years old. All the mothers and unmarried children lived in one single house, divided into three sections. The three co-wives, as expected, did not get along very well. Very seldom were they on speaking terms.

Speaking of speaking terms, it was a communication disorder inherited by more or less all the senior male Bhatras. And it was contagious as some of the wives got it. Polygamy and property were the causes of this disorder.

Bedi was the great-grandfather with three visible wives. The fourth wife, Raji, was a rajput. She lived with her parents, was the only child, and heir to their huge property. A big negative factor for Raji to get married was that she was born with a blind eye and had very little eyesight left in the other eye. The property factor could attract an old brahmin like Bedi to marry her, however. Raji never went to her husband's village, where allegedly nobody saw or spoke about this shady marriage. There was a rumor that Raji's father got this property with some shady deal, anyway.

Raji died after a few years of marriage with no children. Her parents had already died earlier. Now Bedi legally owned her entire property and moved his entire harem and children from Thaili, his ancestral village, to our village, Rajkhet.

In other words, our village was owned by rajputs, so the village was called Rajkhet, the Rajput's Khet (field). The brahmins, namely the Bhatras, came into this rajput village by social default. Nobody in this village or adjacent villages knew much about Bedi's ancestry. Some guessed that his forefathers were Bhattarai living on the border of Nepal and India and moved to Garhwal via Kumaon hills. In Garhwal, their family name Bhattarai was reduced to Bhatra.

However, our rajput ancestry had no connection with the Bhatra brahmins. Nevertheless, we addressed or referred to them as relatives, out of the customary courtesy kinship created for social contact.

Bedi's long genesis was known to everybody in Rajkhet and adjacent villages. His first wife had two sons, Gobind and Sirdhar, and one daughter, Phuli. The second wife had one son, Badris. The third wife had two daughters, Riddhi and Siddhi, and two sons, Bisal and Madan. Each wife and her family eventually lived in separate houses. All girls, after their marriages, left the village.

Gobind had two wives. His first wife died after leaving three sons: Prem Lal, Keshab, and Sundar. Six years after her death Bedi was able to persuade Gobind to marry again.

The story was that at that time Gobind's sons were all big boys. His oldest son, Prem Lal, was more than twenty and serving in the Puri police force. The second son, Keshab, was studying at a college in Merath, a town near Delhi. He wanted to be a lawyer. The third son,

Sundar, was still in high school. Perhaps, Gobind did not feel comfortable with the talk of his marriage while he was planning his oldest son's marriage.

A few months before Prem Lal's marriage, Gobind got married second time to a woman, Ramni, who was as old as Prem Lal. He had two sons and one daughter from Ramni. The daughter, Ratna, was born the day he retired as a forest ranger. Local folks called her "Retirement."

This name had several local interpretations. One was that Gobind would no longer be able to take bribes from forest contractors. The fact that he had a horse, a sign of prestige in the hills, was proof that he was a bribe taker. On his horse, he would survey local forests and women. Now he had neither the horse, nor the mistresses.

Gobind's youngest son Amar, born two years before Retirement, was a classmate of one of Prem Lal's sons. They were an amusing couple for many youngsters who would make fun of them: Uncle and Nephew, same age and same class. The older son, Anjan, avoided us as much as possible.

Badris was Bedi's second wife's son. Uncle Ishan's father, Anrit's grandfather, was this son. Why Uncle Ishan and his father were somewhat different was a social puzzle in and around the village.

Sirdhar, on the other hand, Bedi's son by his first wife, took after his father, as evidenced by his three wives. After Gobind had three more children, he became greedy and took almost all of Sirdhar's land. Sirdhar's death and debt gave him this opportunity. Gobind had given him a couple of forest contracts which went sour. Sirdhar was sued for the losses, but Gobind paid off the debt.

Bedi's third wife's two sons, Bisal and Madan, served as soldiers in the last two years of World War I. A few years later they got married. Bisal had nine children, six sons and three daughters. Madan had two sons. Surprisingly, all were monogamous progeny of Bedi's third wife. Bisal's oldest son, Khemanand, lived in Lucknow with his family. It was around this time that Bisal's next two sons, Shankh and Udai, and both of Madan's sons, Birendra and Brijendra, joined the Indian Army.

The last three sons of Granduncle Bisal were going to our school, ranging from eighth grade to third grade. The third-grader Karun was friendly with me. The other two, Loki and Bhagat, being in higher grades, were more reserved, but still helpful. All of us played soccer regularly in the late afternoons and sometimes extended the game into the moonlit evenings.

In the Bhatra tribe, whether or not each and every individual counted, none was prophet quality. But to give them the benefit of the doubt, maybe God did not have time to think about them, or maybe he thought that the world already had enough prophets. Very few Bhatra adults felt friendly towards each other. What was amazing was that all the Bhatra boys and girls of my generation were not only on good speaking terms among themselves, but at times acted together when there were some confrontational situations with neighboring villages.

For example, Bhatras' cattle would graze in the fields of neighboring villages, almost devouring all the young paddy plants. There would be serious threats from the owners of the paddy fields. The Bhatra boys would challenge them to a fight. Sometimes a couple of Bhatra boys would catch some women cutting grass or wood in their joint forest; in retaliation, they would seize their tools such as axes, sickles, ropes etc. Tribal defense.

I myself had never had any noteworthy conflict with this generation. In fact, Jagjit and Jagriti were like big brother and sister to all the boys and girls of my age in the village. They were Uncle Keshab's children. Their other son, Laksh, was in the sixth grade. Jagjit was in his last year of high school and Jagriti was in the eighth grade. Their mother, Shaila, was not too worried about Jagriti. She considered Jagriti smarter than her sons. (Customarily, parents in this society were expected to be damn worried about their daughters.). Uncle Sundar and his wife Hema had a son Madhav, who was a classmate of Jagriti.

The most unfortunate Bhatra children were Uncle Prem Lal's children as they were not in regular contact with their own cousins.

Among all the Bhatra boys, I found myself more comfortable with Gambhir, Anrit, and Karun, all of them my seniors in school by one or two grades. And all four of us found Bhajnu the most congenial buddy.

Bhajnu was from our village's middle subdivision, strictly an "untouchable" section. His parents were drummers and tailors. The drummer caste or *auji* was very important in this Himalayan society on all auspicious occasions. The two drums, dhol and damau, were played at all eremonies and festive occasions. Bhajnu's father Dhiru and uncle Gyaru were accomplished drummers. They had humiliated many other drummers of this area at several marriages.

In every marriage there would be two teams, with two drummers each—one from the bride's side and the other from the groom's side. The two teams would greet each other by drumming, not in the traditional manner of "namaskar" with palms folded as in prayer, not speaking a single word. The greeting initially would be a fierce artistic competition between the two sets standing in front of each other. But in the end both teams would stand side by side with a friendly exchange. That is, the dhol player on the bride's side would become a partner of the damau player on the groom'side and likewise with the other two. Now they would play together as one team an identical rhythm to celebrate the happy union. Then they would stop drumming, and say greeting words to each other. Ever on speaking terms.

Bhajnu's uncle and aunt had one married daughter. Their immediate neighbors were the mason Bhadu and the baddi Molu. Bhadu and his wife Khunki had a daughter and a son. The daughter was married and the young son joined the army one year before. Young Molu and his beautiful wife Chandni had already earned a good name for their dholak-dance entertainment. They considered themselves very lucky as they had a son and a daughter, both going to Khal Primary School and learning the art of their parents as well.

The rajputs and the "untouchables" of this village were very fortunate in this respect: They had always been on speaking terms with all. Their communicative behavior might have influenced the younger Bhatra generation.

That day, we three boys eagerly waiting for the other boys for the Ram Lila, was enough to show our harmonious relationship. We had been waiting more than half an hour and there was no soul in sight down there. We decided to move up on the trail in a slow pace so that the others could catch up with us.

After a while, we decided to wait again.

Bhajnu and Gambhir were two years senior to me and had already been to last year's Rama Lila. I thought of my mother's instructions. Those instructions presupposed a bigger party. But we were only three. I told them that my mother had a different understanding. But they didn't seem to be concerned at all.

I reminded them after we were already over the ridge of the village of Thaula, almost half way between our village and Puri. I was excited in two ways. It was my first trip to the Ram Lila. The refusal of these two boys to follow Ma's instructions made me equally excited. Joy and fear alternated so much that I suddenly began to walk back home. I increased my speed by the moment.

Bhajnu ran after me, but he could not catch me as he stopped to remove a thorn that had penetrated his foot. He had no shoes. Gambhir must have noticed this. So he began to chase me. He, like I, had canvas shoes, good for running. He caught me and dragged me up with gentle persuasion.

"This is your first time. Nothing bad will happen to you. Just believe in Lord Ram. You are going with us all the way to Puri," Gambhir said.

"Hey, what kind of a rajput boy are you? Don't you know what Ram and Lakshman did at your age?" Apparently, Bhajnu was trying to inspire me.

Anyway, they decided to wait for the others while we ate the stuff Gambhir had brought. Then we walked further up. Here our trail met another trail that connected up to the Mission School and also to Puri further west and up. Then we saw some people from other villages going to the Rama Lila. Yet still no member from our party in sight.

"I really want to go back," I said.

"It will be dark before you reach home. So why not go to the Rama Lila!" Gambhir said in a firm tone even though he was smiling.

"But how are we going to come back alone after midnight?" I retorted in fear.

"Chander, then we will stay with a friend of my Mama ji," Gambhir said in a reassuring voice. His mama or maternal uncle was a government clerk in Puri, but did not live in the town. So I decided half-heartedly to cooperate with them.

Just before reaching the outskirts of Puri, we all peed in a bush.

When we reached Puri, we found eleven men, women, boys and girls from our village and Gwar already there. They were lined up at the end of the hilly part of the Rama Lila audience area, where I saw several small tents with children playing inside and out. Behind the tents, a few yards up, were shops and residential houses from where many people were moving down the hill. Further down on the flat part of the ground was the gorgeous stage. But I was already feeling so down and then Dhan asked, "Where the hell were you three? In the cemetery?"

"We were looking for you!" replied Gambhir.

Most of them did not ridicule us for being late. But the front part, the better part, of the Rama Lila grounds was already occupied by the locals. While our party had been waiting and looking all around for us, the opportunity to sit together as a whole party in the front, near the 'yard' was lost. We told them that we had been going slow because we thought they were late. They took the shorter trail and we took the zig-zaggy, longer, easier trail.

I was feeling terrible inside, even though Gambhir and Bhajnu took the blame upon themselves. The two told the party that I wanted to wait for everybody right at the Bagh Duln, the tiger den.

But that made me feel worse because it also meant that I had caused the delay.

As darkness fell, petromax lamps lit up the stage all around. We sat near the tents. These tents belonged to the more privileged townspeople as I could see from the clothes that they and their children wore. Some of them were eating candies and cookies. Some men and women were sitting on chairs right beside the stage. Gambhir told me that they were big officials.

In front of the stage was a secluded empty area, a small field or yard, obviously a part of the stage since nobody was sitting there except four men on a corner close to the stage. These men were musicians. One had a dholak, a two-sided drum. Another had a pair of tabla drums. The main musician, known as the harmonium master, was giving some instructions to the drummers .

Then the master sang a prayer. After the prayer, he started singing a bhajan (devotional song) joined by the drummers. I could clearly see the fat harmonium player looking at the drummers while nodding his big bald head. He sang another bhajan, then another bhajan. After a pause, he put some thing in his mouth. I realized it was *pan,* a betel leaf with betel nuts, white lime paste, red catechu paste, cloves, and cardamoms with or without chewing tobacco wrapped inside it. Nothing else was taking place on the stage.

So I began to doze. All of us had our own daris and shawls. I spread my dari and laid down on it with my shawl covering me from my head to my toes.

When I got up or rather was asked to get up, I saw everybody standing. Gambhir told me that it was time to go back. So I did not get to watch the night's Rama Lila. Dhan told me that the real Rama story would start the next night. But I did ask him to tell me what I had missed.

"Nothing much. The Narada story was the big thing, all boring." Gambhir said. "You were really tired. I told the others."

I wasn't feeling good at all, but all were in a hurry to go. I also wanted to pee. As soon as we reached the outskirts of Puri, all the lanterns were put aside. We all finished the job in groups—boys and boys together, adult women and women together, and so on. Every group picked up its own lantern (our group's lantern belonged to the Gwar boys) and proceeded on the trail with a slow pace.

After a while, a group started a song, some singers forgetting the tune or words. I even overheard another group enjoying gossip. Some talked about the War, mainly experiences of their relatives.

The boys' group had only five of us—Dhan, Harit, Bhajnu, Gambhir, and myself. They really had fun as they were talking about this or that actor, scene and song. The main talk was about the two attendants of Shiva: how they quarreled and blamed each other using the local cuss words of Garhwali after they were cursed in Hindi by Narada, the old sage who was seduced by and wanted to marry a young woman. I couldn't relate to any piece of the story, so I remained quiet.

But when Dhan made fun of Uncle Prem Lal, who was too old for Auntie Goda, I opened my mouth, "It's not funny."

"Why not?" asked Dhan.

"Because you don't know what I know."

"But you also don't know what we know."

"Now shut up both of you!" Gambhir admonished. Maybe, because he was a Bhatra and his mother was the youngest (third) wife of his father. Or maybe, Dhan and Harit joked because they were from Gwar, not from our village Rajkhet. Who knows, he became serious and there was no more talk until we reached our home.

All the boys literally came to drop me at our verandah, where my mother was waiting for me.

I began to feel uneasy. She asked Dhan and Harit, "Are you two alone?"

"Yes, Chachi ji" Dhan replied to Ma (she was not his real chachi or aunt as my father was not his father's cousin, but people from adjacent villages fall into the category of "relatives").

"Then you both stay with us tonight." Ma said that more or less as a command.

"Yes, we are afraid of the creek area." Harit said.

Gambhir looked at mother and asked, "Can we all sleep together in a room, Bhabhi ji?"

My mother was not really his sister-in-law or bhabhi, but my father referred to his late father as uncle or Chacha ji following the village "relative" rule.

"Yes, you all may. Bhajnu, too. Go in the backroom, upstairs."

Bhajnu looked a little embarrassed. Maybe, because Ma didn't care that he was "low caste." An untouchable sleeping with brahmins and rajputs in the same room! Not allowed in the Hindu system.

But he joined us happily. And I was relieved that this development saved me from my own embarrassment. Ma didn't ask me right away about my first Rama Lila night. I quickly led the boys to the room. There was already a big mandru, a mat made of wheat straw, on the floor. Each of us spread our dari on it and covered ourselves with our own shawls.

I wish Mother had not allowed Bhajnu to sleep with us. Shortly after we had fallen asleep, I began to hear 'dherrrr, dhurrr, fusss, fisss' sounds as if bombs were dropping down and exploding with an awful smell. I got up and wanted to know who was responsible for this. It was Bhajnu. But I didn't want to embarrass him. So I tried to sleep again.

After a while the same noise and smell reemerged in the room. This time Dhan got up and shook Bhajnu by his neck, "What the shit did you eat?"

Gambhir and Harit, too, got up. Gambhir asked, "What's going on between you two?"

"Don't you hear and smell anything? It's from him." I pointed toward Bhajnu.

"Yes, I do. What's the big fuss about it? My mother farts, I fart, everybody farts. Go on, Bhajnu, fart! I gave you those little sweet bombs to eat. What else could you do! If you fellows have to lose your sleep, don't blame Bhajnu. It's my arsas. He ate most of them. Sure, they will explode. Only my mother makes arsas as big as that. I am proud of them. Continue farting, brother!"

Then Gambhir laughed while pinching his nose shut with his fingers and we all laughed. Bhajnu laughed, too.

"Chander!" said Gam, "the Narada story is totally unreal and it's boring. But this one in your room is a real story, much more funny! Thanks Bhajnu! Now let's go to sleep!" Gambhir laid down and covered his entire body with his shawl, part of it tucked under and around his head.

When I got up in the morning, it was already after 10 a.m. Nobody was in the room, no dari and shawl except mine. I went around and out of the house. Except for a lonely Himalayan magpie, gliding with its long beautiful tail, I did not find any noticeable being on our verandah. I decided to go out for toilet and to wash near the spring.

As I was coming up, I saw one man coming out of Uncle Nawal's house. He, accompanied by another man, was carrying a small white bundle in his arms. They were followed by Aunt Kanti, who was wailing loudly. My mother was supporting Auntie with her hands as if saving her from falling down. Then a few more men and women followed. All were crying.

I quickly joined them and learned that Nini had died that morning. She was the only child Uncle and Auntie had. Even though she was four years old, she looked just one year old due to meningitis. Her dead body was being carried away for cremation at the bank of Alakanada, near the town of Srinagar.

By evening Grandaunt, Nini's blind grandmother had died of a heart attack. Then I found out the whole story. While it was still dark in the morning, Grandaunt had tried to go out alone for toilet, feeling her way with a cane. How it happened, I don't remember exactly, but she had stepped on Nini. Thus, the death of Nini.

The next morning a bamboo bier was prepared. The grandaunt's body was wrapped around it. Two men lifted the bier and headed toward the Alakananda river.

Nobody went to the Rama Lila from our village that year. It was customary to observe mourning for a period of time, usually for one month when a funerary rite was performed. Not only in our village, but even some Gwar folks, observed the custom. The two men who carried the bier were from Gwar.

My mother and I slept every evening in Auntie's house, until Uncle Nawal's arrival. He came with three weeks' emergency leave. It was a total surprise since the war in Europe, Asia, and Africa was getting worse as the news would reach Puri and Lansdowne. Uncle Nawal arrived home on a horse. There was no bus transport yet, but it was expected in about two years. One week's leave was wasted in travel alone. But his two weeks' stay at home had a good effect on Aunt Kanti's health. She looked cheerful.

The day of uncle's departure, however, wasn't cheerful. He didn't tell anyone where he was going. All he said that he would be out of India on a new front. We guessed that the new front was Burma. "Is it Burma?" Ma asked him. "Bhabhi ji, like Bhai ji, I am not allowed to say anything about my whereabouts." Bhai ji or big brother (a senior cousin) was my father. Ma had tears in her eyes.

No horse was available in the village. So Uncle got ready to walk to Puri. A few other villagers came to see him off. Gambhir's mother placed a tilak, a sacred red mark, on his forehead for his well-being. Most of them looked serious. Men hugged him while women were crying, but not as much as auntie. Anrit, Gambhir, and I carried some of his luggage up to Puri. Luckily, there was no snow yet.

Then, Uncle rode the horse with his luggage and moved toward the road to Lansdowne, the cantonment where he was to report before going to the war front.

After Uncle Nawal's departure, we began to sleep in one house, sometimes in Auntie's, some times in ours. I thought that this kind of sleeping arrangement was temporary. But it continued for several months until Mother told me that Auntie was going to have a baby soon. I could see now why her belly was growing bigger and bigger. She complained about discomforts and anxiety. I overheard her and Ma, talking about Nini's disease (meningitis). Aunt Goda would also visit and sleep with her when her husband, Prem Lal, was out of town on police business.

A few months later there was sensational news in the village. Aunt Goda had disappeared. It was known openly that Uncle Prem Lal used to regularly beat her. She left no clue as to her whereabouts. There were all sorts of guesses from all sorts of people, but nothing was really known about her new life. Some were even saying that most probably she had committed suicide by drowning in the Alakananda.

One married girl from a nearby village had committed suicide like that the previous year. Her husband was not a wife beater, but his family, especially the mother-in-law and the father-in-law, mistreated her in many ways. The husband was much older than she and he was blind in one eye. Her father had received a good bride price. She was unhappy, not so much about having an older and partially blind husband as about the frequent insults that her father had sold her to them. The in-laws virtually used her as indentured labor. Daily cooking for the family of nine, including the five younger siblings of the husband, working out in the fields and barn, and doing other chores were cause for her miserable end.

The normal custom here was the dowry, not the bride price. But Uncle Prem Lal's age gap had to be filled with bride price, all in cash. He had already been known as a wife abuser starting with his late first wife, who had brought enough dowry and gave him four children—

three sons and one daughter. The oldest son was already more than twenty. The next son about eighteen. And the daughter about fifteen. The youngest was literally the baby brother of these three, just eleven-years old. The daughter, Savitri, and the baby brother, Shyam, went to stay with their father in May, when schools were closed for summer vacation. Most of the household work was now the responsibility of Savitri.

I was happy to have Shyam as one more member of our village football (soccer) team.

Uncle Prem Lal would sometimes sit with Shyam for a study session. Shyam had just finished the third grade. It was surprising when Uncle asked Anrit and me to join the evening study session with Shyam. Anrit and I felt good about his attitude as our fathers were not home.

In the beginning, we found that Uncle Prem Lal would yell at Shyam if he made any mistakes. Sometimes he would say, "Look at Anrit. He is your age, but one grade ahead of you. What's wrong with your head?" and then slap him at the head. But he never touched me and Anrit, except for a few scoldings.

In one study session, he became very mad at Shyam. First, he twisted his arm and kicked him in the butts. Shyam tried to release his arm. But Uncle Prem Lal grabbed him, threw him down on the floor, and sat over his back while hitting his ribs. Shyam screamed in pain and asked for our help. He looked at us. But Anrit and I sat there, as if paralyzed.

Then somehow Shyam got out of his grip and ran out. Uncle Prem Lal yelled at us, "Go get the haram ka bachcha!" I thought he, not his son, was the 'haram ka bachcha' (bastard). We got up and pretended to run after Shyam.

That evening, Anrit felt terrible. The next day, he went to Puri and informed a relative of the children's maternal uncle, who took custody of them after his sister died.

Within a week, Savitri and Shyam were secretly taken away by their maternal uncle.

Uncle Prem Lal, after quick investigation, found that Anrit was the informer. One evening, he came home early and saw Anrit alone on his way from Pan Gadnu. He told him that he needed his help in the nearby watermill. Anrit went with him inside the watermill. There Uncle Prem Lal beat Anrit very badly and left him alone in a semi-unconscious state.

The next morning, Anrit told his mother, who began to spread the news around. But nobody did anything against Uncle PremLal. For Anrit's mother it was impossible to even talk to Uncle Prem Lal, since by relation he was a 'jeth' (older brother-in-law). The two were not supposed to face each other due to strict custom of 'chhaun' or avoidance of senior males on the husband's side.

Then, about two weeks later, we heard that Uncle Prem Lal has been admitted to the Puri hospital in very serious condition. He was found unconscious near the Mission School cemetery and Church, with bruises all over his body. Interestingly, his skin had some traces of ash all over. When he woke up moaning in pain, he had no recollection of his beater. The doctor told him that he would be able to walk within a month.

Meanwhile, the investigators kept looking for his violent victimizer, but could not solve the case. The talk of ashes on his bruised body was a total mystery for anybody who saw or heard about this beating. Some even joked: Ash would be possible near a Hindu cremation ground, not near a Christian cemetery.

Violence near a church was shocking in itself to many. When the school opened in July, many asked me and others from our village if we knew who the culprit was.

Then the month of September arrived and everybody was waiting for the Dashhara vacation. I was determined to see the Rama Lila and not repeat my previous year's actions. Almost everyone of my own age knew the story of the Rama Lila. I felt humiliated for my ignorance.

To my surprise, one evening Jagriti visited me in my house and said, "Chander! You missed last year's Rama Lila. I can get the story for you from the Rama Lila Committee."

I was excited, "O Didi! When can you get it?" I felt that she was really acting like a *didi*, a big sister.

"This weekend. We will read it together. I have read it before. It's better than Tulsidas' story. I don't know the original story. That's in Sanskrit."

"Why is Tulsidas' story not as interesting?"

"Interesting? His book is bad for India, bad for the majority of people."

It was something shocking to me, because Tulsidas' devotional songs were the most popular at any Rama Navami, the birthday of Rama.

"Didi, I don't understand!"

"Brother! Tulsidas' Rama says 'Drums, rustics, shudras, beasts, and women—these all rightfully deserve beating.'...That defames Rama, doesn't it?"

"That's stupid!"

"I am happy to hear this from a man. Men of high castes don't understand the pain of women and people of low castes. Chander! Learn to put yourself in others' shoes, in the shoes of the oppressed people."

I felt so good that Jagriti called me a 'man.'

But I also felt that Jagriti's voice was an awakening, no matter how rude the voice may sound to the men of high classes (interestingly, Jagriti means 'awakening').

She continued, "But don't get me wrong. They say that Rama never said such a thing in the original story. But the story we are going to read is far more interesting. It's called the 'Rama Drama.' It is a story of the past. But at the same time you feel that it is acually happening at this moment. You will see that on the stage. The curtain goes up and down. In between you see the drama unfolding an old, very old story."

In my excitement, I clung to her.

"Don't get too excited yet. Wait when we read it together," she said while pressing me between her arms. I could see her bright beautiful eyes awakening my own to see what follows ahead.

Footnote:

Premindra Singh Bhagat of the Royal Bombay Sappers and Miners was given the Victoria Cross for his bravery in Ethiopia, January 31–February 1, 1941.

Richpal Ram of the Rajputana Rifles was posthumously given the Victoria Cross for his bravery in Eritrea, February 7–11, 1941.

Part II

The Rama Drama

Note:

The folk theater is divided into two interactive parts: the raised stage and the front yard. The area surrounding the yard is for the audience seating. The stage has a front curtain only. The scenes open onto the stage as well as onto the yard. Actors can enter and exit from the corner (side) entrances of the stage or yard or any part of the audience area. Voices, such as divine warnings, are produced from behind the stage. The entire drama is musical (opera) and the texts are in verse with occasional prose. The prose sections are indicated by short spoken dialogs often followed or preceded by "said" or "asked." The nights that have fewer scenes can contain unrelated skits or independent music and dance performances. The languages used are Hindi, Avadhi, Garhwali, and Sanskrit in decreasing order. In other regions, regional languages are used instead. The core story generally follows the versions of Valmiki's *Ramayana* in ancient Sanskrit and Tulsidas' *Ramacaritamanasa* in Avadhi (of the Mughal period), but a great deal of visual and textual variation is allowed here. The most popular Hindi variations are the songs composed by Pandit Radhe Shyam. His style is versatile as it includes traditional Hindustani music and the modern Mughal style of *ghazal* singing in Urdu. Variations in word spelling and pronunciation are common. Every night starts and ends with a chorus consisting of prayers, which may occasionally vary. The text of the story is written in the past tense. The scene directions (in *italics*) are in the present tense.

Chorus

Hail, hail, hail, hail! Mother of the Universe!
Fulfill our wish, O remover of misfortune!
Again and again we call you, Mother!
You will have mercy, remove our shame!
Only then will we have our welfare.
Hail, hail, hail, hail! Mother of the Universe!

Om Namah Shivaya, Salutation to the Lord of
  Good.
Om Namah Shivaya, Salutation to the Lord of
  Good.
Om Namah Shivaya, Salutation to the Lord of
  Good.
Om Namah Shivaya, Salutation to the Lord of
  Good.
Om Namah Shivaya, Salutation to the Lord of
  Good.

1 O *my* mind, sing the hymns of compassionate
    Shri Rama-
  chandra, the banisher of the dolorous fears of
    existence!
  With fresh lotus-eyes and face, hands and feet like
    red lotuses,
2 With the unbounded beauty of unnumbered
    Love gods, with
  the hue of beautiful dark rain clouds,
  His yellow dress shines forth like lightning's pure
    lustre,
  —I worship the husband of Janak's daughter!

3 Him, the friend of the poor, like a sun burning
    up the
  Danavas and Daityas,
  Offspring of Raghu's line, centre of bliss, moon of
    Koshala,

>   Dashrath's son
> 4 On his head a diadem, ear-rings and a tilak, on
>   all his lovely
>   limbs charming ornaments,
> With long arms down to his knees, bearing bow
>   and arrows,
>   in war defeating Khara and Dushana,
> 5 Thus says Tulsi Das, may you, the delighter of
>   the minds of
>   Shankar, Shesha and sages,
> Take dwelling in the lotus of my heart, the breaker
>   of the
>   evil ranks of lust and anger!

THE FIRST NIGHT
Scene 1

(This scene opens on a stage split into two halves. On one half, Sage Narada is sitting in meditation in the middle of a forest. On the second half, Indra is surrounded by gods in his heavenly court where he is sitting on his throne.)

The throne began to shake. "I know, Narada's penance is causing these tremors." Indra, the king of heaven, said to the gods. Then he looked at the two guards, "Guards! Bring a couple of beauties here!" The guards bowed and went out.

The throne began to shake again. "Narada wants to grab my throne. That's why he is doing those austerities." Indra said. He stood up and began to look around.

The guards entered and presented two nymphs to Indra. The two beautiful nymphs, wearing very thin garments, bowed to Indra. He said, "Go with Kama, the god of love. Then you will see Narada and seduce him."

(The curtain drops.)

Scene 2

(*The scene opens on the stage in a forest on Mount Kailasa. Lord Shiva is sitting there in meditation.*)

Narada came up to Shiva from the yard. He was playing his vina. Shiva opened his eyes. Narada bowed to him and sang a song, "The king of heaven noticed my penance and got frightened. He sent Kama to me. The god of love played a lot of tricks with me. His nymphs tried to seduce me. But victory was mine in the end. Their magic failed."

Lord Shiva advised him in a song, "Narada! Do not tell Vishnu what you told me. Keep this secret. Never bring it to your tongue. I beg you not to talk about your victory even if it is talked about. This is the right conduct."

(*The curtain drops.*)

Scene 3

(*The scene opens with Brahma, the four-headed god of creation, sitting in lotus posture at the center of the stage.*)

Narada came from the yard while playing his lute. He went up to the stage and bowed to Brahma. He sang to him, "Lord! The king of gods was afraid of my austerities. He wanted me to be in love with his beautiful nymphs. Kama's tricks failed. I couldn't be trapped by their magic. I refused to be seduced. Victory was mine in the end."

Brahma sang back, "O Narada! Victory and humility go together. This is the right conduct. Keep your victory a secret. Do not mention it even when it is mentioned."

(*The curtain drops.*)

Scene 4

(*The scene opens on the stage where Lord Vishnu is shown seated on a couch on the shore of the 'Khsira Sagara' or Milky Ocean.*)

Narada came from the yard playing his vina. Vishnu saw him and got up to welcome him. Narada came up and bowed to him. Vishnu sang, "Narada! You have done a great favor by visiting me. What could the god of love have done against you? You are now called the Kama Conqueror!"

Narada sang back, "Lord! This was due to your grace that I was able to defeat Kama. Otherwise who could do what I have done!" Narada bowed to him and left.

Vishnu sang, "I will destroy Narada's pride. I will plan a plot that he sees it right. Otherwise, I always show the right path to my devotees. Now I meditate on my Maya."

Vishnu sat in meditation.

In a minute, Maya appeared beside him and bowed. He sang, "O my Maya! Show some feat soon. Create a big beautiful city on Narada's route, even better than my city of Vaikuntha. Let there be beautiful and wonderful palaces, and beautiful markets. The season must be spring with gardens full of plants and flowers. Create beautiful girls and boys. Create beautiful men and women. And Maya! Let there be a king by the name of Shila Sindhu. Show him inaugurating his daughter's pompous 'svayamvara' ceremony in which men compete for her hand in marriage. That slender virgin daughter, or Sukumari by name, must be more beautiful and virtuous than even my wife Lakshmi. When Shila Sindhu happily announces the marriage competition, let many princes be present, ready to marry her." Maya bowed to him.

(*The curtain drops.*)

Scene 5

(*The scene opens on the stage with King Shila Sindhu's court. He is sitting with his beautiful daughter Sukumari on a couch, surrounded by other courtiers*)

Narada came from the yard and saw around. Then he stood in a corner and watched everyone in the king's court greeting one prince after another. Each prince bowed to the king and went behind the court. Narada left the yard.

(*The curtain drops.*)

Scene 6

(*The scene opens on the stage with Narada sitting in meditation.*)

Vishnu appeared in front of Narada. He said, "Narada! You are meditating on me. Here I am. What would you like me to do for you?"

Narada opened his eyes and bowed to him with a song, "Lord! If I have your blessing then I can marry and be happy. First, I need your kind of charming body. Then I will go to see Sukumari for her hand."

Vishnu sang, "Narada! My inerest is in your well-being. I am not lying. You do not have to ask me for a favor. If a patient is sick and does not observe the dietary rules, there would be more pain for him. Then it would be the duty of the doctor to save him as soon as possible." Having said this Vishnu disappeared. Narada looked very happy.

(*The curtain drops.*)

Scene 7

(*The scene opens on the stage with Shila Sindhu and Sukumari sitting on the couch. Princes come in, greet them, and then go behind the court as Sukumari does not ask anyone of them to sit with her. Among the other courtiers are two men, Shiva's guards, sitting beside the king.*)

Narada came in from the yard near the stage. At this time Vishnu also appeared from the other side of the yard. Narada went up and greeted the king and the princess who let him pass. Then Vishnu came up and Sukumari immediately put a garland around his neck. Vishnu sat beside her.

(*The curtain drops.*)

Scene 8

(*The scene opens on the stage with Narada and Shiva's two guardsmen in a forest.*)

One guard sang to Narada, "You saw how Sukumari ignored you and accepted Vishnu as her husband. O great sage! Have a mirror and look at your unprecedented charming face." He gave Narada a mirror.

Narada saw his face and uttered in dismay, "What? I am a monkey!" The two guards laughed loudly.

Narada cursed the two as he sang, "Hear you crooks! You ridiculed me. You will be punished for your ridicule. You committed a sin. You deceived me. Both of you will become demons." Right then Vishnu appeared there. Sukumari was standing behind him. Narada sang to him, "Lord! You made me look like a fool. You committed a sin. I will either lose my life or curse you, too." Narada walked away.

Vishnu sang back, "O great sage! Where are you going? What's the reason for your worry? Why do you look so restless?"

Narada turned back and sang in anger, "You cannot see others' prosperity. Now you need to be careful! You have sinned by resorting to deception, fraud, jealousy, greed, and animosity. With your own will you do whatever you like to do, good or bad. Whatever you do, you are not afraid. Whom would you fear? You took on the form of a prince and earned deception. This is my curse. You will be reborn as a prince. Just as I am sorry, and restless from being separated from Sukumari, you, too, will receive pain when separated from your wife, wandering in her search from forest to forest. Then the kind of face you gave me will help you."

Vishnu then said, "Let it be so." As soon as he said this, Sukumari, his Maya, who was standing behind him, disappeared. When Narada saw her disappear, he looked confused. He wiped his eyes and bowed to Vishnu, "Lord! What am I seeing? Please forgive me, O Spouse of Lakshmi! I beg you again and again, let my curse go in vain."

But Vishnu sang, "Do not repent here, Narada! I earned this curse. Whatever happened is because I willed it so. Repeat the name of Shiva, the lord of Good. He will wipe out all your sins. He will be pleased in his heart by your prayers. Nobody else is my favorite like Shiva. The devotee of Shiva will attain me. Shiva's enemy is my enemy. His enemy will go to hell. So listen to what I say. Meditate on Shiva. Live wherever you like and leave now free from my Maya, my illusive power." The lord vanished.

One of Shiva's guards sang to Narada, "O great sage! We are Shiva's guards. We are brahmins in disguise. Have mercy on us! We are your servants. Please take care of us!"

Narada sang back, "Listen, O Shiva's guards! You will be born in demon bodies, but in a good family, the family of the brahmin sage Pulastya. His son, Vishravas, will be your father. Your mother will be Keshini. You will be called Ravana and Kumbhakarna. You will have two good stepbrothers: Kubera and Vibhishana. But your power will be too fierce. It will shake the universe. You will be freed from this new life with Lord Vishnu's hands. Thus will end my curse. There will be no birth for you after that. Such will be your final position. For your salvation, there will be a way—the incarnation of Rama—just for your sake alone."

(*The curtain drops.*)

Scene 9

(*The scene opens on the stage in a forest where Ravana, Kumbhakarna, and Vibhishana are in meditation.*)

Ravana got up, standing on one leg only. He closed his eyes in meditation. After a moment, Brahma, the four-headed god of creation appeared beside them. He said, "Sons! I am pleased with your penance. You may ask for any wish you have!"

Ravana then stood on two legs and bowed to Lord Brahma. He sang, "Lord! Let me be fearless by conquering gods, demons, demigods, and semi-demons. No humans nor non-humans, not even a man or a monkey, should be able to kill me."

Brahma sang, "Let it be so! You have performed a great penance. So I will now grant you what you have wished."

Then Kumbhakarna sang, "Listen Lord! This is my request. I love to sleep. Grant my wish, kind lord, that I could sleep for six straight months."

"Let it be so! You, too, have performed a great penance. I will grant you what you asked for," Brahma sang.

Then Vibhishana said with folded palms, "My Lord! I wish to be absorbed in God's devotion and spend my life in God's service."

Brahma said, "Let it be so." Brahma vanished.

(*The curtain drops.*)

Scene 10

(*The scene opens on the stage in Ravana's court in Lanka.*)

Narada entered from the yard and went up to Ravana at his court. Ravana greeted the sage with folded palms. Narada sang, "How are you, O Lord of Lanka? How is your family? I haven't heard about you for long time. I am delighted to see you and I like your capital city."

Ravana sang back, "By your grace, O great sage, everything is going fine. Our family is hail and hearty. Your visit delights me. Gods, demons, demigods, humans, and animals must be under my power. This is the boon I have received. Now I am not afraid of anyone, animate or inanimate."

Narada challenged him in his song, "You have received this boon, but you will only be famous if you do something miraculous. All should be able to witness this show of power when you lift Mount Kailasa along with Shiva. Then you may come back to Lanka and enjoy your prosperity and material pleasures."

Ravana accepted the challenge as he sang, "O knower of God! You speak the truth. All gods must know the strength of my hands. I go right now to Mount Kailasa and bring it to Lanka."

(*The curtain drops.*)

Scene 11

(*The scene opens on the stage showing Mt. Kailasa. Shiva is sitting in the middle of the mountain with is wife Parvati.*)

Ravana entered from the yard and sang, "No warrior is equal to me in strength. Now I am going to lift Mount Kailasa and reach Lanka with it in a moment. Nowhere in the three worlds, earth, heaven, and below, is mightier than I in magical strength."

He approached the stage and slowly entered the large hole attached to the bottom of the stage. He raised his head. Suddenly the mountain shook and Parvati went in shock as she sang to Shiva, "O Lord! I am frightened. My whole body is trembling. All the trees are shaking. All the wild creatures are frightened. Who is lifting this mountain?"

Shiva sang, "Go away, you wicked boastful Ravana! You have gone crazy after receiving the boon. You want to test my power?...Now you have started crying 'alas, alas.' Your hands are crushed now. Where is your strength now?"

Ravana cried in his song, "Forgive me, forget my crime. I will leave vice and hold to virtue. Narada made fun of me. He sent me here to lift Kailasa. Save me, save me. I have taken refuge in you. Give me security, O ocean of compassion!"

Parvati heard Ravana's cries, "Lord, forgive Ravana. You are compassionate. He has learned his lesson."

"No, let him remain in this state."

"Please Lord, please Lord. Forgive this fool, O ocean of mercy!"

Ravana ran away as soon as Shiva released the pressure. Then Shiva sang to Parvati, "Uma, whenever demons commit sins, God comes as a human to destroy them and protect the innocent."

(*The curtain drops.*)

Scene 12

(*The scene opens onto Ravana's court in Lanka.*)

Ravana ordered the demon courtiers in his song, "Hear me out, O demons! The gods are my enemies. But even the god of death, Yama, is afraid of me. What do I care for humans! You go out and disturb the sacred ceremonies of the sages and devotees of the gods. Collect taxes from them if they keep practicing their religious services. Enjoy your food and drink, meat and liquor."

The demons cried out, "Yes your Majesty, we will go out."

(*The curtain drops.*)

Scene 13

(The scene opens on the stage with sages in a hermitage.)

Four sages were meditating in lotus posture. Two sages came out in the yard with a fire pot and a plate with sacred grains on it. They sat in the center and lit the fire pot. They started the yajna, the fire ritual. They began to pour the sacred grains over the pot, whispering mantras and uttering "svaha" (sacred pouring).

Then suddenly five demons entered the yard. A couple of them were drinking. One of them announced loudly, "Listen sages! Maharaja Ravana has sent us to collect taxes from you. This land belongs to him. You must leave this land if you don't hand over your taxes."

One demon went up and shook a meditating sage, "You fake! Wake up. Give us your taxes."

"What taxes? We are sadhus. Simple monks like us don't have any possessions."

"Then why the hell are you pouring ghee and grains over the fire? Give us that ghee."

The demon picked up a pot of clarified butter (ghee) which was in front of the sage.

The demon opened the pot and said, "There is no ghee in it. So you cooked up all the delicious dishes with ghee. And now you are telling me that you are simple sadhus." He shook up the sage by grabbing his topknot and yelled, "Come on, come on all of you. Give us your taxes."

Another demon said loudly kicking the plate and firewoods, "We are going to kill you all if you don't give us cash, now." He passed a clay pot to the sage who was in front of the fire pot and said, "Here is the pot. Put your taxes in it. We will be back in a minute."

Then all the demons went away. The sages assembled in their hermitage and whispered to each other. They picked up the empty pot and put it back. Each sage cut his finger and let his blood drip into the pot.

The demons returned from the yard and went up to the sages. A sage handed over the pot to a big demon and sang, "Here is our tax for your king. Tell him that when this pot is opened, his destruction will begin."

"Shut up! Give me the pot!" The big demon said and left the hermitage with the other demons. The sages also left.

(*The curtain drops.*)

Scene 14

(*The scene opens with Ravana in his court.*)

The five demons entered the court through the yard. They bowed to Ravana. He asked them, "Have you brought the taxes? What is that pot for? Where did you get it? Did you contact any sadhus?"

Then the big demon said, "Yes your Majesty, we have brought this pot from the monks. When this pot is opened, your destruction will begin."

"Who said that?" Ravana asked angrily.

"The monks, your Majesty. Do you want us—"

"No, no. Don't open it. Take it to a northern region and bury it there."

(*The curtain drops.*)

Scene 15

(*The curtain opens to a hermitage, showing sages in prayer.*)

The sages stood up and folded their palms. They sang, "Victory, victory to you Lord, leader of the gods, joy-giver to his devotees, protector of the refuge taker. Victory to the benefactor of cattle and priests, to the enemy of demons, the loving spouse of the Ocean's daughter Lakshmi."

The prayer was interrupted by a big explosive sound followed by a divine voice "O sages! Have no fear. For your good, I will assume a human body. With my parts, I will be born as four brothers in the family of King Dasharatha, the star of the royal solar dynasty. For my aid, the gods will be born as monkeys at the Rishyamuka mountain."

When the voice stopped speaking, the sages started singing again, "For the protection of the gods and the earth, the Lord does miracles. No one can understand his secret. Let the Lord who is naturally merciful and kind to the poor, do this favor."

They all exited, saying "Victory to God, victory to God, victory to God…"

(*The curtain drops.*)

Scene 16

(*The scene opens on the stage with Dasharatha's court in the city of Ayodhya.*)

A minister, Sumantra, approached Dasharatha, the king of Ayodhya, through the yard. The king looked sad on his throne. His face was down. Sumantra bowed to him and said, "Your Majesty, you look sad."

"Yes friend, I am consumed by this concern. I have reached the last quarter of my life and yet I have no son. Who will be responsible for running the kingdom?"

"Your Majesty, you need counsel. I will bring our royal teacher Vasishtha immediately."

Sumantra left the court while Dasharatha sang, "What good is your wealth, what good is your power, what good is your home if you have no child! Tell me O Creator, what wrong did I do to earn this destiny? In my old age, there is no hope for me. Help me, God…"

Sumantra entered with sage Vasishtha from the yard. The king stopped singing and bowed to his guru. Vasishtha blessed him and said, "I have heard from Sumantra. Your concern is genuine. We should arrange for a child-giving fire ritual with sage Shringi. Let us invite him."

Scene 17

(*The scene opens on the stage with a fire pit from which flames are coming up.*)

Sage Shringi was surrounded by Dasharatha's three wives, namely Kausalya, Sumitra, and Kaikeyi. The sage uttered "svaha" with the sacred mantras while pouring food over the fire pit. Then he gave some milk pudding to each queen. They ate the pudding. "You will have sons," said the sage and he left.

(*The curtain drops.*)

Scene 18

(*The scene opens on the court of Dasharatha. The king and the three queens are seated on a couch. Kausalya and Kaikeyi with one baby boy each are on the right side of the king. Sumitra with twin boys in her arms is on his left side.*)

The singers led by the drummers entered from the yard and moved toward the court. They were singing the song "Hail! Hail! Mother of the Universe." While the music was playing, Vasishtha, the royal sage, entered the yard and went upstage. The music stopped. All bowed to the royal sage. He placed his hand over the head of Kausalya's son and said, "I bless you, Rama!" Then he placed his hand over Kaikeyi's son, "I bless you, Bharata!" He went across to Sumitra's twins and placed his hand on the first boy's head, "I bless you, Lakshmana!" and then to the next boy, "I bless you, Shatrughna!"

The music started again with loud shouts of "Let's all say: Victory to Rama, Bharata, Lakshmana, Shatrughna." There were big explosive sounds and fireworks from all directions. The drummers played the dhol and damau drums in the yard with fireworks in progress. Then everyone left the yard.

(*The curtain drops.*)

Scene 19

(*The scene opens on King Janaka's court in the city of Mithila.*)

Janaka, the king of Mithila, was seated on the throne surrounded by his courtiers when a guard and a minister appeared on the stage through the yard. They bowed to the king who asked them, "What's the news?"

The minister said, "Your Majesty, it is very difficult for me to say this. There is a big drought. People do not have enough food. The astrologers say that there will be rain and food if the king himself plows the land."

"Sure, I will do so right now," the king answered.

(*The curtain drops.*)

Scene 20

(*The curtain opens with queen Sunayana and courtiers in Janaka's court, busy talking.*)

Janaka entered from one end of the yard with a pair of oxen yoked to a plow. He exited from the other end.

In a few minutes, he approached the court from the yard with a clay pot in his hands. He stood beside the queen and showed the courtiers the pot saying, "I found this clay pot in a furrow when I was plowing a field just now. Look at it!" The pot slipped from his hands and rolled down behind the floor. Suddenly, the cries of a baby were heard there.

Janaka ran to the spot where the pot was broken open with a baby in it. He called the queen with excitement and joy, "Sunayana, come over here! We have a new daughter!" The queen came across the court from behind and held the baby in her arms with tears in her eyes, "We will call her Sita which means furrow. She was found in a furrow."

There was big applause from the courtiers, "Let us say: Victory to Sita!" They all left the court. Explosive sounds or fireworks were heard from behind the court while the chorus sang "Hail, hail, hail, hail! Mother of the Universe!"

(*The curtian drops.*)

THE SECOND NIGHT
Scene 1

(*The scene opens on the stage with sage Vishvamitra in his hermitage performing the sacred fire ritual.*)

Vishvamitra and his three disciples pronounced the mantras with the words "Om" and "svaha." As they poured grains mixed with ghee in the fire pit, a rowdy noise was heard. About half a dozen demons came from the yard onto the stage. Some of them began to kick the walls and floor and some poured water over the fire. One demon, Maricha, dragged Vishvamitra off the stage. Another demon, Subahu, began to beat two disciples. Another disciple ran away while crying "Help! Help!"

Vishvamitra, followed by the fleeing disciple, reappeared on the stage. Maricha grabbed the neck of Visvamitra, "We told you again and again not to do these worships. Now say "Om" again?"

The disciple behind him tried to rescue him, but another demon grabbed him by his dhoti from behind. Another demon yelled, "Hey! Here is some ghee." All the demons went to him and began to drink ghee while spitting into the fire pit. Vishvamitra walked away with his disciples while saying, "I am going to see Dasharatha for help. This routine must stop."

(*The curtain drops.*)

Scene 2

(*The scene opens with Dasharatha in his court.*)

King Dasharatha was seated on his throne when a guard entered the stage and bowed to him, "Your Majesty, sage Vishvamitra is here. He has requested your company."

"Oh! The great sage has come to bless us. Sumantra! Please bring him in respectfully."

Sumantra descended and exited. He came back with Vishvamitra. The king and his courtiers walked to Vishvamitra and greeted him. They all sat.

Then Dasharatha said, "Your Holiness, I am honored with your presence. You must have come with a purpose."

"Yes, I need your help, Dasharatha. I am in serious trouble."

"I will do anything right away to help you. It is my privilege and duty."

"In a part of your kingdom, Maricha and Subahu bring their gangs very often. They beat us, loot the travelers, destroy our hermitages. We just cannot live in peace."

"O great sage! My army will accompany you and punish the culprits at once."

"No, I don't need your army. Your two sons, Rama and Lakshmana, are enough."

"Your Holiness! I myself can come with my soldiers, but ask not for Rama and Lakshmana. They are still boys of tender age. How can they fight those horrible devils?

Moreover, I had them in my old age after long despair. It's impossible for me to live without them. I cannot risk their lives." Dasharatha sang very slowly.

Vishvamitra sang back, "O great king! Your sons are old enough to marry. They are not ordinary boys. They are born with divine power and purpose. They are here to finish the demon terrorists. You have to give Rama and Lakshmana to me. That is the only way to protect us. And remember, I will keep teaching them as long as they are with me."

Then Vasishtha, the royal teacher, arose and said, "Dasharatha! Vishvamitra is right. Let him have Rama and Lakshmana."

"All right, guru ji, whatever you say," said Dasharatha.

(*The curtain drops.*)

Scene 3

(*The scene opens on the stage with the hermitage where Vishvamitra and his disciples are performing the fire ritual.*)

Vishvamitra and his three disciples came down with the fire pot. They sat down and started pouring holy grains over the fire uttering "Om" and "svaha" with mantras.

Rama and Lakshmana appeared from the yard and went in front of the hermitage. Then a ruckus was heard from behind the stage. The two brothers walked toward the direction of the noise and looked behind the stage. Rama said, "I see a big demoness followed by two robust demons."

"Son! That demoness is Tataka with her two boys, Maricha and Subahu. They are coming to kill us," alerted the sage, "You have to kill Tataka first."

"But Guru ji, that's a woman. It's unethical to lay hands on a woman, no matter what!" Rama said.

"You call her a woman? She has killed many innocent men, women, and children, looted their belongings, left many behind in pain with no houses for them to live. She has weapons. I know the law, never kill a woman or any unarmed person. But then this bandit queen will continue her bloody activities. You are a prince. You are representing your father. To protect the innocent from any kind of terrorist is a ruler's dharma."

Suddenly, Subahu entered and jumped on Lakshmana. Lakshmana yelled at him, pushing him back. Rama warned him, "Stop or I am going to shoot!"

Then Tataka jumped on Rama while Maricha began to drag Vishvamitra. Rama pushed Tataka aside and said, "Stop your cruel acts! Go away, never return to this place!"

She sang, "I am Tataka. I beat men like you with *tat tat* sounds of slapping and eat them alive. Once you are in front of me, you are under my warm jaws." Then she picked up her ax and ran toward Rama who killed her instantly with his arrow.

Subahu had almost killed Lakshmana with his sword. But Lakshmana shot him fatally with an arrow. Maricha challenged Rama.

Rama sang, "We are young brothers. But we are archers. You wicked insensitive enemies of the innocent! You have tortured the sages too long. Your time now is limited."

Maricha sang back, "You are boastful and stupid. You killed Tataka. What's so great about that? We demons are too powerful. Now face your death." He threw a spear at Rama, who escaped quickly and flung the demon away with an arrow. Maricha looked like he was flying up and behind the stage.

There was big applause from everywhere "Victory to Rama, victory to Lakshmana" After these repetitious applauses, Vishvamitra addressed Rama and Lakshmana, "Both of you, like your ancestors, have done a great service to dharma. Now let us go to Mithila to enjoy the svayamvara of Sita."

They all went away to see the svayamvara or marriage competition.

(*The curtain drops.*)

Scene 4

(*The scene opens on the stage with an old forest hermitage. A big rock is in the center.*)

Vishvamitra followed by Rama and Lakshmana entered the yard and moved toward the stage. They stopped near the rock.

Rama sang, "Your Holiness! Why is this rock here? What could be the reason for it?

This hermitage must have been a place for austerities. What is this shining red rock here for?"

The sage sang, "This is Gautama's wife, Ahalya. She became this rock with her husband's curse for loving Indra, who looked like Gautama. This rock needs the touch of the dust of your feet. O Rama, have mercy on her."

Rama touched the rock. Out of it came Ahalya with folded hands. She sang, "Victory to Rama! Victory to Rama! The Rama incarnation of the Lord has released me from the curse. Now I will go to heaven and will never return here. Victory to you Lord, joy-giver of all."

(*The curtain drops.*)

Scene 5

(*The scene opens with a garden on the stage and three girls singing the prayer in praise of Parvati, Mother of the Universe.*)

Rama and Lakshmana entered the yard. They looked toward the garden. When the prayer song stopped, Lakshmana sang to Rama, "O great Prince! Look at the girl in the middle who sang the prayer with her friends. She is so charming. Look at her crown so beautifully shining upon her face. How charming are her movements and looks! What could she be here for?"

Rama sang in reply, "Brother! That girl is king Janaka's daughter for whom the svayamvara will take place tomorrow. She is here with her friends to pray to Gauri, the shining Mother Goddess. The princess has brightened the garden with her radiant beauty. My mind is earnestly attracted by her out-of-this-world charm."

The princess and her friends looked at the princes intermittently. Then the brothers went away. Sita and her friends walked to the shrine at the corner. They bowed to the beautiful statue of the goddess.

Then Sita sang, "Victory, victory to the darling daughter of the king of the Himalaya mountains. Victory to the sweetheart of Shiva. Victory to the mother of Ganesha and Karttikeya, to the Mother of Universe, whose body flashes like the lightning. Mother! Even the gods do not know your beginning, middle, and end, your infinite aura. You know my wish. Let me be in his heart who is in every heart."

A divine voice came from behind the statue, "Listen O Sita! This is my true blessing. Your wish will be fulfilled."

(*The curtain drops.*)

Scene 6

(*The scene opens on Janaka's court in Mithila.*)

Janaka was seated in the middle, on his throne. He was surrounded by his courtiers and a bard. Vishvamitra, Rama, and Lakshmana went up on the stage through the yard. All bowed to the sage. The two brothers touched the feet of the king. Janaka asked the sage in his song, "O great sage! Who are these boys with you? I am eager to know about them from you. In what city were they born? What are the names of their parents? Their brows are like bows, their eyes are beautiful, crowns bright on their heads, one is tanned, the other light-skinned, tender aged. What a handsome pair!"

The sage sang back, "O King! The two boys with me are Rama and Lakshmana, King Dasharatha's sons. They are like the sun and the moon. They protected my hermitage from demons. They are here to see Rudra's bow."

"Oh yes, I am honored to have the sons of the great king, Dasharatha. Please be seated. We will show you the bow," said the king. He and a minister exited.

As the sage and the two brothers sat on the chairs provided there, suitors from different sides of the yard began to appear and move toward the center with great pomp and show.

Then a decorated cart came into the yard. It was pulled by several strong-bodied guards. Just when the cart reached the center of the yard, the king with his minister and bard came out from the other end of the yard. There was big applause when the king placed Shiva's big and beautiful bow, which he was carrying in his hands, on top of the cart. Then he went upstage and sat on his throne. Everybody was standing on the stage giving the king big applause. King Janaka asked the bard loudly, "Bard! Announce my vow out loud!"

"Yes, your Majesty," the bard said, and approached the cart.

He sang the vow, "Royal suitors! Hear the vow wholeheartedly. The gods and demons get frightened by looking at Rudra's terrible bow. Mighty kings tremble at its sight. Whoever breaks such a bow here will become famous in the three worlds and will take Sita as his bride."

Then, one by one, the suitors attempted to lift the bow. Some suitors' attempts looked humorous while some others' outrageous, but no suitor could move the bow a bit, let alone lift it. Then came Ravana. First he ridiculed the other suitors for their failure and then he boasted about his strength. Suddenly an explosion was heard. A divine voice followed it instantly, "O Ravana, your daughter in Lanka is abducted by a demon. Kumbhakarna is sleeping, Vibhishana and Meghanada are absorbed in their penances."

Right after the voice, Ravana announced, "I have to leave immediately, but I will take Sita away some other day." Then he left the yard.

When nobody was able to accomplish the feat, Janaka got up and sang in sadness, "Today I found that this earth is devoid of mighty men as no one could lift the bow. Now Sita cannot select anyone as her spouse. So friends, you all go home!"

No sooner had Janaka said this than Lakshmana got up angrily as he sang, "O King! No one says such words where any male descendant of Raghu is present. You said inappropriate words even when you knew the crown jewel of Raghu's dynasty is present here." Then he turned to Rama and sang, "If you give me your command, I can lift the cosmos in a second. My Lord, with your grace, what does this old bow mean to me? With your aura's power I can break this bow like the stick of an umbrella, my Lord. I swear by your feet, Lord, if I don't do so, I will never again touch my own bow."

Rama replied gently in his song, "Lakshmana! Do not be angry. Just listen to me. So many mighty men are seated here in shame as they could not even move the bow. Let us do what could be fruitful."

Then Vishvamitra interrupted, "Lakshmana! Just hold your patience. Rama! You get up. Break the bow of Shiva and take away Janaka's despair. The king is sad, so he said wrong words. He didn't know your manly strength."

Rama got up gracefully and bowed to Vishvamitra and Janaka, "Please give me your blessings to break the ancient bow of Shankara."

The two elders said, "We bless you, son!"

Rama majestically walked down to the cart and easily lifted the bow. He looked at Vishvamitra and Janaka and bowed to them. They both nodded their heads. Rama strung the bow and it fell down instantly into two pieces making a big explosive sound. Big applause was heard from all directions for several minutes. Sita, carrying a beautiful garland in her hands, came out from the other entrance. She was followed by her mother, Sunayana and several other maids. She raised her hands holding the garland and sang, "Lord! Accept this garland from your bride, Sita. Accept this *pan* chew to sweeten your mouth."

Rama sang back, "Place, dear Sita, this garland on my neck. Give me the *pan* chew."

Sita placed the garland around Rama's neck and gave him *pan* from a plate held by Sunayana. Rama bowed to Sunayana, touching her feet. She placed her hand on Rama's head and sang, "The mighty prince of Raghu's dynasty broke the bow. My Sita placed the garland on him. He won Sita's hand with his own valor. Friends, rejoice with this meeting!"

Everyone came down from the stage to join Rama and Sita. The other suitors stood there with folded palms. Rama touched the feet of Vishvamitra and Janaka. Lakshmana touched the feet of Rama, Sita, and Sunayana.

Janaka asked his ministers, "Friends! Please send the message to the great king of Ayodhya. Prepare for the wedding."

Then all of a sudden, from one entrance of the yard Parashu Rama entered with an ax in his hand. Janaka and Vishvamitra moved toward him and bowed to him. He blessed them by raising his hand. Sunayana and Sita followed likewise. When Sita touched his feet, he said, "Live long with fame, be married to the greatest among men." Then Janaka introduced Rama and Lakshmana to him. The two brothers touched his feet. He blessed them by saying, "Live long. May unequaled fame be yours."

After the blessings, he looked around and asked Janaka, "O King! What is the reason for this big crowd here?"

Janaka said to him very humbly and joyfully, "Your Holiness, how fortunate we are that you have honored us with your presence at this great occasion!"

"What is the occasion?" Parashu Rama asked.

"This is Sita's svayamvara," answered Janaka.

Suddenly, Parashu Rama looked at the broken bow there. He angrily asked Janaka, "Who broke my guru's bow? I am going to destroy him right away!"

"Your Holiness, please forgive me for my vow—"

Rama interrupted and sang, "Your Holiness, he who broke the bow of Shambhu is a slave of yours. Whatever order you give, I will follow it."

"Then hear me out, Rama! Whoever broke this bow is my enemy like Maharaja Sahasrabahu. Bring him out, or I will kill, like him, all these rajas and princes immediately."

No sooner had Parashu Rama said this than all the suitors ran away.

Then Lakshmana came forward and sang to Parashu Rama, "Your Holiness! We broke many bows in our childhood. You never became mad at us like this. Why are you so attached to this old bow? Please tell us the reason."

Parashu Rama became furious as he sang, "Hey, you little prince! Hold your words. You idiot! Looks like your death is near. You are stupid not to know that this is Shiva's bow. I am angry because you are talking like that!"

Lakshmana replied, "You are proud of your ax. Don't show it off. I am not afraid of it."

Vishvamitra intervened, "Your Holiness! He is only a boy. Please forgive him."

"This boy is little, but is a crook and ignorant. I told him the reason. He is too young, otherwise I would have killed him."

Rama intervened by his song, "I am the one you should be angry with, your Holiness. My name is Rama. Your name is Parashu Rama, bigger than my name with your ax. When King Janaka became helpless, I picked up the bow. It fell apart, while I was stringing it. So please give me whatever punishment you see fit."

Parashu Rama sang, "I doubt that you could have done that. But if you claim so, then here is my bow. Rama! Pick up this bow and string it. Let my doubt be destroyed. This bow came to me with God's grace. If you string it, then I will know who is God, the spouse of Lakshmi." He handed over his bow to Rama.

Rama bowed to Parashu Rama and strung the bow instantly.

Parashu Rama folded his palms, bowed to Rama and then went around Rama three times (in a clockwise or right direction). After the circumabulations, he said with folded hands, "Lord! I know now who you are. I rightfully give you back all my powers. I leave now for my mountain resort and I will never use weapons again."

Parashu Rama left the yard. There was big applause. Janaka repeated his order, "Ministers! Send the great news to the mighty king of Ayodhya. Please prepare for the wedding of Rama and Sita."

All went away.

(*The curtain drops. The chorus song "Shri Rama Chandra kripalu bhaja mana..." is sung behind the curtain.*)

THIRD NIGHT

(*The night begins early with a public procession of the bridegroom's party coming from the town in the yard. The party is led on foot by the dhol-damau drummers. They are followed by Vasishtha, Dasharatha, Sumantra, and other courtiers on horses. Rama, Bharata, Lakshmana and Shatrughna follow as the bridegrooms on horses. Other courtiers and citizens follow them on foot. Then from behind the stage comes Janaka's party in the yard to welcome Dasharatha's party; everybody in this party is on foot.*)

The drummers playing the dhol-damau led Janaka's party down to the yard to greet Dasharatha's oncoming party. The two parties faced each other with the drum music coming from both sides. Bells, gongs, conches, and horns were played. The guests were honored with garlands and flowers. The two kings and others hugged each other. The princes bowed to King Janaka who blessed them. Then the musicians of the two parties led everyone out by the decorated side gate.

Scene 1

(*The curtain opens with Rama and Sita facing each other at the altar with a fire pit in its center. They are surrounded by the two kings, queen Sunayana, priests, Vasishtha and Vishvamitra.*)

The wedding mantras from the Vedas were recited. Rama and Sita poured the holy grains in the fire pit and walked around it seven times. Each time Sita stepped on a corner stone. The seven steps were uttered by the bridegroom for the bride in the following order: First step for pleasures, second step for health, third step for wealth, fourth step for general welfare, fifth step for progeny, sixth step for the seasons, and the seventh step for friendship.

Then Lakshmana, Bharata, and Shatrughna were wedded likewise to Urmila, Mandavi, and Shrutakirti (Janaka's daughter and nieces) respectively.

Then the elders blessed each couple. Sunayana and Janaka wiped their tears as they hugged the couples. Vishvamitra blessed the brides and bridegrooms and said to Dasharatha, "O King! I take your leave. And I leave with you your two sons whom you entrusted to me." They all bowed to the sage.

(*The curtain drops.*)

Scene 2

(*The scene opens on the stage with the court of Dasharatha in Ayodhya.*)

The king asked his minister beside him, "Sumantra! What is the latest news of our kingdom?"

"Your Majesty! Like the king, like the subjects. All are happy."

"I am concerned!"

"What's the reason, your Majesty? Yes, you do look concerned."

"Sumantra! I am too old. I should now declare Rama as the crowned prince. The sooner the better. You announce my decision and let there be preparation for Rama's coronation."

"Yes, your Majesty." Sumantra went out in the yard.

(*The curtain drops.*)

Scene 3

Sumantra appeared in the center of the yard close to the audience and announced loudly, "People! Rama's coronation will take place soon. Prepare for the celebration. He repeated this proclamation at all ends of the yard. He suddenly saw Manthara, Kaikeyi's old hunchbacked maid, coming out from the other end of the yard. She sneezed a couple of times which was a bad omen. She looked at Sumantra who was walking quickly toward her. She asked him, "Dear Sumantra! Why are you in such a big hurry?"

"Rama's coronation will be soon. The king has proclaimed 'Let there be celebrations!' Please prepare for it."

"Yes, I will have my own magic for the celebration." Manthara said this and went in the other direction. Sumantra went away in the other direction.

Scene 4

(The curtain opens with Kaikeyi in her palace.)

Manthara entered and bowed to Kaikeyi who was on her couch. The queen sang, "My dear Manthara! You look sad. What's the reason? Did somebody say something bad to you? Yesterday you were so happy. You are my dear maid."

"O Queen! A big celebration will take place in every home. Rama is going to get the throne. I am your dear friend." Manthara sang back.

"You are indeed my dear friend. We are fortunate, very fortunate for this news. Here is my gift for you. This necklace of mine is yours." As Kaikeyi sang this, she gave her the necklace.

But Manthara handed the necklace back to her and sang, "What will I do with your necklace, O Queen! Please take your necklace back. I am your dear friend."

Kaikeyi said to her, "Yes, you are my dear friend."

"Then listen, O Queen! You are forgetting. Soon Rama will rule. That's what the king has decided. Bharata will have trouble. He will not get the capital. You simply like your couch and sleeping is your favorite thing to do. And your son has gone away, out of the country." Manthara sang.

"Rama will rule. What's the harm in that? This is the royal family tradition. The king has considered this to be the right thing. Don't talk foolish. Your words feel like arrows. Get out you foul-mouth! Rama and Bharata are both dear to me. If you speak harshly again, I will have your tongue removed." Kaikeyi sang this in an upset tone of voice.

"Please forgive me. I made a slip. I am unable to bear your loss. I said this in your interest. If Rama rules, dear Queen, you will be ignored." Manthara sang back.

"In the name of Bharata, tell the truth with no deception. Tell me the reason. You are expressing disgust at a time of delight." Kaikeyi inquired in song.

"Dear Queen! Why do you ask me? You don't know what's happening even now. Even animals understand their gains and losses. I lose nothing, no matter who becomes the king. I don't become a queen instead of a maid. But placing the royal mark on Rama's head is sowing the seed of your misery." Manthara sang.

"All right. I understand now. Tell me what I should do," asked Kaikeyi.

Manthara answered in her song, "You remember, long ago the king wanted to fulfill any two wishes of yours. You asked him to wait until some time in the future. Now is the time. First, go sulk in your palace, then ask him to grant you two wishes. Let Bharata be king and have Rama go to the forest for fourteen years."

(*The curtain drops.*)

Scene 5

(*The curtain opens with Kaikeyi sitting on her bed.*)

Dasharatha entered the chamber. But Kaikeyi looked the other way without greeting him. He sat beside her and sang, "O my beloved! You have a beautiful face, beautiful eyes, and a beautiful voice like that of a cuckoo. Your walk is so graceful. Why are you angry? Tell me the reason."

But no response came from her. The king sang again, "Dear! Why are you sitting so upset? I am wondering whether someone put a spell on you. Your anxiety causes me pain, like that of a fish without water.

Did someone speak foul, or taunt you? Tell me frankly, did someone take away something? I swear by Rama. I am at your service. It's yours—whatever you ask for. Trust me. Ask for anything."

Now Kaikeyi opened her mouth as she sang, "Dear! You just say 'ask for anything,' but you never give or take. You said I could ask for two wishes. I doubt I will get them."

The king laughed and sang, "Now I understand the secret. Look, I forget. That is my nature. But do not accuse me. Ask not for two, but for four wishes. This always has been the tradition of Raghu's dynasty: Lose your life but not your word."

"If so, then these are my two favorite wishes: Give Bharata the throne. And send Rama to the forest for fourteen years."

When Dasharatha heard her song, he looked stunned and sad. Then he sang, "Rama and Bharata are my two eyes. I swear by God. Until now, you always said that you loved Rama. What evil intent has entered your heart now? Certainly, I will send the messenger to bring back Bharata and Shatrughna. Let your son be the ruler. But I say, let Rama stay home. I will not survive without Rama. You know my nature."

"You may try to persuade me countless times. But your magic will not work. You do exactly what I asked for, or I will die. Know what defamation would be yours." She sang this in a very firm tone. Dasharatha fainted and dropped on the bed.

Then suddenly Rama appeared there from the side entrance and saw his father in that condition. He bowed to Kaikeyi and asked her in his song, "Mother! Why is Father in shock? Please tell me. Did I do something wrong? I am terribly sorry to see Father in this condition. Please forgive me if I committed any mistake. Whatever is the cause of his unhappiness, please eliminate that."

Kaikeyi replied in her song, "There is no such reason for him to be angry. But you must know how sad he is for you. Listen! The king had granted me two wishes long ago. Today I asked him to fulfill them: give forest exile to Rama and the throne to Bharata. The king is lying unconscious because of his love for you, for dharma. If you really want to accept his sentence, you may do so."

Rama sang back at once, "Mother! Fortunate is a son who obeys his mother and father. Unfortunate is that son who does not obey them. Mother! By obeying your order, I am going to make my life successful."

Kaikeyi sang again, "I told you that there is no other reason, but I explained to you. It is not possible for you to be at fault. Listen Rama! You must convince your father in every way. Tell him clearly that you will observe his words. Let there be no infamy for him in his life's last quarter."

Rama touched his father's feet and sang, "Dear Father! Please pardon me for my arrogance. I am just a boy, so forgive any impropriety on my part. You are sad for such a little thing. Why didn't you tell me before? I am delighted to follow your order."

(*The curtain drops.*)

Scene 6

(*The scene opens with Rama sitting on a couch in his chamber.*)

Sita appeared from the side entrance and greeted Rama. He simply nodded and signaled to her with his hand to sit down beside him.

Sita sat and sang, "My Lord! Why are you so serious? Do you have a tough job to do? The priests have already fixed the time for your royal anointment. But you don't appear to be joyful. What happened, my lord?"

Rama waited for a few moments and then sang, "Listen, O Sita! My dear father has ordered my anointment for my forest dwelling. Long ago Mother Kaikeyi was to have her two wishes granted by him. So he has decided to implement them. I will live in the woods for fourteen years and Bharata will have all the royal work. Please live here in comforts and never cause any discomfort to anyone."

Sita sang softly, "What are you saying, my lord? Your words rend my heart. I can't hold my tears. I will go with you in the woods. I will step ahead of you crushing the thorns on your path." Rama covered his eyes when he heard Sita's determination.

Then Kausalya appeared there from the side entrance. She sang, "I am so happy, dear Rama! When is the auspicious time for coronation? Eat something and have a good drink before you find out. Let my hope come to fruition."

Then Rama sang to her, "Father has awarded me the rule of the jungle. There I will have more important work to do. This is my destiny, Ma. Give me your permission with a happy heart. I have eaten here so long. Now is my time to live in the fierce forest."

"But, son, you are so dear to your father. He becomes happy at your every move. That is why he announced the auspicious occasion. But tell me what went wrong?" Kausalya asked him in her song.

Rama replied in his song, "Mother Kaikeyi asked Father for two wishes. Royal throne for Bharata, jungle exile for me. This is great for me. I will see sages performing penances there. Give me your permission to make my life fruitful. I will come back after fourteen years."

"Alas! The movement of karma cannot be stopped, no matter what. While announcing the coronation, he granted her two wishes. Fortunate is the forest. Unfortunate is Ayodhya when you leave Raghu's rule. O my beloved Kaikeyi! What will you show next? My fate spoiled my life. Where is happiness for me now? The king has rewarded me with the rank of a beggar. I had only Rama as my helper. He has separated me from him, too." Kausalya sang as she kept wiping her tears.

Rama put his arms on her shoulder and sang, "Pleasure and pain, loss and gain are written, and cannot be erased. Think like this. This was written for me in my destiny. There will be great happiness for me in the forest. Listen, Ma! Don't cry."

(*The curtain drops.*)

Scene 7

(*The scene opens in Rama's chamber with Rama alone.*)

Lakshmana appeared from the side entrance and bowed to Rama. He immediately sang, "Listen, Brother! Father is too old. He was just saving face. Alas! How could he give Kaikeyi her wishes? Why couldn't he see Rama as the joy of the Raghu family? How will Rama live among the animals of the jungle? Father didn't observe the tradition of the family."

"Lakshmana! You know all the rules. This was written in my destiny. How could our parents be blamed? Just think a little with your heart. It is our dharma to obey our father. This is considered the best conduct in the scriptures." Rama sang to him with a soft voice.

"Father gave you exile, O Ruler of the Raghus, out of his womanly love. You rule with no obstacles. I will sit here with my bow. Think of my helpless sister-in-law and think of Kaikeyi, our father's beloved. I will kill all of them in a moment. My words will not be worthless. Even if Dasharatha, our father, turns out to be a troublemaker, I do not see any wrong to send him to heaven." Lakshmana sang in a very terse tone.

"Do not blame it on Father. Forgive him, forgive me. Our job is to be pleasant to him. What is destined to me will not go elsewhere. This is my understanding that you should listen to me, please." Rama sang again in a gentle voice.

"Listen, my lord! I am your servant. There is no livelihood for me without you. I do not know any teacher or mother or father. Lord! You know my nature. They gave you forest living. Why wouldn't I feel pain when I hear this? I will go with you, my brother. I am going with you. What will I do here in Ayodhya? Without you, all places are empty. You will suffer alone in the forest. You should agree with me about this, my life-bearer! Sita is my mother and you are my father. I will go with you." Lakshmana sang back.

"Look, Lakshmana! Our brother Bharata is not even here in Ayodhya. Brother Shatrughna has also gone with him. Father is already sad with his own pain and then the public, too, will be sad. There will be a disturbance in Ayodhya. How will I find comfort in this?" Rama sang.

"Lord! You have to take me with you. This servant is the master of your feet. Where they go, there goes this servant. If you leave him behind, he will die." Lakshmana sang.

"Lakshmana! You must talk to your mother Sumitra and wife Urmila," Rama said.

"My lord! I will convince them. I am going with you," said Lakshmana.

(*The curtain drops.*)

FOURTH NIGHT
Scene 1

(*The scene opens in Kaikeyi's chamber. Dasharatha is lying on the bed. Kaikeyi is sitting beside him. Kausalya and Sumitra are seated on the other side of the bed.*)

Rama, Lakshmana, and Sita led by Vasishtha entered the chamber from the side entrance. All greeted each other. Other men and women began to pour into the yard near the stage.

Dasharatha sang after being blessed by Vasishtha, "Alas! What has destiny done to me! Everything is upside down. The day for construction turned into destruction. Here is the forest for Rama and Lakshmana and there goes my beloved Sita with them."

Then Rama said in his song, "Father! Give me your blessings. At the time of joy, please do not be dismayed. I will prove your word. I am ready to leave. This is definite. If you will not let me go, dharma will not be served and you will be left in shame."

Kaikeyi got up and handed Rama a package of clothes while saying, "Rama! If you don't wish to go to the forest, the throne is yours. Otherwise, put on these garments of forest dwellers."

Rama said, "Mother! Undoubtedly we are going to the forest."

Then Rama and Lakshmana started to put on the garments. Sita asked Rama for her garments, which he gave her. She tried again and again, yet failed to wrap the garments around her body. She asked Rama, "How do ascetics wrap these garments?" She broke down in tears. The other women were crying, some covering their faces or wiping their tears. Some were heard saying "Dear Rama! Sita does not deserve this exile nor these mendicant's garments" or "Let her stay home."

Then Rama began to wrap the garments around her body.

As Vasishtha watched Rama helping Sita, he cursed Kaikeyi, "Kaikeyi! O you stupid Kaikeyi! You are a disgrace to this royal family. You deceived the king. You have not stayed within your domain. You immoral woman! Lady Sita ought not to go to the forest. She will sit on the throne of Rama. A wife is the soul of her husband's body. Sita as the soul of Rama should rule his territory. Or we should all go with her. Even Bharata and Shatrughna will go and serve their brother Rama in the forest. Then you can live and rule this territory by yourself with nobody by your side. Kaikeyi! Do not force Sita. You did not ask the king for her exile. He exiled only Rama."

People began to shout loudly "Shame on the king" or "Shame to Dasharatha."

Then Dasharatha sat up and spoke with a deep sigh, "Kaikeyi! Sita does not deserve ascetics' garments to go to the forest. Our teacher Vasishtha is right. You fallen woman! What wrong has this soft sinless Sita done to you?" He leaned back on the bed.

Rama went quickly to his father's side and said, "Father! We now leave for the forest. Sir! My great mother Kausalya is old now. She never complained about you. You must live well so that she could bear my absence." Dasharatha fell flat on the bed.

Sita and Lakshmana came forward and with Rama they touched the king's feet. Then they bowed to all and moved down to the yard where people were standing. People were heard shouting, "Shame, shame" etc.

Then Rama raised his hands and sang, "Farewell, men and women!" Sita sang the next sentence, "May all of you here live happily." Lakshmana sang the last sentence, "Please do not be sad." They turned around and repeated their farewell sentences again and again until they left the crowd behind.

(*The curtain drops.*)

Scene 2

(*The curtain opens with a boat, partially sunken in the back and surrounded by boatmen. A chariot appears in the yard beside the stage.*)

Sumantra, Rama, Sita, and Lakshmana got out of the chariot and approached the boatmen. The leader of the boatmen, Kevata, greeted them.

Rama sang to Kevata, "O Nishada Raja Guha! We have to cross the Ganges. From there we will leave for the forest. My father has given us a fourteen-year exile. I have nothing to offer you for favor, except this ring." Rama offered him the ring.

But Kevata sang back, "No, my lord! I cannot take you across the Ganges right away. First, I have to wash your feet. Otherwise, my boat would go to heaven. That's the effect of your feet's dust. Without my boat I will be helpless."

Kevata washed Rama's feet. Rama hugged him. Then he sang to Sumantra, "Sumantra! Now you can return. Take the chariot back. Tell Father 'You did your dharma.' Tell Bharata 'Take care of the honor of the Raghu family. Rule by the law.' Tell my mother 'Do not ponder over this. Keep people happy.' This is Rama's request."

Sumantra said, "My lord! I cannot go back without you."

"No, no! Sumantra! You have to go back and tell my message to everyone."

Sumantra wiped his tears and bowed to each of them. He returned to the chariot and went away.

Guha (Kevata) led the trio toward the boat. Lakshmana escorted Sita. All four sat on the boat.

Then Sita sang, "O Mother Ganga! This is my prayer for you, with folded hands. Victory to you, victory be yours always. May Rama fulfill the promise to his father. May we all offer you worship. Victory to you, victory be yours always, Mother, destroyer of sins."

(*The curtain drops.*)

Scene 3

(*The scene opens on the stage with Rama, Sita, and Lakshmana in a forest.*)

Sita said to Rama, "Lord! This forest is so beautiful. But the sun is too hot. I am tired of walking. My feet have blisters. Is there some water to drink?"

Rama said to Lakshmana, "Lakshmana! Sita is thirsty. Could you look around for fresh water?"

"Yes, my lord! I go to fetch water."

Lakshmana came down the yard and sang, "Can anybody tell me where to find fresh water? Sita is thirsty. What a reversal of destiny! Such a great princess desperate for water! Can anybody tell me where to find fresh water? Sita is thirsty."

Lakshmana went far in a corner and struck a hole in the ground with his arrow. He placed his pitcher over the hole and filled it with water. He brought it back to Sita. The trio came down the yard and walked away.

(*The curtain drops.*)

Scene 4

(*The curtain opens with the hermitage of sage Bharadvaja with his two disciples.*)

Rama, Sita, and Lakshmana entered the yard. They went up to the hermitage and bowed to the hermits. Bharadvaja blessed them by placing his right hand on their heads and sang, "Rama! The hermits are very fortunate to see you here. Please give us an opportunity to serve your feet. Please stay here."

Rama sang, "Your Holiness! You are gracious. You have given us honor with your kind words. We are your servants. But we have to move ahead. Please tell us where to make our own cottage."

Bharadvaja replied, "Rama! These two disciples will take you to Chitrakuta hill."

The two disciples and the trio came down and exited from the yard entrance.

(*The curtain drops.*)

Scene 5

(*The curtain opens on the hermitage of sage Valmiki.*)

The trio entered the yard and went up to the hermitage. The three bowed to the sage. Valmiki sang, "Listen, Rama! How have you come here? You are so soft and so is Sita. This forest is tough and frightening. Why are you roaming on foot? Tell me the reason, O Banner of Raghu's family!"

Rama sang in reply, "O lord of the sages! You are the seer of all the ages. The world is like a berry in your hand. With my father's words, we left home for the woods. Thus a meeting with you became possible. Kaikeyi devised this plan: The throne for Bharata and the woods for us. I will build a cottage here. So I could live here for some time, O abode of kindness!"

Valmiki sang, "Don't say this, O lord of Raghu's family! You are the protector and joy-giver to the saints. Make Chitrakuta hill your residence. Things will be easily available for you there." They bowed to the sage.

(*The curtain drops.*)

Scene 6

(*The scene shows Sumantra walking from the far corner toward the yard.*)

Sumantra came in the yard and sang, "How do I show my face in Ayodhya? What do I say when the king asks me? Things went wrong just when they were going so well. What happened in no time! What control does one have over destiny! Rama, Sita, and Lakshmana went to the jungle with me and I came back home. Why doesn't my life leave me?" He moved slowly toward the stage.

(*The curtain opens on the court of Dasharatha who is lying on a bed, surrounded by his three queens and Vasishtha.*)

Sumantra walked up to the court and bowed to all. Dasharatha sang, "Dear Friend! Tell us about Rama's well-being. Where are Rama, Lakshmana, Sita? Did you bring them back or see them off in the forest? Tell me quickly, son, what path they took. At the time of coronation, I pronounced forest-exile. And they were not upset at all upon hearing that. My life didn't leave me at their departure. Who could be a dumb sinner like me!"

Sumantra sang back wiping his tears, "The first day, we camped on the bank of the Tamasa. The second day, on the bank of the Ganges. There Guha did great service, brought the boat for crossing. Rama saw that I was overwhelmed. With firm control, he said sweetly to me 'Offer my respects to Father. I touch his lotus-like feet again and again—'"

Dasharatha interrupted, "Alas! Rama! Alas Rama! Listen, O Kausalya! Long ago, there lived an old blind couple. Their obedient son Shravana went to the banks of a river to bring water for his blind parents. I, from a distance, mistook him for a deer and shot him dead. Then I informed his parents. They put a curse on me 'Like us, you will die at the separation of your beloved son.' They died. Now I go, Kausalya!"

Dasharatha's cries were heard as he died: "Alas Rama! Alas Rama!" Everyone wept.

(*The curtain drops.*)

FIFTH NIGHT
Scene 1

(*The scene opens with Kaikeyi in her chamber.*)

Bharata and Shatrughna entered the chamber from the side entrance. They bowed to the queen. She hugged both of them. Bharata looked sad with his head down. Kaikeyi sang, "O Bharata, my son! You are dearer to me than my life. Why are you sad? Is everything fine in my parents' country? Tell me quickly. I am concerned."

Bharata sang, "All is well in your parents' home. Tell me what's well in my home. Where is Father? Where are the other mothers? Where are Rama, Sita, Lakshmana?"

"Son! I have taken care of everything. Poor Manthara became a helper. Something went wrong in the middle due to destiny. The king placed his feet in heaven—"

As Bharata heard this, he fell down on the floor while uttering, "Alas Father! Alas Father! Why wasn't I here with Rama? Mother! What was Father's sickness? Tell me. What was the cause of his death?"

Kaikeyi attempted to lift Bharata as she sang, "Listen, dear Bharata! Get rid of your sadness. I have arranged the coronation for you. Rama went to the forest for fourteen years. Sita and Lakshmana joined them. The king took the pain on himself. Now compose yourself and take care of the kingdom. Everything is done by destiny."

Bharata got up and sang, "I am leaving your kingdom. You sent Rama, Sita, and Lakshmana to the forest and gave me the kingdom!"

Kaikeyi sang back, "I became a widow for your good and denigrated my face. Now you, too, accuse me. Karma is hard. It's not your fault."

Bharata sang, "Why did you let Rama, Sita, and Lakshmana go to the forest? O Mother! What a horrible sin you have committed! You have put a blot on our family. You sent Rama, Sita, and Lakshmana to the forest. You gave pain to the entire family. Now I will be a beggar and join them."

Just when he was about to go out, Manthara entered the chamber. Shatrughna kicked her as he sang, "Get out of here. Where did you come from, O heartless woman? You have set our entire family on fire. And now my brothers have become beggars."

(*The curtain drops.*)

Scene 2

(*The scene opens onto Kausalya's chamber. Kausalya is seated on a couch.*)

Bharata and Shatrughna entered the chamber from the side entrance. They touched her feet. She blessed both of them. Bharata sang, "Mother! When will I see my father? Where are Rama and Sita in the forest? Could anyone in the whole world be more unfortunate than I? I am the cause of this misfortune."

Kausalya sang, "Rama abandoned his royal outfit by his father's order. He went to the woods with immense joy. Bharata, listen! Compose yourself and abandon pain. Follow the elders' orders. Rule and take care of the people."

Bharata sang back, "Listen, Mother! I beg you with folded hands. There is no life for me without Rama. Rama, Lakshmana, and Sita, clad in ascetics' garments with no shoes, are roaming in the forest."

Vasishtha entered the chamber from the side entrance. All greeted him with bows. He blessed them with his raised hand. Bharata said to him, "Sir, I have decided to go with Rama."

Vasishtha sang, "Let us perform funeral rites for the king. Do not grieve. Loss and gain, birth and death, fame and shame—all of them in the hands of destiny. Thereafter we will all go to meet Rama."

(*The curtain drops.*)

Scene 3

(*The scene opens on the stage with Rama, Sita, and Lakshmana in Chitrakuta cottage.*)

Sita sang, "My lord! Last night I had a dream, somewhat sad, somewhat joyful. A big team with Bharata came here, all looking grim due to my lord's separation. Among all the unhappy men and women I saw my mother-in-law, so miserable in mind and body."

Rama sang, "Lakshmana! This dream does not look good. It does not look like a good move. What could be the reason for Bharata's coming here? I do not know what plan he has in mind. This is my concern."

Lakshmana sang, "You, all-knower, are the crown jewel among all. My understanding follows yours. But you are guileless by nature. You don't understand Bharata's crookedness. Having devised a cunning move with his troops, he is coming here to make his rule thornless. But allow me to foil his plans. I will destroy Bharata along with the other brother and their army like a crop in the field.

Rama sang, "Listen my dear Lakshmana! There is no better brother than Bharata that I have ever heard of or seen in the whole world. I swear by you and Father. There isn't a clean and good brother like Bharata anywhere."

They saw from the far corner an approaching team headed by Bharata and Shatrughna. Both dressed as monks. They reached the yard near the cottage. The trio came down to greet the team. The brothers embraced each other and cried. Rama, Sita, and Lakshmana touched the feet of all the mothers and Vasishtha. All embraced each other. Sumantra and Guha bowed to the trio and cried.

Rama sang, "Bharata! Tell me how is our father as I don't see him here. I have great concern for him."

Bharata replied in his song wiping his tears, "Lord! How do I say this! Listen! Father abandoned his life with your separation."

Rama bent his head down and covered his eyes. Lakshmana wept.

Kausalya sang, "Rama! Listen! Your father went to heaven. Destiny has given us a tough time. Your father died and here I am alive. So many misfortunes did destiny give us. Who knows what it has planned next!"

Rama raised his head and sang, "Alas! What the Creator has done to us! So many misfortunes dropped at once: father to heaven, exile for us, destruction in Ayodhya. My heart breaks when I see my mother's condition. This is my family's total destruction."

Then Vasishtha sang, "Listen, Rama! You are the knower of all. Have courage as you are the store of all virtues. Son! You are in everyone's heart. You understand things that are well or ill in intention. Listen to what the people and mothers with Bharata have to offer as a solution."

Rama sang, "O Lord of the sages! I hear your words of good intention. I act with your hands. Whatever your order is for me, I will follow that wholeheartedly."

Then Vasishtha turned to Bharata and sang, "Listen, Bharata! Don't hesitate. Ask for what you have thought in your mind. Speak your heart to Rama, the ocean of kindness. Whatever Rama's order, you must follow that in its entirety. This is my opinion."

Rama sang to Bharata, "Listen, Bharata! Whatever your heart's desire, let me fulfill it, Brother! Do not be sad. Compose yourself. Utter those words that could save dharma. And then our teacher has commanded me that I must do what you wish."

Bharata sang, "Lord! You are asking me when you already know the hearts of all, O ocean of kindness! Please, O ocean of kindness, do what is good for me. Then I will have no regrets."

Rama sang back, "My dear Bharata! You are an authority on dharma. You understand the tradition, the laws, and the scriptures. I have full trust in you. Nevertheless, say what suits you."

Bharata humbly sang, "Lord! This is my humble request. Please accept it accordingly. We two brothers will go into the wilderness. You will return to Ayodhya."

Rama sang, "If I forego my father's words and return to Ayodhya then dharma will not be served and I will earn shame. My time of exile will pass soon and then I will return. Think like this and take care of the family and Ayodhya."

"No my lord! I cannot sit on the throne. My job is to serve at your feet."

"Here, take my sandals with you. You can keep them on the throne. Now I urge you all to return."

Bharata accepted the sandals.

(*The curtain drops.*)

Scene 4

(*The scene opens with sage Atri and his wife Anasuya in their hermitage.*)

Rama, Sita, and Lakshmana entered the yard and went up to bow to the hermit couple. Atri offered them water and Anasuya served fruits on leaf plates.

After breakfast, Anasuya sang to Sita, "Dear Sita! This is the dharma of a wife. Never think of any other man. The woman who cheats on her husband goes to hell for long time. In her next life, such a woman becomes a widow in her young age." Then she offered Sita a necklace. Sita touched Anasuya's feet and accepted the necklace.

(*The curtain drops.*)

Scene 5

(*The scene opens on the stage with sage Sutikshana in his hermitage.*)

Rama, Sita, and Lakshmana came up from the yard and bowed to the sage. He said, "I am very grateful that you came here. Please let me know what service I can offer to you, Lord!" He offered water and fruits as he said this.

Then Rama said, "O great sage! We are very fortunate to meet sages like you. We want to visit other sages, too."

"My lord! Very near here is the hermitage of sage Agastya. I will show you how to get there." They all walked out.

(*The curtain drops.*)

SIXTH NIGHT
Scene 1

(*The scene opens onto Panchavati in a new cottage. Rama, Sita, and Lakshmana are busy working separately.*)

Shurpanakha entered the yard and walked up to Rama. She sang, "Wonderful! There is no man like you and no woman like me. Destiny made our contact with understanding. The man fit for me is none else, not even if I search in the three worlds. This is why I remained a virgin up to this day. My heart feels like that having seen you."

Rama sang back to her, "O Beauty! Listen to my words! Over there is my younger brother, Lakshmana. No sooner would he see a charming beauty like you than would he propose to you, dear!"

She went to Lakshmana and sang, "My lord! Accept me, accept me. I am so charming. Please accept me. I am Ravana's sister."

He sang back, "Listen, O beautiful woman! I am Rama's servant. You met him just now. He is the mighty lord of Ayodhya. He can do whatever he feels fit. He is the gem of Raghu's family. He may accept you. Listen, O Beauty! You are fit for him."

She went to Rama and sang, "Even the shining moon felt ashamed and hid himself when he saw my beauty. Indra was enchanted and sages felt hot when they saw me. But what can I do, dear Rama, my mind is lost upon you. Make me your wife soon. Without you my heart is sinking."

Rama sang, "Listen, O beautiful lady! Why have you come back to me? Go, Lakshmana will accept you. He will again see your exquisite beauty and propose to you immediately now. I already have a wife, Sita, over there. For this reason I will not propose to you."

She went singing toward Lakshmana, "Look boys! Who is more beautiful than I in this world? My brother is Ravana. And also Khara, Dushana, and Trishira with him. Lanka is all golden."

Lakshmana sang, "Listen, O beautiful woman! Over there is my dear lord, Rama. You are not speaking words with right thought. You look like an evil demoness. If you come back to me again, I will put you to shame."

She became furious and said, "I will go to your lord and kill his woman." Lakshmana saw Rama signaling to him. He cut the tip of Shurpanakha's nose with the blade of his arrow.

She ran away crying.

(*The curtain drops.*)

Scene 2

(*The scene opens on the stage with Khara, Dushana, and Trishira in their court.*)

Shurpanakha entered the yard crying and went to the court. She sang, "Brother, Brother! Help, help! My nose is cut. I was sightseeing in a forest. I met Rama and his beautiful wife Sita there. His brother Lakshmana cut my nose. It's your dishonor, brothers!"

Dushana sang in anger, "Your nose is cut. Your face is all blood-soaked. Dear sister! I will give them a taste of this insult."

(*The curtain drops.*)

Scene 3

(*The scene opens with Rama, Sita, and Lakshmana in their cottage.*)

Several demons entered the yard with Khara, Dushana, Trishira, and Shurpanakha and marched toward the cottage. Then Khara stopped and sang to Dushana, "Tell the brothers this: 'Hand over your woman if you wish to live.'"

Dushana went up and sang to Rama, "Khara saw you and with his kindness has sent you this message 'Hand over your woman to us and we will let you live.'"

Rama sang, "Today, it is your good fortune that your master thought so. We are Kshatriyas and have come to this forest to hunt. Come for a battle and show your skills. Pity on an enemy is great timidity."

Dushana returned to Khara and told him what Rama had said. Khara sang, "March on my young fighters! Take out the swords from your waists and hit them hard! Strike them with your spears, lances, maces, and arrows!"

The demons attacked Rama and Lakshmana. After a brief battle on the stage and in the yard, Rama and Lakshmana killed all the demons. Then Shurpanakha ran away from the yard.

(*The curtain drops.*)

Scene 4

(*The scene opens on Ravana's court.*)

Shurpanakha came from the yard and went up to Ravana. She sang while crying, "Brother! Alas! My nose is cut. I went to a forest for sightseeing. There I met Rama. He had Lakshmana cut my nose."

Ravana sang, "Dear Sister! Tell me quickly who these low men are. They don't know someone like Ravana."

She sang, "These are the sons of Dasharatha, the king of Ayodhya. They are like lions who have come in the forest to hunt. Khara and Dushana and Trishira heard my plight. They went to kill the two brothers. But my brothers and our entire force have been slain. Those brothers have a beautiful woman, very suitable for you, Brother!"

Ravana sang, "They killed my brothers. Now, Sister, you see my valor. I will take full revenge."

Then he addressed Maricha with his song, "Listen, Maricha! Come with me. We will go where the two men of Ayodhya are living. You will become a deer in disguise to lure them out. And then I will carry their woman away."

Maricha sang, "Listen, O Ravana! Those you call men and woman are the rulers of the universe. Rama is the loving lord of Lakshmi. He is everywhere. Do not become their enemy. Do not earn infamy by fighting them. Those two youngsters went to protect the worship of the sages. They hit me with an arrow there and I fell thousands of miles away here. There is no happiness in being their enemy. Think rightly with all your attention. Why are you going to kidnap another's wife?"

Ravana sang angrily, "How do you dare give me a sermon? Is there anybody anywhere as brave as I am? Come with me or I will kill you. Are you stupid, trying to give me wisdom?"

Maricha said, "Brother! If I have to die, then it is better that I die there. Let me be killed with God's hand and fulfill your wish."

(*The curtain drops.*)

Scene 5

(The scene opens on Rama, Sita, and Lakshmana in their cottage.)

A gold-skinned deer passed near the cottage in the yard. Sita saw it and sang, "Listen, my lord Rama! This deer skin is beautiful. Catch this deer. I want to see whether it is skin or gold."

Rama got up and said, "All right. Listen, Lakshmana! Demons roam in this forest. Take care of Sita and I will hunt the deer."

Rama came down and began to chase the deer. They both disappeared.

Then a voice "Alas Lakshmana!" was heard by Sita and Lakshmana. Sita sang to Lakshmana, "You heard this voice. I know your brother is in trouble. He may be surrounded by demons. Go help him quickly!"

Lakshmana sang, "He, by whose one wink the cosmos is dissolved, cannot be in trouble, not even in a dream. The Raghu's lord has entrusted you to me. Won't I be blamed for leaving you alone here?"

Sita said, "Lakshmana! I have understood your intention. There is some insincerity in your mind. You want harm to your brother."

Lakshmana said, "Mother! Definitely some harm is about to happen. Otherwise, why would you say such words! Sure, I will go now. But do not cross this line."

Lakshmana quickly drew a line in front of the door and left the cottage.

Moments later, Ravana dressed as a monk appeared in the yard. He sang, "To see the unseen, sing god's praise. We do this, so we are called monks and saints. We spend our lives in doing selfless deeds. Devoid of lust and anger, we smear our bodies with ashes."

Ravana moved toward the door of the cottage and sang, "A jogi is waiting here at the door! I have been hungry and thirsty for a long time. Now I am waiting here!"

Sita came out at the door and sang, "O Yogi! Here, take alms. I have brought this for you. We are forest-dwellers. All we have are roots and fruits."

Ravana replied, "O beautiful lady! I cannot accept these alms bound by this line here. Please step over the line and give me the alms."

Sita crossed the line and offered him alms. He grabbed the corner of her garment and dragged her further out. Then he sang to the screaming Sita, "O Sita! Do not be dismayed. Listen! I am Ravana, the king of demons. Lanka is my residence. You will now go with me. Do not be afraid. All my queens including Mandodari will accept you as their head queen. This cottage does not fit your status. You will live in my huge palace."

Sita sang back, "You fool, bragging in vain about your power. You saw me alone and spoke words of deception. Get out of here, you sinner! Do not touch my garments. You will suffer consequences after my lord returns."

Ravana angrily sang, "There is nobody like me in this world. There is no stopping my power. You are talking of ordinary people. You have no idea of my strength. I will devour your husband, won't even drink a drop of water to swallow his flesh."

He lifted Sita on his shoulder. She cried and sang, "O Lord! King of Ayodhya! Due to what fault of mine have you forgotten kindness? You are the destroyer of the pain of whoever takes refuge in you, O sun of the lotus of Raghu's dynasty! Alas Lakshmana! This is not your fault. I received the fruit of my anger towards you. Is anybody out there? Tell my lord about my plight. Request him to take care of me quickly."

Ravana took Sita away from the cottage and entered the yard. Suddenly from the other corner came Jatayu the eagle. He heard Sita's cries and attacked Ravana. After a brief fight, Ravana cut Jatayu's feathers and left him wounded on the ground. He ran away with Sita. Jatayu cried "Rama, Rama" in painful voice and slowly moved inside.

(*The curtain drops.*)

Scene 6

(*The scene shows a forest on the stage with Rama and Lakshmana.*)

Rama sang, "O Brother! You left Sita alone and came here taking my words in jest. Demons are near, they roam in the forest. My guess is Sita isn't there."

Lakshmana sang back, "Lord! This is not my fault. Mother Sita said to me in anger 'Your brother is in trouble. Lakshmana, go quickly, be with him.' Tell me whom I should obey! Mother Sita is there. You, my brother, are here."

Rama sang, "Brother! I was deceived. It was Maricha in the form of the deer. 'Alas Lakshmana, help me'. Thus he uttered these words loudly."

Lakshmana sang, "Yes, Sita became restless when these words fell on her ears. I ignored them, but she was displeased. I helplessly obeyed her and came to see you."

(*The curtain drops.*)

Scene 7

(*The scene opens with the Panchavati cottage.*)

Rama and Lakshmana entered from the yard and went up the cottage.

Rama sang when he didn't see Sita in the cottage, "Alas Sita! Mine of virtue, beauty, character, discipline, and sincerity! Are there any birds, deer, or bees, around here? Have any of you seen Sita the fawn-eyed beauty? Dear Sita! Appear here quickly! Why can't we see you?"

They suddenly heard a voice saying "Alas Rama!" They went to the far corner of the yard and saw Jatayu dying. Jatayu said, "Lord! I am Jatayu. Ravana brought me to this condition. That crook carried Sita away to the south. I have held my breath to see you. Now I depart, merciful lord!"

Rama and Lakshmana sobbed and cremated Jatayu.

(*The curtain drops.*)

Scene 8

(*The scene opens on the stage with Shabari in her cottage.*)

Rama and Lakshmana came from the yard and moved toward the cottage. Shabari said, "Lord of the devotees! Come over here to my cottage! Share fresh berries with me. You have done a great favor to me."

Rama and Lakshmana went up to her. She bowed to them. Then she presented them with fruits on a plate. She herself tasted part of a fruit and offered it to Rama, "Taste it Lord! It's very sweet." She placed that part in Rama's mouth. "Oh yes, it's very sweet," Rama said.

She offered another fruit, "Taste this!" Rama tasted, "No, it's sour. But tastes good." She offered to Lakshmana in the same manner. They all ate on the same plate.

She said, "Thanks my lord! You ate with me, an untouchable woman."

Rama said, "Shabari! I make no distinction. That is my nature."

(*The curtain drops.*)

SEVENTH NIGHT
Scene 1

(*The scene opens on the stage with a view of hill Rishyamuka.*)

Rama and Lakshmana were resting on two hill rocks. Hanuman, disguised as a brahmin priest, came from the yard and went up to where Rama and Lakshmana were resting. He sang to them, "Who are you two? One dark-skinned and the other light-skinned? You are roaming here like the Kshatriyas. You are walking in this rough land with your soft feet. Lords! Why are you traveling here? You have tender, charming, and handsome bodies. Why do you tolerate the intolerable forest heat and wind?"

Rama replied in his song, "O Brahmin! We are from Ayodhya. Who can erase what destiny has written! We are the sons of Dasharatha, the king of Kosala. We have followed his order in coming here. By name, I am Rama and he Lakshmana. We are brothers.

There was a beautiful woman with us. That was Sita, my wife. A demon has kidnaped her. We are looking for her in this forest."

Hanuman touched their feet and sang, "I have seen the lord of Ayodhya. My sins from past lives are all finished. I have now tasted good fruits of good deeds."

Then he said, "Lord! I am Hanuman, the monkey. Let me take you to my master, Sugriva. He will be happy to meet you."

Hanuman lifted the two brothers on his shoulders, took them in the yard and then exited from the other end.

(*The curtain drops.*)

Scene 2

(*The scene opens on a hill at Sugriva's hideout. Sugriva is surrounded by his other fellow monkeys.*)

Hanuman entered the yard with Rama and Lakshmana on his shoulders. He dropped them in front of Sugriva, the lord of the monkeys. He said, "My lord! These are the princes of Ayodhya, Rama and Lakshmana." Sugriva bowed to them.

Then Rama sang, "O king of the monkeys! Tell me why you are hiding here. Abandon sadness, my friend, with my strength. I will help you in every way."

Sugriva sang, "Lord! Valin and I are brothers. The love between us cannot be described. He found some fault in me every time he saw me. He felt more and more differences. Then he beat me like an enemy, took away all my possessions and my wife."

Rama sang, "Listen to my words, Sugriva. By nature, I don't suggest deception. My friend! Fight him and I will see how strong he is. I will kill him with one arrow. Then you will help me to search for my wife, Sita."

Sugriva said, "I promise, my lord, to help you. Here are some jewels that fell from a flying car."

Rama said, "Lakshmana! See these jewels."

Lakshmana saw the jewels and said, "Brother! These are Sita's jewels.

Rama said, "Sugriva! Go now to fight Valin."

Sugriva bowed to the brothers and left.
(*The curtain drops.*)

Scene 3

(*The scene opens on the stage with Valin's court.*)

Sugriva approached the court from the yard. He hit the floor with his mace and challenged Valin, "O Vali! I challenge you for a duel. Or else I will kill you."

Valin got up and said, "Let's go in the courtyard. And I will smash you."

A duel with maces took place between the two monkey brothers. Sugriva fell down and got up, several times. Finally he ran from the yard. Valin returned to his court.

(*The curtain drops.*)

Scene 4

(*The scene opens with Sugriva's hideout.*)

Sugriva entered the yard and walked up to his hideout. There he bowed to Rama and Lakshmana. He sang, "Lord! Valin defeated me. I am very badly hurt. You didn't help me."

Rama sang, "Sugriva! You and your brother looked alike in the fight. Because of this confusion, I didn't kill Valin. Here, take this garland. Put it on your neck. With this on, I will recognize you in the next fight. Now you will see my valor."

(*The curtain drops.*)

Scene 5

(*The scene opens on Valin's court.*)

Sugriva entered the yard and went near the court. He said, "O Vali! I am ready to fight again. Come down." He hit the ground with his mace.

Valin got up and came down to the yard where Sugriva was standing. The two monkeys began to fight. Sugriva fell down. Rama shot Valin from behind a tree. Valin fell down and looked at the tree where

Rama was standing with a bow to shoot him again. Other monkeys came down from the court and surrounded Valin. Angada sat beside his dying father. Rama also came to him.

Valin looked at Rama and sang in pain, "Lord! You descended here for dharma. But you shot me like a hunter. How am I your foe and Sugriva your friend? What was your reason for shooting me, Lord?"

Rama sang, "Listen, you fool! Brother's wife, a sister, son's wife, all these are like daughters. To kill a male who looks at them with lust incurs no sin."

Valin sang, "Lord! I have committed sin. You alone can redeem me from it. This is my last moment. My salvation is under your control."

Rama sang, "Listen, O Vali! This is my nature. I never intend ill of those who take refuge in me. Ask for any wish you like. I have no hesitation for you."

Valin sang, "Lord! Now look at me with mercy. Give me the boon I request of you. May I have the love of your feet in whatever life I am born with. Here is my son. Hold his hand and make him your devotee."

Valin died. Lakshmana, holding the hands of Sugriva and Angada, said, "Sugriva! You are the king and Angada is your heir-apparent."

Then they all carried away Valin's dead body for cremation.

(*The curtain drops.*)

Scene 6

(*The scene opens with Rama and Lakshmana in their cottage.*)

Rama sang to Lakshmana, "Brother Lakshmana! The rainy season is over. Autumn is here. So far there is no news of Sita. Sugriva has forgotten me after regaining his rule, treasury, throne, and wife. Lakshmana! Ask him to fulfill his promise. If he ignores it, say to him, 'The path the slain Valin went by is not narrow. Keep your promise, Sugriva. Don't follow the path of Valin.'"

Lakshmana said, "Yes, Brother! I will tell him immediately."

Lakshmana left the cottage.

(*The curtain drops.*)

Scene 7

(*The scene opens onto Sugriva's court at Pampapura. Hanuman and Angada are seated beside him.*)

Lakshmana entered the court from the yard. Sugriva bowed to him. The other monkeys also bowed.

Lakshmana sang to Sugriva, "Tell me, O king of monkeys! Have you started the search for Sita? Rama is very sad without Sita. This is why he killed Valin. We developed a friendship with you in many ways. On top of that, we gave you the kingdom of Pampapura. Having ownership now of the kingdom, you have forgotten us. It makes me very angry when I see you sitting here. I can turn your rule upside down and burn everything here."

Sugriva said, "Lord! Please forgive me. I am a great fool. We will go right away in search of Sita. Let us inform Lord Rama."

They left the court and exited through the yard.

(*The curtain drops.*)

Scene 8

(*The scene opens with Rama in his cottage.*)

Lakshmana accompanied by Jambavan, Hanuman, Angada, and other monkeys entered the yard and went up to the cottage. They all bowed to Rama.

Sugriva sang to Rama, "Lord! Due to your very powerful maya, even sages get confused. Lord! Have mercy upon me. I am an ordinary monkey full of desires. Now the weather is clear, lord of the world! I am sending out all the monkeys everywhere."

Rama sang back, "O monkey king! Send all the monkeys around and bring back information of Sita's location. Without Sita, I have no life. Now make every effort."

Then Sugriva said to the monkeys, "Go in all directions and find Sita as soon as possible."

Rama sang to Hanuman, "O son of the Wind-god! Tell dear Sita how sad I am day and night. Have patience. Do not despair. I will come to rescue you. Tell her this message and give her this ring of mine for proof."

Rama gave his ring to Hanuman who sang, "Lord! With your blessing, I can uproot all of Lanka. I can burn it down in seconds, reduce it to ashes, and mix it with dirt. So long as there is life in Hanuman, the search for Sita will surely continue."

Rama and Lakshmana stayed in the cottage. Others came down and exited through the yard.

(*The curtain drops.*)

Scene 9

(*The curtain opens to the seashore where monkey chiefs along with Jambavan have assembled.*)

Jambavan said, "We have searched all the places that Sugriva requested. But nowhere do we see Sita."

Angada said, "And we'd rather die if we cannot find her. How fortunate was Jatayu who died for her!"

A voice came from behind, "Hello! Who are you that mentions my brother's name? I am Sampati, Jatayu's brother. Alas! He died!"

Jambavan said, "We too are looking for Sita. Lord Rama has sent us. We cannot return without locating her."

Sampati sang, "Over there is Trikuta hill in Lanka. Ravana lives there fearlessly. Over there is the Ashoka garden. Sita sits there in despair. If anyone among you can cross the ocean and land in the garden, then you will achieve Rama's goal. I am too old. Otherwise, I would have avenged my brother's death."

Jambavan said, "Dear friend Sampati! Thanks for your information. You have saved us. We will avenge your brother's death. We salute you."

Then Angada said, "Jambavan! I can go across. Do not doubt. It will take me a few seconds."

Jambavan said, "I do not doubt. But let Hanuman go first."

Hanuman sang, "O Lord of the bears! Hear my word! I will cross the salty ocean in seconds and finish Ravana and his court. I can uproot the hill of Trikuta. But tell me what exactly I should do."

Jambavan sang, "Dear Hanuman! Do this much. Go there, see Sita, and bring any information about her. Then Rama, the lotus-eyed, will go with all of us. He will bring Sita back after slaying the demons and Ravana."

(*The curtain drops.*)

Scene 10

(*The scene opens in the far end of the yard prepared as the Ashoka Vatika 'sorrowless garden.'*)

Sita came out and sat on a rock in the garden under a tree. She was accompanied by a demoness, Trijata.

Then Ravana came from the other end through a gate. He was accompanied by some demons. They sat on a bench near Sita.

Ravana sang to Sita, "O beautiful Sita! Look at me for a while. Pay attention to what I say. Do not make a fuss. Your husband has forgotten you. He hasn't started to search for you. I will make you the head queen. Mandodari and the other queens will be at your service in the palace. I will kill you if you don't accept my proposal."

Sita sang back, "O Ravana! Whom are you threatening? I have no fear of death at all. You may brag about your golden Lanka. But for me your palace is less than a lump of clay."

Ravana sang angrily, "Sita! You have insulted me. I will cut off your head with my sword. No good will come of you if you don't accept my word today. I will kill you in two months if you didn't propose to me. Listen, all you demons! Continue torturing Sita." He got up and went away with the other demons except Trijata.

Sita looked depressed as she uttered, "O Raghunatha! Free me soon from here." Then she covered her face with her hands and sobbed.

Then Trijata sang with her hand on Sita's shoulder, "Dear Sita! Do not cry. I saw this in a dream. A monkey burned down Lanka. He killed several demons. Ravana rode a donkey. He was naked and bald. Then his head and hands were cut off. Vibhishana became the king."

Sita raised her head and sang, "Trijata! Listen to my request. I have to tell you about my plight. I want to die. It's hard for me to bear this terrible pain. Ravana is cruel and arrogant. He has been torturing me regularly. I cannot touch this evil demon Ravana, not even with my foot. Why would I propose to him?" Sita leaned back with her eyes closed. Trijata quietly left.

Suddenly, Hanuman dropped a ring on Sita's lap. She picked up the ring and looked at it. Then she said, "This is Rama's ring. Lord! Where did this ring come from?"

Hanuman sang from the tree, "There is Ayodhya's king from the dynasty of Raghu. He is Dasharatha's son, well known for his valor. Rama, with Lakshmana and Sita, accepted the word of his father and went into exile. One evil demon came and abducted Sita, my mother. Rama roamed here and there in search of her. My lord, Rama, sent me to give you his message."

Sita looked up and sang, "You told your beautiful story. Why don't you come down, brother? Having heard your word, I feel some comfort now, as if there's new life in a dead body."

Hanuman jumped down and bowed to Sita. He sang, "I am Hanuman, the messenger of Rama. I am telling you the truth. God is my witness. Mother! The two brothers of Raghu's dynasty sent me for news of you. I brought this ring for proof. Now do not worry. Have faith. Brave Rama will come as soon as he hears the news."

Sita sang in excitement but softly, "Tell me about his well-being. Are my lord and his brother happy? The lord of Raghu's dynasty is the abode of happiness. He gives pleasure to all. Does he talk about me? What wrong did I do that my lord hasn't thought of me yet?"

Hanuman sang, "Mother! Lord Rama and his brother are well. The Abode of Mercy is sad due to your suffering. Wait for some more days,

Mother! The brave scion of Raghu will come with monkeys and will take you away after vanquishing the demons."

Then he said, "Mother! I am hungry. Please allow me to eat some fruits. I haven't eaten for days."

Sita sang, "Dear son! This garden is guarded by big powerful demons. Who knows what these demons would do if they see you. Quietly eat any fruit that has fallen down."

Hanuman said, "All right. Whatever you say, Mother! I go now to look for such fruits."

He went around and picked up some fruits. He ate a few pieces and threw the rest away. Then he broke some branches. A couple of demon guards came and threw rocks at him. He beat the demons. They ran away. Meanwhile, he destroyed the garden.

(*The curtain opens on the stage with Ravana in his court.*)

Ravana was seated on the throne. His two sons, Akshaya and Meghanada sat beside him. The gardener entered the court and said to Ravana, "My lord! There is a big monkey in the Ashoka Garden, and he has destroyed it. He ate fruits and uprooted the trees. The demon guards tried to stop him. But he beat them back."

Ravana said to his son, Akshaya, "Akshaya! Go catch that monkey!"

"Yes Sir," said Akshaya.

Akshaya entered the garden and challenged Hanuman, "You little monkey! Come down or I kill you."

Hanuman didn't come down. Akshaya aimed an arrow at Hanuman, but missed. Then Hanuman jumped on top of Akshaya and killed him in a wrestling duel.

A demon guard ran to Ravana at his court and said, "My lord! Akshaya has been killed by that monkey!"

Ravana said in anger, "What? Akshaya killed by that monkey! Meghanada! Let us avenge your brother's death. Catch that monkey and bring him here alive! We will make him dance in our court before we kill him."

"Yes Sir!" Meghanada said.

Meghanada went to the garden. He looked around and then saw Hanuman on a tree. He sang, "Hey, you mean monkey! You are a crook and a pain. Why did you kill the demons? You don't know that I am Meghanada. Now you will see how we'll kill you."

Hanuman sang back, "You rogue! Worthless is your bragging. You don't know my might. I can grab your legs and drop you into the ocean. Then I will see your bravery. You haven't met a brave one yet. That's why you are talking nonsense."

Meghanada quickly threw a magical rope around Hanuman and dragged him down. He tied him up and then walked him to Ravana at his court.

Ravana looked at Hanuman and said in anger, "You rouge monkey! Where are you from? You don't know the power of my arms. Haven't you heard about me? I see you are a fearless crook. For what crime did you kill the demons? You rogue! Aren't you afraid of losing your life?"

Hanuman replied in his song, "Listen, Ravana! I have been sent by the lord of the world. He broke Shiva's bow at the court of Janaka and humiliated you and the kings there. He has killed such powerful warriors as Khara, Dushana, Trishira, and Valin. I ate fruits because I was hungry. I killed only those demons who attacked me. For this reason, your son tied me by trickery. I understand your power. Don't be an enemy of a brave whom gods and demons fear everywhere. Send Sita back to him!"

Ravana sang, "Hey monkey! Hold your tongue! You haven't understood my power yet. It's time for you now. Who can help you now? You are in my prison. Who you are praising was banished because of his wickedness. Listen my fellow demons! Kill this monkey now!"

Vibhishana got up and said, "It's not right to kill a messenger. If you wish to punish him then just burn his tail."

The demons wrapped Hanuman's tail with rags and set it on fire. Hanuman was released. He jumped up and went out.

Shortly a blaze was seen behind the court.

(*The curtain drops.*)

Hanuman returned to the garden and bowed to Sita. He sang, "Mother! Give me some object like the one Lord Rama gave me for you. With his grace and your blessings, I have burned Lanka. See the blaze. I have killed many demons. There is a mess out there."

Sita sang, "Hanuman! You are the abode of wisdom and energy. Give my message and greetings to my lord, 'Lord! You are merciful, a helper of the meek. I am now in great danger. If you do not come within two months, Ravana will kill me for sure.'"

Sita gave Hanuman her crest jewel. He bowed to her and left the garden. Then Sita exited from the other end.

(*The curtain drops.*)

EIGHTH NIGHT
Scene 1

(*The scene opens on the stage in Kishkindha hill where Sugriva, Jambavan, Angada, and the other monkeys are seen with Rama and Lakshmana.*)

Hanuman entered from the yard and went up on the hill. He bowed to Rama and Lakshmana and greeted the others with folded hands.

Rama asked him, "Dear Friend! Have you bought any news of Sita?"

Hanuman replied by his song, "Lord! Her eyes filled with tears. Janaka's daughter said these words, 'I am at your feet in thoughts and words. Why have you abandoned me?' O merciful lord! I cannot describe the awful plight of Mother Sita. Here is her crest jewel for you."

Rama held the jewel in his hands and kissed it with tears in his eyes. He embraced Hanuman. Then he sang to Sugriva, "My dear brother Sugriva! Let's attack Lanka. Make no delay. Give order to all the monkeys."

(*The curtain drops.*)

Scene 2

(*The scene opens on the stage at the seashore with Rama, Lakshmana, Sugriva, Hanuman, Jambavan, Angada, Nala, and Nila.*)

Rama looked toward Nala and Nila, the two brothers who knew how to build bridges. He said, "Nala and Nila! Now you will make plans to build a bridge from here to Lanka. In the meantime, I offer my worship to Lord Shiva."

Nala and Nila got up and bowed to Rama. Nala said, "Yes, my lord! We will start the plans right away." They went out.

Rama and Lakshmana sat before the stone symbol or *linga* of Shiva and meditated for a few minutes.

Then Nala and Nila returned. Nila said to Rama, "Lord! We have informed all the monkey workers about our bridge plan. The bridge will be ready soon."

Rama said, "Nala and Nila! I have prayed to Lord Shiva. With his grace, we can cross any ocean. Start your work."

(*The curtain drops.*)

Scene 3

(*The scene opens with Ravana's court. Ravana is with Mandodari, Vibhishana, and others.*)

Mandodari sang, "My dear lord! Return Sita. Take refuge in God if you wish welfare. He is the lord of the world against whom you have developed animosity. This understanding is unwise understanding. Lord Rama has come at our door. Hanuman has made Lanka a desolate place. Yet you ignored all this. Return Sita with dignity."

Ravana sang, "Mandodari! Who in this world is as powerful as I am? Any man? Any ascetic? Any brave? Whom all fear, his wife is now fearful. That's a joke!"

Then he turned his face toward his courtiers and sang, "My courtiers! Hear me out! We have news that Rama's army has crossed the sea to our shore. Now tell me what action we must take. Do everything you can to find the right approach."

Then Vibhishana stood up and sang to Ravana, "My brother! If you kindly allow me then I will give you my advice. If you wish to have your welfare, great fame, wisdom, and happy state of affairs, then return Sita, another man's wife. Brother! Rama is not just a human king. He is the lord of the whole universe. He is Time itself."

Ravana sang back angrily, "Rogue! You are praising our enemy! You crook are near your death. Tell me, stupid! Is there anyone in the whole world whom I could not win with my might? Get out from here, you crook! And meet him whom you are calling brave." Ravana kicked Vibhishana.

Vibhishana left the court. After he disappeared, Ravana said to a courtier, "Keep an eye on Vibhishana's movements."

(*The curtain drops.*)

Scene 4

(*The scene opens on the stage with Rama's camp at the Lanka seashore.*)

Hanuman entered from the yard with Vibhishana. They walked over to the camp. Hanuman went up and bowed to Rama, "Lord! Over there is Vibhishana, Ravana's brother. He wants protection from you."

Rama said, "Hanuman! He is most welcome. Bring him over here!"

Vibhishana came up when Hanuman signaled to him. He bowed to Rama and sang with folded hands, "Lord Rama! I am Ravana's brother, born in the family of demons. I have heard of your fame. You are merciful. The one you favor loses all miseries. Please save me. I have come to seek refuge in you."

Rama sang back, "Listen, my friend Vibhishana! I never intend to harm anyone who has sought my protection. I will make you the king of Lanka."

Then he said to Lakshmana, "Lakshmana! Place the coronation mark on Vibhishana's forehead."

Lakshmana said, "Yes, my lord!" Then he placed a red mark on Vibhishana's forehead. Vibhishana bowed to Lakshmana.

Then Rama sang to Angada, "Dear friend Angada! You are the abode of power. For my sake, go to Lanka. Tell our enemy to do what we will. Show him fear, good will, and the law. And quickly bring news of Sita!"

Angada got up and bowed to Rama. He said, "Yes, my lord! I will do as you command me."

Angada left the camp.

(*The curtain drops.*)

Scene 5

(*The scene opens on the stage with Ravana's court.*)

Angada leapt into the court from the side. Ravana was startled and sang, "Hey monkey! How did you get here? You are standing fearlessly in my court. Don't you know Ravana's might in fight?"

Angada sang in his reply, "My father had friendship with you. I came here for that reason. You have done wrong by abducting Sita. You have brought shame to the family of sage Pulastya, your grandfather. Now, follow my advice and Lord Rama will forgive you. Bring Sita in front and present her to Rama. Bow to Rama. He is the gem of Raghu's dynasty. Say to him, 'Lord! Save me!' The lord will listen to your call for mercy and make you fearless."

Ravana sang in anger, "O mean monkey! Hold your tongue! You fool don't know me, the enemy of gods. Tell me your name. Who is your father? Why did I have friendship with him?"

Angada replied in his song, "I am Angada, son of Valin. I met you before with my father. Now I am Rama's messenger. I have come here to meet with you."

Ravana sang, "O Angada, son of Valin! You are a disgrace to your family. You are a messenger of a monk. But I ask you to tell me Valin's welfare."

Angada sang, "Tens of days have gone by since Valin's demise. You have asked me about his welfare. Let me tell you about what Rama's opposition does. Because of that, Rama killed him."

"O rogue! I am listening to your harsh speech. I understand polity and dharma. The law says that no one should kill his enemy's messenger. So for that reason, I won't kill you, stupid, my opponent. But I am going to throw you out of here."

Ravana grabbed Angada by his foot and tried to lift him up. He couldn't move his foot even a bit.

Then Angada sang, "You rogue! Why do you hold my foot? Why don't you hold Lord Rama's foot, with no guile in your heart? By holding Rama's feet, you will overcome your troubles of this and the other world."

Then Angada leapt out of the court and disappeared.

(*The curtain drops.*)

NINTH NIGHT
Scene 1

(*The scene opens with Ravana's court.*)

Ravana sang to his son Meghanada and the other courtiers, "O my braves! Go surround the monkeys and bears of Rama's army in all directions. Eat them all. Look, with no effort of yours, destiny has delivered food to your home. Not only should you take the lives of those monkeys, but catch the monks, ascetics, and the other worshipers alive."

Then he said to Meghanada, "Son Indrajit! I am proud of you. You conquered Indra the king of gods. Now, take your army and conquer them all."

Meghanada got up and sang to the courtiers, "Get up my young warriors! Have your swords tied to your waists. Bring out spears, maces, bows, and arrows and hit our foes hard with them."

All got up.

(*The curtain drops.*)

Scene 2

(*The scene opens on Rama's camp.*)

Lakshmana sang to Rama, "Lord Rama, listen! The demons have come out to inflict injuries upon us. If you command me, I will send them all to Yama, the god of death."

Rama sang back, "Dear Brother! Go and slay those crooked demons. Fulfill the wishes of the sages. These demons have given them so much pain. They deserve quick punishment."

They all got up. Lakshmana sang, "Sugriva! Ask your brave warriors to be ready. Ask them to cause havoc in the battlefield. Let Hanuman be at the front of the monkey army. Let the bears go in the east. Let Angada give support to all from behind. Let us shout 'Victory to Rama' and slay those demons."

(*The curtain drops.*)

Scene 3

(*The scene starts in the far end of the yard.*)

From one side, the forces of Meghanada entered. He challenged as he sang, "Where are Rama and Lakshmana, the two brothers who are famous in the world as archers? Where are Nala, Nila, Jambavan, Sugriva? Where are Hanuman and Angada, the mighty ones? Where is Vibhishana, the enemy of his own brother? Why can't I see him?"

Then from the other side came Lakshmana and his forces. Lakshmana sang, "Hey you rogue! Why are you standing there fearless? Don't you know me? You crook! Abandon any hope to live! You have given the sages a lot of trouble. Having violated ethical conduct, you have acted with deception. Now you reap the results of your actions, O mean enemy of gods!"

Then Meghanada aimed at Lakshmana with his bow and arrows. Lakshmana did the same. They came close to each other. Meghanada hit Lakshmana with an arrow. Lakshmana fell on the ground. Two monkeys carried him away.

The battle stopped and all went away.

Scene 4

(*The stage opens on Rama's camp.*)

The two monkeys arrived at the camp with Lakshmana unconscious in their arms. Rama got up and held Lakshmana in his arms and sat down. Vibhishana said to Rama, "Lord! There is a physician in Lanka. His name is Sushena. He will understand what kind of injury Lakshmana has. Someone has to bring him here quickly."

Rama said to Hanuman, "Hanuman! You are the son of the Wind-god. Please bring Sushena here as soon as possible!"

Hanuman saluted to Rama and said, "My lord! I go right away." He left the camp.

Rama sang to Lakshmana, "Lakshmana! Open your eyes. If you don't, I will die then. It will definitely happen so. Your mother entrusted her one son to me. How can I return to Ayodhya without you? What answer will I give her? That I lost my dear brother for my woman?" Rama cried.

(*The curtain drops.*)

Scene 5

(*The scene opens in the yard.*)

Hanuman and Sushena entered from the far end. Hanuman sang to him, "O Doctor! Let us go as fast as possible. Otherwise, Lakshmana will lose his life. Examine him and let me know what kind of medicine you need for him."

Sushena said, "Hanuman! I will do my best for Lakshmana."

They walked faster toward the camp.

(*The curtain goes up on the stage. Rama, with Lakshmana in his arms, is shown in the camp.*)

Hanuman and Sushena approached the camp. They bowed to Rama. Sushena immediately examined Lakshmana. He said to Hanuman, "O mighty Hanuman! You go to the Dronagiri mountain in the north. There in the middle range you will find the *sanjivani* plant. The sooner you bring that plant here for medicine the more hope for Lakshmana's life."

Rama said to Hanuman, "Hanuman! Do whatever you can to bring that plant here."

"As you command, my lord!" said Hanuman. He bowed to Rama and left.

(*The curtain drops.*)

Scene 6

(*The scene opens on the stage with Bharata in his cottage in Ayodhya.*)

Hanuman appeared flying over the yard with a big bag on his shoulders. He moved faster away from the cottage. Bharata shot him down with an arrow. He came down to see the wounded Hanuman. Hanuman uttered "Alas Rama!" repeatedly.

Bharata asked him, "Friend! Who are you, calling Rama's name?"

Hanuman said, "I am Hanuman. I am the son of Pavana the Wind-god. Rama is my lord. There was a fight in Lanka between Lakshmana and Meghanada. It is because Ravana kidnaped Sita whom he hasn't returned yet. So we have a war. Lakshmana is wounded badly by Meghanada. I am taking this medicine for him. I have to return now very fast."

Bharata said, "Dear Hanuman! I can fly you on my arrow."

Hanuman said, "With your blessing, I can move as fast as your arrow. So I take your leave." Hanuman bowed to Bharata and ran to the other end of the yard.

(*The curtain drops.*)

Scene 7

(*The scene opens with Rama's camp.*)

Hanuman entered from the yard and went up to Sushena. He bowed to both and showed the bag. Sushena checked the bag and took out a plant. He rubbed some leaves in his palms and applied them to Lakshmana's wound

In a couple of moments, Lakshmana opened his eyes and looked around. Then he said, "Who brought me here? I was in the battlefield."

Rama said to him, "Lakshmana! Meghanada hurt you with his power arrow. Now you are all right. I go with you to fight."

(*The curtain drops.*)

Scene 8

(*The scene opens with Ravana and his courtiers in a chamber where Kumbhakarna is sleeping on a couch.*)

The courtiers shook Ravana's brother Kumbhakarna with shouts of "Wake up." He woke up after several attempts. Ravana sang to him, "O Brother! How do I put it? I am ashamed of myself to tell you this. Rama left his capital and came to the forest with his brother Lakshmana. They cut Shurpanakha's nose. Then I abducted Sita, Rama's wife. Rama and Lakshmana have an army of monkeys headed by Sugriva, Hanuman, and Angada. They have killed a lot of demons. Now you must take some action. Otherwise, this calamity is going to finish us all."

Kumbhakarna said, "As you command me. I will go into action right now."

He came into the yard and sang, "I shall eat Rama. So shall I Lakshmana. I shall eat Hanuman and Angada. Sita I shall chew raw."

Meghanada came down and joined him. They and the other demons assembled in the yard and then left.

(*The curtain drops.*)

Scene 9

(*The scene opens with Rama's camp.*)

Kumbhakarna, Meghanada, and the other demons appeared from the other side of the yard. Kumbhakarna yelled, "Rama and Lakshmana! Come out to fight! I will kill you." Accompanied by their army, Rama and Lakshmana came out. A fierce battle followed. Rama fatally shot Kumbhakarna with an arrow. Then Lakshmana fatally shot Meghanada and cut off his hand with another arrow. The hand was flung far away. Then Lakshmana cut off the head of Meghanada. The head fell on the stage. Some demons pulled away the dead bodies of Kumbhakarna and Meghanada. All left.

Scene 10

(*The scene opens on Rama's camp.*)

Sulochana, Meghanada's wife, came out from the yard. She was crying and moving toward the camp as she sang, "O my ruthless destiny! Mercy has left you. My husband had gone to fight and no news came from the battlefield. When his hand fell in my arms then I knew about his death by Lakshmana."

She came up near Vibhishana who was beside Rama. She bowed to Vibhishana who sang to Rama, "Lord! This is the daughter-in-law of Ravana. She must be looking for the head of her husband Meghanada."

Sulochana bowed to Rama and sang, "Lord! You know everything. You understand the good and the bad intentions of all beings. Have mercy on me. Please give me the head of my husband! Then I will have my funeral with his head."

Rama sang, "Here I give you his head. We could have saved him and let him rule Lanka for a long time. But he wanted to fight. Please ask me for any favor!"

She sang, "Lord! You are generous. You can indeed grant me any wish. You are the compassionate lord of Raghu's dynasty. But nothing is stable here. All I want is to die on my husband's funeral pyre."

(*The curtain drops.*)
(*A blazing light is seen later behind the stage to indicate the funeral.*)

TENTH NIGHT
Scene 1

(*The scene opens on Ravana's court.*)

Ravana sang to his courtiers, "I have increased animosities with my own power. I will answer to the enemies who have invaded us. Now whoever does not want to go into battle, may stay at home. Whoever loves his wife and home, does not have to come with me to fight the enemies. We move now to the battlefield."

(*The curtain drops.*)

Scene 2

(*The scene takes place in the yard.*)

Then from one side of the yard Ravana and his army of demons entered. Rama's army appeared on the other side of the yard. Ravana came near Lakshmana and sang, "You crook, you killed many mighty demons. Now you see my valor. I have been looking for you. Fool! Today is your end."

Lakshmana sang back, "O wicked Ravana! Why do you say such nonsense? Even now you have not come to your senses. We have killed your sons. I am going to kill you with the same bow with which I killed Meghanada."

Rama came forward and joined Lakshmana who had already aimed at Ravana. A battle between the two armies followed. A fierce battle between Rama and Ravana continued for some time. Then Vibhishana came near Rama and signaled to him. Rama then aimed an arrow at Ravana between his heart and throat. It hit Ravana very badly as he fell down.

Rama and Lakshmana went to him. Rama said, "Ravana! We warned you a long time ago: Peace is worthier than war; forgiveness is fairer than fighting. But this is your last moment. Say anything you wish to say."

Ravana said, "I have nothing to say. I am dying. I am going to your place. I will meet you there." Ravana breathed his last breath.

Hanuman lifted up the dead body of Ravana. Vibhishana said, "I am sorry, brother Ravana! Because of your foolhardy behavior you came to such an end. You could have become a peacemaker. But you chose to be a terrorist. I wish nothing like this would have happened. I am sorry that I have to perform your cremation because of this sad end."

Rama said to Vibhishana, "Vibhishana! We will join you. Death ends enmities. Our purpose is over. With you and like you, I must perform his cremation."

They all left the yard.

(*The curtain drops.*)

(*A big blaze is seen across the audience area to indicate the burning of Ravana's body*)

Scene 3

(*The scene opens with Rama's camp.*)

Rama sang, "My friends Angada, Nala, Nila, Jambavan, Sugriva, Hanuman, and all others! Go with Vibhishana to Lanka's palace and place him on the throne. Following my father's word, I shall not enter any city yet. I will send Lakshmana with you to bring Sita here."

They all left from the side of the camp.

(*The curtain drops.*)

Scene 4

(*The scene opens with Rama's camp. He is surrounded by a few monkeys.*)

From the yard a small procession entered with Sita on a palanquin. Vibhishana, Lakshmana, Hanuman, and Sugriva placed the palanquin in front of Rama. Sita came out of the palanquin and bowed to Rama. He turned his face away from her.

After a few quiet moments, Sita sang softly, "My lord! Your mate is standing here. What fault have I committed that you turn away your face? Will you not take me home with you, my lord? If you do not reply now, I will abandon my life now. Sita's future is in your hands."

Rama said angrily, "Sita! You have lived in Ravana's home. What will people say if I take you home?"

Then Sita sang with tears in her eyes, "O Tiger among men! Behaving with anger like an ordinary man, you have given priority to my womanhood only. You didn't consider the proof of my hand that you held in tender age. You considered all my devotion and character secondary."

Then Lakshmana sang, "Dear Rama! Please listen to me. Sita is pure and pious, my lord! Let us take her home, my brother! Do not test her."

Sita said to Lakshmana, "Lakshmana! I will offer my proof. Prepare a pyre for me."

Lakshmana said, "No. Mother! I cannot do that."

Sita said in tears, "Lakshmana! Look, my lord is quiet. So you must do it."

Lakshmana and the others went out and prepared a pyre in the yard.

Sita came down and sat atop the pyre. It was lit by Lakshmana. All watched the fire with sadness and horror on their faces, while Rama kept his cool. But Sita was not burned at all. Then a voice was heard with a big blast from behind the camp "O Rama! I am Agni, the god of fire. I couldn't burn Sita because she is pure and chaste. Accept your dedicated wife!"

Rama came down. Sita got up. The two embraced each other. Then Rama said, "I believed all along in Sita's purity. But for her proof to you, I behaved like this. We take Sita home."

(*The curtain drops.*)

(*The chorus follows: "Hail, hail, hail, hail! Mother of Universe" and "Submit, my mind, to God, Rama Chandra the compassionate!"*)

THE ELEVENTH DAY CELEBRATION
The Bharat Milap

The Bharat Milap "Bharata's Meeting" (Bharatamilapa in Sanskrit) is celebrated in the afternoon. Two colorful processions are prepared. One procession is with Rama, who returns to Ayodhya at the end of fourteen years of exile. Rama, Sita, and Lakshmana are carried in a decorated open palanquin. Ahead of them go the musicians, usually drummers and horn players. They are followed on foot by the monkeys and bears of the Rama army.

The other procession is headed by similar musicians with Bharata and his party consisting of Shatrughna, Vasishtha, Sumantra, and the three mothers, etc.

Then at a designated spot, the two processions meet. First, Bharata and Rama meet and embrace each other, thus known in Hindi as the Bharat Milap. Other relatives, elders, and ministers also meet each other likewise. There is applause in Hindi with "Swagat" (svagata 'welcome' in Sanskrit) from all around "Swagat to Ram the lord of Ayodhya, Swagat to Sita the mother of all, Swagat to Lakshman the protector." Then Rama announces in Hindi, "Please welcome our pet friends, Hanuman, Sugriw, Jambawan, Angad, and all others including Wibhishan, the king of Lanka! Without them, this meeting would not be possible." The guests receive garlands with repeated applause in Hindi such as "Jay Mahawir Hanuman, Jay Widwan Jambawan..." (Victory to Brave Hanuman, Victory to Wise Jambavan...). Then the two processions become one and proceed to the Vishnu temple, where the celebration ends with music and prayers. Tulsidas' song "Shri Ramachandra kripalu bhaja mana..." (Meditate, mind, on kind lord Rama the Moon...) is repeated throughout the procession with intermittent applause in Hindi "Bolo! Sita, Ram, Lakshman ki jay" (Say! Victory to Sita, Rama, Lakshmana). At the end the most popular chorus song is heard everywhere:

> Raghu's Lord! Raghuson! King Rama!
> The purifier of the fallen! Sita! Rama!
> ("Raghupati Raghava Raja Rama,
> Patita Pavana Sita Rama")

Part III

The Fall Years

Chapter 4

▼

1943–44

Finally came the Rama Lila month with its autumn glory. This was going to be my first year of watching the Ramayana story on the stage at Puri. I was prepared for it. Jagriti and I had even acted out some scenes to feel the story as a drama. Compared with the *Ramayana* epic the *Rama Drama* was too short. But Jagriti kindly gave me a rough translation of a one-page Sanskrit summary as follows:

"King Dasharatha of Ayodhya had four sons from his three wives. Kausalya, the first wife, gave birth to Rama. Sumitra, the second wife, had twins: Lakshmana and Shatrughna. Kaikeyi, the third wife, gave birth to Bharata. All four princes were nice, handsome, and brave. Young Rama and Lakshmana protected the hermitage of sage Vishvamitra from the fellow demons of Ravana, the evil king of Lanka. Later, only Rama could break the bow of Shiva to win in marriage the hand of Sita, King Janaka's daughter. The other princes were married to Sita's sisters. Dasharatha announced Rama, the oldest son, as his heir apparent. But Kaikeyi forced the king to exile Rama for 14 years and declare her son as the heir apparent. Sita and Lakshmana accompanied Rama in exile and Dasharatha died in shock. Bharata refused the throne, but took care of the kingdom as Rama's regent. Shurpanakha, Ravana's sister, met the exiled trio in a forest and insisted that Rama marry her. Lakshmana became upset and cut her nose. Angry Ravana took out his friend Maricha in a plane to kidnap Sita. Disguised as a golden deer, Maricha ran by the cottage of Sita. She wanted the deer. Rama and Lakshmana went after him. When they returned, Ravana had already abducted Sita. The monkey king, Sugriva, and his army helped Rama. Hanuman, a deputy of Sugriva, located Sita in a garden of Lanka when Ravana was threatening to kill her soon because of her refusal to marry him. After Ravana left, Hanuman promised her to bring Rama soon to free her. Then Hanuman burned down Ravana's capital and went back. Rama and Lakshmana, with the help of Sugriva's army and Ravana's brother Vibhishana, killed Ravana and other demons. Then Sita was brought to Rama. But he didn't accept her, as he doubted her character. Sita chose to burn herself to prove her chastity. But the fire couldn't burn her at all. Then Rama trusted her. They all returned to Ayodhya as the exile period was over."

My greatest achievement this month was that I didn't sleep at any night of Puri's Rama Lila (I saw a few, children and adult, sleeping there occasionally). The last night was memorable. While we were returning home around 2 a.m., we heard this Garhwali song, a benediction:

> *He Beda-mukhi Barma!*
> *Mukh kholi bol de!*
> *Kai ki chhan dandi,*
> *Raunteli kanthi?*
> "Hey Veda-mouthed Brahma!
> Open your mouth and speak out!
> Whose are these mountains?
> The panoramic peaks?"

We had no problem in recognizing Bisram's voice. Where was he? We looked around. We saw the cloud-free mountains and snow-white peaks. Who created these majestic mountains all around us? The creator was the four-headed god of Creation, Brahma, whose four mouths are the four 'Vedas,' the first scriptures of 'knowledge.' He alone is the knower. He alone can see all around at once with his four heads. Tell us Lord! Who owns them, the Himalayas?

This year's Rama Lila was really my first understanding of Dashhara, the set of ten nights, including the following day of Bharata's meeting (with Rama) or Bharat Milap. I was in the third grade at Mission High School. The school's first year class started with the third grade. Uncle Nawal and Aunt Kanti were blessed with a new baby. He was named Vijay, which means 'Victory.' They hoped that with Vijay's birth we were going to win the War in Europe, the Middle East, Africa, Asia, and the Pacific Islands.

We received very little news about the War. Our school teachers gave us some news, but in very general terms. Their main interest was in whether or not we were doing well in class. In spite of having a lot of homework, we boys would make time for a late afternoon game such as football (soccer), gulli-danda, field hockey, and kabaddi. The only time we didn't play these games was either during the days of the Rama Lila or on snowy winter days.

Right on the first evening of the Rama Lila, I met some of my new classmates from Puri. One boy's father was also a member of the Rama Lila Committee. The inauguration speech of the new chairman of the Committee had some mention of the War, for which he received applause. (I could not understand his speech at that time, but years later it appeared in a compilation distributed at the time of his farewell party.) This is what he said:

"Brothers and sisters! As the new chairman of the Rama Lila Committee, I welcome you all. It is not a matter of chance, it is by God's grace that my name is Raghav Dhyani. I am a lawyer by profession. But as my name says, I really meditate on Lord Rama. I fully believe in his rule of law." There was laughter and applause from the audience. At least I did know then that Raghava meant Raghu's son or Rama and dhyani meant doer of *dhyana* 'meditation.'

I suddenly remembered that one of the Bhatra girls was married to a Dhyani. I did not recognize this Dhyani because he was dressed like

Jawahar Lal Nehru, in a black sherwani as his top coat and white tight pajamas. No Nehru white topi (cap). Dhyani ji didn't need one as he was not bald. The Nehru outfit was rare in the hills. But modeling after Nehru ji, another Himalayan brahmin, reflected Dhyani ji's national pride. Maybe, Gambhir was related to Dhyani ji. I could not be related to him as I was not a brahmin.

Then Dhyani ji continued his speech, "Rama's Lila or God's Game is Mother Nature's stage. See the big colorful canopy over this theater." He paused as he raised his head while pointing with his hand toward the canopy. The canopy was glittering with so many flowery designs. He started again, "Now look way out there to the north, under this starry sky, the snow-covered line of peaks, peaks after peaks. From that line, you see countless mountains hanging down like curtains. In front of those curtains and behind those curtains, it's all Lord's Drama, his Nature's Lila. Rama is enjoying all of it. Which is why he is called Rama, the enjoyer. All of us here are trying to imitate his joy, his game." He paused to wipe his tears with a handkerchief. "These are really tears of joy."

Most people stood up and gave him big applause.

He started again, "Those curtains in the north continue further and further, all the way to Europe. There Ravana has been born again. His name is Hitler. He is killing innocent men, women, and children. Many of our young men from Kanyakumari to Kashmir, from Calcutta to Cutch have joined to defeat his evil forces. And the evil forces from Japan. They will be destroyed. Have faith in our own thousands of Himalayan braves. These braves are fighting the war to save the innocent, to destroy the evildoers, to reset dharma. Rama through our braves will punish these demons, the demons in human bodies."

There was thunderous applause. "Now we start the Lord's Lila. Everybody say: 'Hail Rama!' All said after him "Jay Ram."

At the end of the tenth night, a giant size effigy of Ravana was burnt outside in a walled area. There was a loud popping noise from the firecrackers inside the burning effigy.

The next afternoon was quite dramatic, not on the stage, but on the main road. This was the Bharat Milap day. It was, as customary, celebrated as the meeting of two parties.

From one fork of the main road came Bharata and his party with a big Puri crowd as if they were the Ayodhya folks in Ayodhya. Several boys from our village and Gwar including myself, Gambhir, Anrit, and Bhajnu were in the crowd.

From the other fork came Rama, Sita, and Lakshmana with men dressed up in monkey or bear suits as if returning from Lanka. The two brothers, Rama and Bharata met. Bharata fell at the feet of Rama. Rama lifted him up with his arms and hugged him. Flowers fell upon them from all sides. Gunshots welcomed their meeting. The dhol and damau were played by Bhajnu's father and uncle. They were accompanied by four Scotch bagpipers. With the bagpipers, a special style of dhol-damau drumming, known as 'Ram Dhol,' was played. Lord Rama's dhol played as Scottish drums!

Suddenly, we saw a man behind the Rama army of monkeys and bears who looked like Uncle Ishan, Anrits's father, who had disappeared to become a monk. But he was dressed up as if still the postmaster of Puri. Gambhir immediately asked Anrit, "Look over there! Doesn't that man look like the former postmaster?"

Anrit crossed over Rama's army while we stayed behind. Then the man ran toward Anrit and hugged him. Gambhir remarked, "This whole celebration is 'bap-beta milap.' Now let us see how 'pati-patni milap' goes!" After the father-son meeting or bap-beta milap, we were really hoping for the husband-wife meeting or pati-patni milap.

Indeed, there was a husband-wife meeting, apparently on continuing basis.

The next week at Aunt Radha's wedding, we all saw Uncle Ishan very active. Aunt Radha was Grandaunt Guna's only child. Gambhir was her stepbrother. The other stepbrother was Dilip, Grandaunt Mira's son; he and his family lived in Agra, where he was a government accountant. Gambhir, even though younger than Radha, had a major role to play. Traditionally, the father gave away the daughter. Since the father was long dead and the big brother was away, Gambhir was the only male in Granduncle Sirdhar's family.

All of Granduncle Sirdhar's three wives had their own contribution to Aunt Radha's marriage. The first wife, Mira, arranged the marriage, that is, she found the bridegroom, Mool Chand. Grandaunt Lathi, Gambhir's mother, was in charge of the food. Grandaunt Guna was least active; she was gentle and nice, but very incompetent in practical matters.

Except for the adult males of Granduncle Gobind's family, the entire village was active in this wedding.

The village of Gwar was also active. Each family sent one adult male to work with food preparation. They brought fresh leaf plates in addition to other food items.

Bhajnu's father and uncle were the drummers; they also tailored clothes for the bride. Molu and his wife Chandni, our village baddi (bard) family, provided the dholak (a drum) dance entertainment.

Even a few rajput families from Kandy and Thaula were represented at the wedding. One of them sacrificed a ram whose meat was being prepared for the feast. (All Bhatra brahmins ate meat.)

One of my own contributions was saved by Jagriti. Grandaunt Guna asked me to get some cow urine for a ceremony of purification. I didn't ask her what sort of pollution was there for which I had to bring cow urine. Grandaunt Lathi had a cow. With a pot in my hand I waited for the cow to urinate. It was more than an hour, but I returned back with the empty pot. The priest looked unhappy. Jagriti volunteered to bring cow urine. I was upset by my failure. She let me accompany her. "I guess you've never seen how others get cow urine on demand?" she asked me with a smile.

"No," I answered like a blind.

"It's very easy," she said as she shook my head softly. I felt relaxed.

We went to the same cow. I had the pot in my hand. Jagriti massaged the urinary organ of the cow with her hand for a few seconds.

The cow raised her tail and urinated. I filled the pot. That was my holy gift. Thanks to Jagriti!

Every family came with a utensil as a gift for the bride. There was no dowry. The widowed mother of the bride could not have afforded it. The bridegroom's uncle, Kailas, was an idealist. Mool's father had died when he was three years old. Kailas ji took care of Mool and his mother.

We expected a big barat, bridegroom's party. Kailas ji came with the bridegroom and a kuli (porter), with no drummers, no bagpipers, not even a horse to carry the bridegroom. In the Hindu tradition, the bride and the bridegroom are carried on separate palanquins, called *dola* or *doli* and *palki* respectively. Kailas ji was active in local social reforms.

There was news about him that when Mahatma Gandhi and Pandit Jawahar Lal Nehru nationally condemned discrimination against the harijans in these hills, he decided not to use the dola-palki tradition at all. The local untouchables here called themselves 'silpkar' or 'shilpkar' (Sanskrit *shilpakara* 'artisans') instead of the new name 'harijan'(God's people) given by Gandhi. But 'harijan' was definitely better than 'dom,' which the 'bitth' or the higher castes used. The silpkars attempted in the past to use the dola-palki tradition for their own brides and bridegrooms.

The attempts usually created a bad pattern. The higher caste males would come in gangs to stop the silpkars' barat, the marriage party. When the silpkars would try to move ahead, the gangsters would throw down the bride and the bridegroom and beat not only them but their entire party. They would run away for their lives, leaving their things behind. Those things would be looted by the gangsters.

Because of such discriminations, the harijans here and nationally were becoming vocal about their rights. Many had already converted to Islam and Christianity. The converts attracted others as they found equality in their adopted religions. The Arya Samaj (Aryan Society), a well-known Hindu reform group founded by Swami Dayananda in the nineteenth century, was also active in the "purification" (conversion) of anyone, including the untouchables, and declared the convert an Arya or Aryan, a noble person.

The Aryan Society believed that anybody could become an Aryan and adopt the Vedic religion. No discrimination due to "race, ethnic, caste, gender, or region." Such were the ideals of the Society, which were meant to counteract the influence of Islam and Christianity. It was strange that although Hitler wanted to create an Aryan society, he never followed the Aryan interpretations of this Society.

The higher castes hated all conversions of Islamic, Christian, Arya Samaj, or any other type. There was a new war emerging between the "high" and the "low" castes.

The recent interim Congress Government was very much aware of the plight of the harijans. But the higher castes, in spite of the order of the interim chief minister of U.P., kept discouraging the silpkars from having the honor of using the dola-palki carriages for the bride and the bridegroom. (The chief minister was ironically Pandit Govind Ballabh Pant, a native brahmin of these hills!).

Mool, anyway, did not deserve any such honors. He flunked and flunked and flunked in his high school years. The reason was the type of company he kept. They all lived in Puri and became a gang of six to ten teenage boys. They would frequently ditch their classes, bully other classmates, disrespect the teachers, and smoke bidis. In the gang, Mool was the robust, hard core rogue. At midnight, they would raid adjacent villages for fruit.

One night, some gang members were caught red-handed in the orchard of Granduncle Gobind . He came out and yelled at them. A couple of them grabbed him. Fortunately, his second son, Keshab, who later became a practicing lawyer in Puri, heard his father yelling. He brought his gun and pointed it at them, ordering them to lie down. They wouldn't. He fired a shot and all of them fell flat on the ground.

Suddenly, Uncle's son Laksh woke up and came out. Since he was a student at Mission High School, he had no problem recognizing all of them. Then Aunt Shaila, his mother, also came out and saw the boys lying there. By this time other villagers, too, began to assemble. Some of us thought that Uncle must have shot a wild animal. Aunt Shaila asked the 'grounded' boys to get up and eat as much fruit as they liked.

So they were let go.

The next day Laksh and his father notified their parents, who were all very prestigious persons of Puri. Luckily, Mool missed that night's raid. But other gang members exposed him when questioned by the parents. Mool denied any connection with them.

With that reputation, Mool was lucky to be considered fit for the honor of being a bridegroom. Morever, Uncle Ishan gave him a postal clerk job in Puri. The bride, too, was lucky that it was socially very difficult for a poor widow's daughter to get married and so soon. Radha was only seventeen. She was born when her mother was her age.

Mool's small barat (bridegroom's party) and all the folks from our side sat in the front yard for the feast. One interesting event during the feast was that Uncle Ishan sat beside Kailas ji, both old friends. Uncle Ishan was in his normal clothes, a shirt and trousers, like Kailas ji. The food servers, all from the bride side, came one by one with one item each to serve the guests. The meat server gave meat to Kailas ji and skipped Uncle Ishan.

"Hey, you didn't give me that item! Why?" Uncle Ishan asked the server. The server was a rajput from Kandy. He turned back and showed him the pot, "Pandit ji, this is meat from our ram. See those big meat pieces in Pandit Kailas ji's plate. You have those three big ash marks on your forehead. I'd be a sinner to serve meat to a saint." To show respect, the rajputs and other non-brahmins addressed senior brahmin males as 'Pandit ji.' It was clear from those three ash marks, the tripunda, that Pandit ji was initiated in a Shaivite (Lord Shiva's) sect.

A devout Shaivite here used to smear his entire body with ashes and even remain almost nude with barely a loincloth on his body (Shiva the ascetic has been pictured so in mythology). But otherwise a tripunda or three ash marks on the forehead were considered enough for lay followers.

"You can give me just the soup," said Uncle Ishan softly to the server.

The server smiled and began to pour the soup slowly so that no meat piece could drop on his plate. The moment a couple of pieces were about to drop, the server held them back with the serving ladle.

"Don't block whatever is coming along with the soup!" quipped Kailas ji.

"That's right," said Uncle Ishan. They all laughed.

Then Kailas ji asked him "How did you manage to get your food when you were a jogi?" I saw a smile of mischief on his face.

"Religious people are gullible. Even if a fakir farts, they hear or smell spirituality in it. In exchange they give him more free food." Uncle Ishan replied and we all laughed.

Then around 1 a.m. came the astrologically determined auspicious time, the 'muhurt,' for the wedding. The bridegroom was awakened by a man with a series of gentle knocks on the door. Mool opened the door and picked up his turban and sehra (the crown decorated with strings that hang over the face of the bridegroom or bride). He immediately asked, "Where is my uncle?".

"He is sleeping in the orchard under a tree," the man replied politely.

"Why?"

"He just dozed off there. We won't disturb him."

"And here I've been dozing off on a comfortable bed! I am not moving to the altar."

The man went to wake up his uncle, Kailas ji, and told him about the whole thing. Kailas ji immediately went to see Mool and said, "I slept there because I enjoyed the orchard and fresh air. Let's go."

"No, I feel insulted. I was in the bed and my uncle under the tree, with not even a dari! I am not going to the altar."

His uncle failed to persuade him. The priest, the bride, and the others were kept waiting at the altar. Somebody informed Uncle Ishan about the bridegroom who was acting like a stubborn mule. He came running to see Mool. Everybody knew that it was he who had given the post office job to Mool. So he would have more leverage. He came and said very politely, "Mooli, let's go. Radha's mother is crying! The priest is afraid of losing the muhurt. That's a bad omen." (*Mooli* sounded like an affectionate variation of *Mool*, but it could also mean 'radish', thereby implying a chewable or worthless individual!)

"Sir, I am not coming."

When the standoff continued for few more minutes, Uncle Ishan asked all of us to march toward the Vedi, the altar. He told us that it was not proper to insult the bridegroom in front of the bride's relatives. When the two were left alone in the room, Uncle Ishan closed the door. In about five minutes, the two came out of the room. Uncle Ishan escorted Mool because he was limping slightly. We wanted to see his face, if it was happy, but it was covered by the shiny crown strings (sehra).

At the altar, the priest seemed to be very unhappy as he was pronouncing the bridegroom's wedding mantras very loudly as if he were shooting him with verbal bullets.

For example, at one point the bridegroom became a little hesitant when the priest asked him to touch his bride's heart. The priest had already pronounced the Vedic mantra for 'heart touching.' Then the priest grasped his hand and, with a jerk, placed it over the breast of the bride. Mool pulled his hand back slightly. It was not clear whether he felt embarrassment or some sort of pain.

Anyway, the wedding was concluded with no further possibility of adding more injuries to insult!

But the bridegroom's uncle, Kailas ji, looked very serious throughout the wedding. At the end the priest led the wedded couple out to look at the polar star, Dhruva, and his female companion star, Arundhati, to symbolize their stable (and shining) marriage. Mythology holds that these stars are always together—a heavenly model of monogamy, which is not the custom of most Bhatras. There was a good chance for the model to succeed, as Mool was not a Bhatra in this marriage. And who knows how Uncle Ishan had inspired Mool.

Then at the altar I heard a dialog between Kailas ji and Uncle Ishan. Kailas ji appeared to be somewhat dissatisfied with the priest as he said, "Bhai, your priest is a rude man. The heart touching ceremony is the first tender moment between the bride and bridegroom. I didn't like his mantra shouting. Did you see how he pulled Mool's hand! I think he was hurt."

"Bhai ji, I tell you, this priest is no phony religious leader. Right now he is performing the marriage stability ceremony. He means it. Look at his own marriage, the same wife. He is Rama. Now what would you say about those Sharmas from Kot?"

"But young Kot Sharmas don't have many wives. You Bhatras do!" He laughed.

"But no Bhatra is a practicing priest. The Sharmas are still fooling the people," Uncle Ishan said as he also laughed. "But I understand your point. Some day India will be a free country. And then make a law: No man can marry another woman without divorce."

"I am sure the Bhatra men will break that law. They will force their wives to say, 'But we are happy.'" Kailas ji laughed again.

"Yes, the Bhatras are stupid." Uncle Ishan said as if confessing.

Kailas ji did not laugh at this time.

Exchange of insulting jokes and foul words between the relatives of the bride and the groom at the time of wedding was a very special feature of our marriages. Except for the dialogs of these two gentlemen, I heard no jokes.

Even this light-hearted criticism of the Bhatras wouldn't have been possible if men like Uncle Prem Lal, Granduncle Bisal, Uncle Keshab, and Uncle Sundar were present. They might have threatened Kailas ji with their guns.

Uncle Keshab's gun power had increased many folds after he became a lawyer. His influence with the local administration was quite visible. So was his white horse. Like his father, he used the horse not just for riding but also for hunting. While good lawyers from here such as Govind Ballabh Pant were using their legal knowledge to fight the British rule, Uncle Keshab was friendly to the British deputy commissioner. The commissioner, like his other fellow English officers, was very fond of hunting.

For local people it was unusual that an Englishman learned hunting from a yellowish brown man. They were familiar with the name Jim Corbett, an Englishman world-famous for killing the worst man-eating tigers of this region. According to our village story, a hunt made the commissioner and his English colleague, a young magistrate, believe that Uncle Keshab and his brother were superior to them.

Sundays were the usual days reserved for hunting. One morning, the four friends rode their horses and divided themselves into two teams. The commissioner and Uncle Keshab went toward the Adhwani forest and the other two to the Bhatra forest. After going up and up along the creek of Pan Gadnu, the two waited to see if a tiger would come for water around noon.

Finally, the magistrate saw a bear instead, above the creek. Without consulting his partner, the magistrate fired a shot at the big animal. The bear ran toward him. The magistrate hurriedly climbed an oak tree. Apparently, he didn't understand bear behavior. The black giant climbed the tree and grabbed his pants. The magistrate yelled for help. The bear fell down, not because of his yelling but because Uncle Sundar fired two shots at the beast.

Later the magistrate asked the commissioner why the two brothers scalped the bear the other day and took home certain parts beside the skin. He didn't know the answer either. The magistrate concluded that mountain men loved bear organs! He didn't understand the men's behavior either.

However, the magistrate helped Uncle Sundar get his coveted position as chief forest officer. Unfortunately, Uncle Keshab could not receive the title of "Rai Bahadur" (Royal Brave), an honor given to the most important man of the region for his loyalty to the British Raj.

Many Rai Bahadurs were hunters of some sort.

But there are hunters and there are hunters. One of the hunters known in this region was Shri Ram Sharma, a brahmin from Agra. He hunted here mainly for tigers. But then he began to hunt British officers and their bases of power such as electricity stations, bridges, armories, and government buildings in the plains. This just happened last year. The news reached here through his close local friends.

In 1942, Mahatma Gandhi's "Quit India" movement against the British meant "do or die" for many Indians. It was the time for Shri Ram Sharma to test his hunting skills. Even Gandhi and Nehru, the two topmost leaders, were personally familiar with his character and caliber, not to mention his courage.

On December 7, 1942, he and his fellow revolutionaries met in Agra at a designated place in the morning. In spite of their differences, they finalized their program—where and when to use bombs, dynamite, guns etc. By late afternoon, the Agra police found out from a communist that Shri Ram Sharma was there. The house was surrounded immediately. Luckily, his older brother, Bala Prasad, had already dumped all the bombs, dynamite, and secrets in a garbage heap nearby. The plans were also burnt. Officers went inside and checked the whole house, but found nothing suspicious. They ignored the nearby garbage dump. The revolutionaries were free to leave the house unsuspected. All left.

When Shri Ram Sharma and his friend Pitambar Datt Pant were about to leave, two of his acquaintances appeared out of nowhere, even though all the others had been told that he was not available to meet anyone after 4 p.m. Out of courtesy, Mr. Sharma sat inside and talked to them for about one and a half hours. It had grown dark outside. He just wanted to leave the house. Outside he saw a police officer under the electric light. He told his friends. They destroyed all the papers they had and waited to escape. But when they came out, they found about four hundred officers surrounding the house and all their escape routes. Shri Ram Sharma and his friends went up to the second floor. He still had the draft that had the targets throughout the plains of U. P. or the United Provinces of northern India. Then a police officer came to meet them when they were attempting to escape via the stairs. They pretended as if they were leaving for home. The officer told them that he had orders to search the whole house. They complied and asked his permission to go home for dinner. He let them go.

They went out through the back door and saw in a room across the way a woman kneading dough on a pot in front of the kitchen oven. The room had a clay lamp giving very dim light. Standing at the door was a slim man, the woman's husband, with a friend. Mr. Sharma entered the room. He told them that his name was Shri Ram Sharma and he wanted their help to save him from the police outside. He also told them that he could have climbed the tree in front of their house and jumped to the other side of the wall, but that he was sick. The couple went along with his alternate plan. He put on her sari and began to knead the dough. He burned the draft and other remaining papers, but kept 1,500 rupees that Mr. Pant had given him earlier.

Suddenly he heard the sound of heavy police boots moving toward him. He asked the couple and the other man to stand between him and the approaching officers. Three officers, all Indian, came and saw the open door. First they hesitated. But then they grabbed the husband and his friend. The husband, in spite of a brutal beating, did not reveal Mr. Sharma's identity. But the other man did. Which woman? One of the officers came closer to the unusually heavy-built woman. Sharma looked heavier than his size because in a rush he wore the sari over his own clothes.

In seconds, the three officers beat Sharma so brutally that he lost hearing in one ear. He slumped down and was dragged out like a dead animal. Later he found himself in jail with his colleagues. The famous freedom fighter and lawyer, Mr. Kailas Nath Katju, was going to represent him.

This true story of Shri Ram Sharma's sacrifice for India's freedom had another meaning for his Pahari friends here. The friend who gave him 1,500 rupees and one of the three officers, who brutally beat him, were both Paharis from this region. Sweet and sour fruits from the same tree!

Another sweet fruit from this tree was Mr. Umrao Singh of Baingwari. He was not like the famous hero Chandra Singh Garhwali, who in 1930 became the first Indian soldier of the 20th century for refusing the British order of firing at the Peshawar crowd (mostly Muslims of Afghan origin). Umrao Singh was one hundred percent a Gandhian freedom fighter.

Mr. Umrao Singh passed through our village the previous year before he went to jail. The entire village lined up to see him. Such a handsome and serene face, exuding peace, not hatred. We threw flowers over him. Some touched his feet, some garlanded and embraced him. Many cried. In our village, it was a very emotional moment, a moment that was linked with India's freedom. *Vande Mataram*, I salute Mother (India). Everyone was shouting this Sanskrit line taken from Bankim Chatterjee's song of national freedom. We kept on repeating *Vande Mataram, Vande Mataram* until he disappeared from the village.

The Bhatras, like Keshab and Sundar, were neither sweet nor sour fruits. Sacrifice for India was not in their careers, which were looking good with the wild animal sacrifices they were making to propitiate the English rulers. But they were not against any freedom fighter. Mr. Umrao Singh was never heard to say a word against such Bhatras. Nor were the Bhatras ever heard to disrespect Mr. Singh.

For my mother, Indian soldiers who were fighting in the World War made the highest of sacrifices. She talked often about the four Bhatras as well as about Bachan, a mason from our silpkar community, my father, and Uncle Nawal, all fighters in the War. Not to mention the other Indian soldiers. It is the participation of thousands and thousands of Indian soldiers that would gain India her freedom from the British government. She said many times, "This gain did not mean a damn thing to the dead soldiers!"

But Mother could not appreciate the new sacrifice made by some boys that June. They burned or tore to pieces their high school certificates (diplomas) in response to Gandhi's call. "What are these boys up to?" she asked Aunt Shaila, whose son Jagjit had also graduated from the Mission High School, "Shouldn't these boys check with their parents? The parents spend money on their education." Mother and Aunt Shaila had been educated up to middle school, so they understood the value of a modern education.

Aunt Shaila replied in a relaxed voice, "Jagjit already knows about them. He just laughed at their actions."

Like father like son!

My father had graduated from the same school I was attending. He and Uncle Nawal had two more years of college and then received more education at their military academy. As Mother told me, Father never thought of ever joining any group or party that was against the British Raj. His opinion was that the best thing to happen to us was to have gotten the British style of education. With this education, he hoped, we could be like them, organized and hard working.

This educational philosophy was given by the greatest and most respected Garhwali educator, Mr. Choufin of Gadoli. Due to his instruction, many of his high school graduates were already showing the signs of leadership.

I believed firmly in following my father's footsteps, at least in regards to school. There was no doubt that the English were very particular about modern education in India. In our school there was a clear sense of secular education, even though our first class was Bible class. After that class, no religion was praised or criticized. The school was inspected regularly for its quality education.

One month before our academic year was over, an English school inspector came to inspect the school. This was an annual routine. Since the school began from the third grade, he started his inspection of our class first. We were all excited about his visit. The class teacher had already given us a lecture on good behavior. I had never seen any Englishmen in my class. All the teachers were Indian, even the principal (whose official title during those years was the 'head master')

We all entered the class as soon as the bell rang and sat very quietly because the inspector could come in at any time. We were well prepared for him, even in our clothing.

Most of us put on shirts and pants or shorts (sweaters and jackets from November). Otherwise, colored pajamas were very common. The teachers, however, always wore shirts, pants, sweaters, and jackets. Only the principal put on a necktie once in a while. And only the Sanskrit teacher put on a Nehru jacket or Jodhpur coat, tight pajamas, and a Gandhi cap or a turban. No teacher, except the P.T. (physical training) teacher, was ever seen in shorts. No male teacher ever wore a dhoti. There were only two female teachers, both Christian, in the whole school and they put on saris. There were very few girls. Our class of about thirty students had only two girls and they wore loose pants with a tunic or *shalwar-kurta* suits. Some students were barefooted because they could not afford shoes.

After about ten minutes, we heard a big bang. The inspector had banged his head on the door top. He was in a short-sleeved shirt and shorts with good hiking boots. Our school doors were made for the Paharis, who were not as tall as the plains people, let alone the English inspector. Did we laugh! The teacher, however, did not laugh. In fact he gave us a stern look.

The inspector, however, quietly went in the back of the room and sat on a chair. And there was a big crackling noise. We looked behind us. The inspector was trying to get up from the floor from his supine position. We all laughed again. (Even the teacher had a misleading smile below his long moustache.) These chairs and desks were made for third-grade Pahari kids. The inspector was the tallest and broadest man I had ever seen in my life. With the size of the Englishmen, the Allies were bound to win the War. So we joked later.

In the month of June the monsoon rains came. So did my report card called a "Result Card." Mother's eyes teared seeing that I had successfully passed the third-grade battle. I knew, like the rains, that her tears were a mix of pain and pleasure. How would my father have reacted? My Ma and I would never know. (How he must have enjoyed the Normandy D-Day victory of the Allies in June! The greatest general of the Axis forces, Rommel, had been fooled!)

On July 26, a press release was issued by the publicity officer of the maharaja of Tehri Garhwal State: Shri Dev Suman had died on July 25 in the Tehri prison due to his hunger strike.

Suman was only 28. For many days, his widow was not even informed. She didn't get to see his body for it was thrown in the river immediately in the evening. No funeral. His brothers tried but couldn't find the body.

This was devastating news for the Garhwalis of both Garhwals: Tehri Garhwal and British Garhwal. The former was ruled by a maharaja and the latter by the British. I was from the British Garhwal. But my grandmother, like my grandfather, who had died long before I was born, was from Tehri Garhwal. My father was born in Tehri, the capital of the maharaja. The British protected the maharaja, a favor continuing under a treaty from the past maharajas. The favor was given because the British took over half of the State. This half, the British Garhwal, was already influenced by Gandhi's "Quit India" freedom call. The other half, the Tehri State, began to respond to Gandhi's call. In British Garhwal, that meant to "do or die" against the British.

But the maharaja was opposed to cooperation with the Indian National Congress. Instead he supported the British regime. He suppressed many attempts of those who urged him to dissociate himself from the British and improve his corrupt rule. They were imprisoned by him. Shri Dev Suman was one of them. The maharaja was not very different from the other maharajas of India, more than five hundred in number, corrupt and British lackeys.

This maharaja had two queens, officially. Nobody could tell exactly how many other mistresses, concubines, and slave women and their children he was associated with. The average citizen of Tehri Garhwal was burdened with all sorts of taxes. Suman was one of the rising stars in the national movement. Even Nehru recognized his leadership quality at such a young age. He became active in the reform movement of his home state. The maharaja ignored the pleas of Suman and his colleagues of Praja Mandal, a civic organization of Tehri State. He found good excuse to put Suman in the infamous Tehri jail.

This jail was not suitable for humans. A prisoner lived in a tiny cell, dark and dirty. Without proper toilet facilities, the prisoner had to squat behind the prison walls with heavy chains around his feet. There was verbal abuse followed by brutal beatings of weak naked bodies, smelling awful. Very poor and limited quantity of food was given and hopeless medical care. No talking was allowed among the prison inmates. If any complaints were heard, more abuse.

Many Shri Ram Sharmas and Shri Dev Sumans suffered in Indian jails what others suffered in Hitler's concentration camps.

July 25, 1944, the date of Suman's death, was considered by many in Garhwal as the death knell of the maharaja rule in Tehri.

But for India, the more important news came in early September that Japanese forces definitely had a terrible setback in Kohima and Imphal, the two towns near the Burmese border.

Footnote:

Prakash Singh of the Punjab Regiment was given the Victoria Cross for his bravery in Burma, January 19, 1943.

Lal Bahadur Thapa of the King Edward VII's Own Gurkha Rifles was given the Victoria Cross for his bravery in Tunisia, April 5–6, 1943.

Chhelu Ram of the Rajputana Rifles was posthumously given the Victoria Cross for his bravery in Tunisia, April 19–20, 1943.

Gaje Ghale of the Gurkha Rifles was given the Victoria Cross for his bravery in Burma, May 24, 1943.

Chapter 5

1944-45

The Rama Lila of 1944 was literally cold and windy.

Nevertheless, more people came that year to watch. This was because the new motor road between Buba Khal pass and Puri town had been completed and the villagers around this road had an easier walk. Regular bus service was still not available for this purpose. People from our village could not use the new road because it was way up, close to the mountain top.

Some of my classmates were happy because they could use this road and would get less tired. For most people, the bridle roads or the trails still remained the only routes to town. I felt sorry for those classmates who usually slept in class and were beaten by some insensitive teachers. Those teachers didn't care that they slept because they had walked more than four miles one way. Some of them did not sleep, but still got beaten for not completing their homework. They had no way to do their homework after such a long mountainous walk in one day.

For example, Sobat was slapped by Mr. Vaishnav, the fourth grade history teacher of our class. Mr. Vaishnav asked him, "Who is the emperor of the British Empire?"

With some hesitation, Sobat answered, "King George."

"George who?"

Sobat remained silent. The teacher stood at Sobat's desk. "Did you hear me?"

"Yes Sir."

"Then answer. George who?...George I, George II, George III, George IV?...Who?"

"George IV, Sir."

Obviously, he must have thought that the teacher stopped at the last George. So he was slapped.

Then the teacher asked me. "George VI, Sir," I answered it easily because my father was officially serving in the army of King George VI. If it were some other question, who knows if I would have met the same fate as Sobat. The teacher slapped Sobat again. "You are much older than Chander. You should have done better than he. We sing here 'Oh, Worship the King!' You should know who that king is."

Yes, it was true that all the students sang or heard this song every morning when assembled for the prayer, the first activity of the school day. But it was hard to remember whether it was George IV or V or VI. So many Georges. Couldn't they have their own names? Why are they numbers, not nouns? Many of us talked among us that the British monarchy should be abolished for these reasons. But some teachers talked about its end with the war because royalty was like a caste. Why should one caste be higher than the other? Everyone must earn his or her worth by work, not by birth or inheritance.

Some resented worshiping any human and did not sing the King song at all. They preferred to sing Iqbal's national anthem *sare jahan se achchha Hindustan hamara* 'Our India is better than the whole world.' But Iqbal also supported a nation for the Muslims, separate from Hindustan, the land of the Hindu. Therefore some thought that there shouldn't be a national anthem at all because it encouraged separatism in any case. There were those who dreamed of a united world some day: National anthems are demonic prayers which disturb the divine dream of an undivided world.

I knew why Sobat was slow in his studies. He told me that he never had time to open his books on regular school days. He walked to the school every day, more than ten miles' round trip. He looked sad after class. Maybe, he felt humiliated as the oldest in a class of about thirty students. It was not only a Hindu teacher like Mr. Vaishnav who slapped him, but also a Christian teacher who slapped him on both cheeks in another class. (Almost all the teachers were Hindu in this Christian school).

Some students lived in the dorm mainly to avoid the long hike to school. They would, during vacations or holidays, walk to their villages at varying distances, usually more than ten miles one way. Such students were not seen watching the Rama Lila. That was the time when they would share domestic chores with their parents.

Those who couldn't afford the dorm expenses simply dropped out of school. The number of students in the last two years of high school would not be the same as in the previous two years of seventh and eighth grades. Some failed not because they were stupid, but because of these lengthy walks or having to help their parents or because of the bad weather during final exams.

High school examinations were conducted in the month of March, the same as in the plains of U.P. The month of March was not too hot in the plains whereas the town of Puri faced the battering cold winds coming from the highest range of snow-covered mountains standing just in the front. Many students wouldn't be able to write in their exam books because their fingers were frost bitten. Several students would fail the U.P. High School Board Examinations because they couldn't complete the test on time.

Those who could afford it would leave for the U.P. plains colleges. Some dropouts and even total illiterates would go for jobs in the plains where they were willing to take on such menial jobs as cook, watchman, peon, janitor, waiter etc. Lucky dropouts were admitted to the army or police force and lived in the plains. With such low-paying jobs, the *Paharis* or high landers had a "low" image among the *desis*, the lowland people.

I didn't know this until our class teacher Mr. Bahuguna told us. For his college education he had to live in the plains. Our question to him was why he wrote his family name as Bahuguna. The Pahari name was Bughana, a high caste Brahmin name. Then he explained in detail how some strategies were adopted to change the attitude of the plains people. (It's doubtful if they really worked.)

Some brahmins, for example, became priests or babas (holy mystics) in the plains. So the holy name, for example, would be Swami Ramananda or Ram Das, or even as shorter as Swami Ram or Rama (from the holy Himalayas). Obviously, the sacred name of Rama or Ram is pan-Indian. But others adopted more generic names such as Sharma, Vashishth, Chaturvedi, Vaishnav, or Upadhyay, etc., all very common brahmin family names in the plains. Some even gave an unrelated twist to make their names more elegant or acceptable sounding. For example, Bughana changed to Bahuguna, Juyal to Jayal, Kandwal to Kandpal, and so on.

Some dropped their family name altogether, defending the drop to others that they did not believe in the caste system. But at the time of their marriages you wondered why they arranged for a spouse from the same caste group. There was nothing peculiar about this last pattern in the hills. Many prominent national leaders such as Rajendra Prasad, Narendra Dev, Lal Bahadur Shastri, etc. had already done so with their family names, dropping or replacing them. To replace the family name Shrivastava by Shastri was like replacing Sheraton by Scientist if Mr. Sheraton had a science diploma. Of further interest, Mr. Scientist's children would also be called Mr. Scientist or Miss Scientist, not to mention Mrs. Scientist, whether or not anyone of them have any science diploma.

"But there are exceptions, very good exceptions," he added.

The exception was the famous Hindi writer who lived in Allahabad and added his pen name as "Pahari" to his odd sounding name

"Ghildyal." Writers in Hindi literature books or magazines would put the honorific word "ji" after his name. Thus, Pahari ji, or his full name, Rama Prasad Ghildyal Pahari ji. But this honor was not enough to destroy the images of "high" and "low," based on the high and low regions. Not even when the first interim chief minister of the entire U.P. was a Pahari, Govind Ballabh Pant (the other Pahari name was Sumitra Nandan Pant, the most distinguished Hindi poet). At that time, the interim government under British rule was over. There was no chance to avoid the war.

"Another war, just on this basis, is possible," Mr. Bahuguna predicted. "For a hill person to go up is to go down in the plains. Anytime, snow or sunshine."

The war, that is, the World War, was moving everywhere in favor of the Allied forces. News like this began to float around, even on the Burmese Front. Earlier we thought that the Japanese would devastate the north-eastern region of India. They had helped create another army, the Indian national Army or the I.N.A., headed now by the charismatic leader Subhas Chandra Bose. The Japanese released all Indian prisoners of war to Mr. Bose. The prisoners, among them thousands of Garhwalis, began to fight against the British Indian forces. Indians began fighting Indians in the War. They would say in Hindi *kale kale lar rahe hain* "Blacks are fighting blacks." Many Indians considered themselves *kala* or black compared to Europeans. A European was always *gora* or white. (Only a few knew about real European and Indian diversity.)

"Indians-against-Indians" did not happen in the First World War. But then we were told that many Americans of German, Italian, and Japanese origin were fighting against Germany, Italy, and Japan. We were very familiar with names like General Montgomery, General Rommel, and General Tojo. The American general Mr. Dwight Eisenhower seemed to play a more important role in Europe than these three (the British, the German, and the Japanese). Another American, General MacArthur, was also becoming a more and more familiar actor in the East Asian theater. The three political names, Churchill, Stalin, and Roosevelt, were too familiar; for Indians, all these names were *gore* or 'white' names.

Some Indians considered this war to be a Mahabharata war in which the warring factions were cousins. The devastating epic war of the Mahabharata lasted eighteen days. Could it be that World War II would end soon? Many thought that the Axis demons would soon meet their doom. Mussolini had already been dethroned by his own Italians. May be it was for the Germans and the Japanese to do the same with Hitler and Hirohito. There were others who had praise for them.

From that year's Rama Lila I learned that the story is not always the whole story. Two scenes were affected by the weather.

The yajna or worship of sage Vishvamitra was being protected by Rama and Lakshmana. The sage was dressed up in ochre robes, a kurta shirt and a dhoti. That year it was too cold. The sage was allowed to have a shawl. The dhoti was very unsuitable as it allowed the winds to pass up through the leg openings. Fortunately the sage sat with his two disciples in front of the fire pot of worship. Good warmth.

Then suddenly one female and three male demons appeared with their swords. Rama and Lakshmana warned them by pointing their bows and arrows at them. But the demons didn't give a damn. The sage was pouring holy grains over the sacred fire pot by repeating *svaha*, the Sanskrit word for the holy offering, which the demons didn't like at all. They grabbed the sage by his topknot and threw him down. Then they grabbed the two disciples in the same way. The two young disciples attempted to loosen the demonic grip over their bodies. In the skirmish, the disciples' pajamas began to pop out from their socks, which neatly covered and hid the pajama leg openings under their long dhotis. This unhistorical dress was done to keep the cold winds from blowing up their legs. One demon yelled at the two in Garhwali, while laughing wildly, "I will tear out your pajamas. I will prove, you are not true pundits!" The whole audience laughed with such fun-loving demons.

But in the end Rama and Lakshmana killed the two and let one go.

The other scene was the bow-breaking for Sita's hand in marriage. Many kings, including Ravana, came to break the bow.

There were two maharajas in this competition. Both wanted Sita to be their maharani (head queen). They appeared drunk, but it was clear that they were local maharajas because they spoke Garhwali. They both began to argue using some foul words with one another. One said, "Listen you....son of a dumb donkey!...I go first...to break the bow." The other stopped him and said loudly, "Where is she?...Your mother? You drink that bitch's milk...while, while I break...The bow, the bow." Neither would let the other go near the bow as they were fist-fighting.

Then another maharaja came as a mediator and said, "Look, I tried to break the bow. But I couldn't move it one bit. Why don't you both try to lift it up? If you can lift it then try to break it. If you break it then you will fight each other. The winner gets Sita's hand." Such advice would have looked more proper if it were from King Janaka, Sita's father. Anyway, the two went near the bow and picked it up. Immediately four men came out from inside and dragged them out of King Janaka's courtyard! According to the story no suitor was even able to move Rudra's or Shiva's bow, let alone lift it up. Only Rama was expected to pick it up and break it. That was how it became clear that those two actors were really drunk.

But when Janaka saw that the two had been ejected, he came forward and addressed the suitors, "O princes! The bow you just saw was an imitation to test the sobriety of the Pahari princes. The real bow of Shiva is the one with which Sita used to play. Only Sita can bring it out." Then he turned to Sita, "My dear Sita! Bring now the real bow of Rudra. Place it there for these nice brave *desi* princes."

Sita did bring out another bow. There was big applause from the audience as well as from the actors.

We heard later that the two maharajas (local actors) had apologized. They told the Rama Lila Committee chairman that they had had some drinks because it was too cold outside.

As the year of 1944 was coming to a close, the news became better and better. The schools of Puri closed for winter vacation, from Christmas Eve until February 14. On Christmas Day, to our surprise we saw Uncle Nawal back in the village. He had gotten leave for three weeks to see his new baby, Vijay. How come, my father never got leave like this! Uncle Nawal explained that he was in the supply line whereas my father was on the front. That meant the other War participants from our village were also posted like my father as none of them had gotten leave either.

On Christmas Eve it snowed a lot. In our Mission School church there were prayers for the safety of our local soldiers and world peace. More important, it was a white Christmas. Almost every day it snowed.

Then the day of Uncle Nawal's departure came. Clouds had filled the whole sky. Fog had overtaken every space around us. The sun had no courage to come out. Snow, very heavy snow was everywhere. Every tree looked like it was made of snow. There were no signs of our trail to Puri. Mother told me early in the morning, "Chander! Go get Gambhir. In one hour, you will both go with Nawal to Buba Khal."

"Buba Khal? Why not to Puri?" I asked her. The Buba Khal pass was about twice as far from our village than to Puri.

"Puri is completely closed. All snowed in. The motor road is burried under snow. But a truck is available on the other side of Buba Khal. About one mile down from there."

"One mile further down from there? Ma, it's a very bad time to go that far. Can't he wait one more day?"

"You stupid, Uncle Nawal is not going to school. He has to be present at his military job. Go get Gambhir!" she said in a rough commanding voice. The local schools were closed whenever serious weather problems occurred.

But I didn't have to get Gambhir. He had already come to Uncle's house to help him pack his bags. Lathi dadi, Gambhir's mother, was also helping.

I understood the reason. The motor road on the other side of the pass was situated on a less snowy slope. But on this side there were layers and layers of snow.

We three reached the pass and then stopped inside a teashop, the only shop open. With the tea we had some hot snacks, courtesy of Uncle Nawal. The shop owner told us that the truck was not one mile away, but more than three miles away. The pass had been covered by thick layers of snow, even further down. Two more passengers heading for that truck had already left about one hour ago.

We hurried up. From there, it was all downhill and much less snow. The road was clearly visible. When we reached our destination, we saw that several men were pushing the truck down the road. Uncle Nawal yelled, "Hey, wait for me!"

Fortunately, the truck didn't move enough to cause a stir or brrrr in its engine. Then we three joined and gave the truck another push. The truck rolled down a few yards and the engine finally started. Uncle Nawal jumped on the truck. And slowly, it went off down the road.

We stood there a few minutes. Then Gambir said, "Let's go." He paused. "You know, you and I are part of the Great World War. We helped a soldier!"

I was not feeling any thing like that. My father was on the front line.

We went back to the teashop and ate more snacks. Uncle Nawal had given us one rupee each before he left. That was a lot of money at that time. We forgot about our misery of having to walk through the snow for miles and miles.

When Gam and I had gotten up high enough, we saw our side of the pass. There was no sign of any improvement in the weather. We knew that it could be dark before we reached home. We were not carrying a flash light or a lantern. It was possible that we could get confused in following the trail. It was hiding deep down under the snow, as if afraid of the bone-chilling beatings of the gusty winds coming from the front line of the snow-clad mountain range. "There's no sign of the trail yet," Gambhir said, "Let's slide, or we will be late or lost."

Our clothing was not as heavy as that of Uncle Nawal. He had long military boots, partly covered by his long heavy top coat. His army hat was good for head protection. We had only sweaters, khaki pants and canvas shoes. Sliding over thick snow! No big deal for us Himalayans; even in shorts and shirts, barefooted, we had slid down snowy mountains many times before.

We both began to slide down using trees as bases. But several times we missed them and fell far from our targets. Gambhir made a big leap when he saw a tiger. The tiger ran away as both of us yelled, but Gam's leap turned out to be more risky. He had hit a rock and there was a big bump on his forehead. But luckily no bleeding. Luckily the bears were not a problem as they were in hibernation. Our hands with frostbitten fingers had blood here and there. The real pain was in our butts because they bore the brunt of the sliding.

Surprisingly, we reached home way before dark. Our mothers were waiting for us with Aunt Kanti. They saw our bruises. Lathi dadi looked at the big bump on Gam's forehead. "What happened to your head?" she asked him. "We fought." I answered.

First she paused in disbelief. But then she became angry and moved her eyes toward me, "Why did you quarrel? Did Gam say any bad word to you?" She must have thought that I hit him in anger with a rock. Gambhir laughed, "Ma, he didn't hit me. We both fought in the highest second world war!"

There was one casualty in our village during the first week of March. Dhiru, Bhajnu's father, died. An ox gored him over the rim of our village gorge, the 'bhel.' He fell down below in the creek. Fortunately, Uncle Ishan was home that day. He and three other men from Gwar took him to Puri's hospital on a stretcher.

The hospital allowed Bhajnu and his mother Jaima to stay with Dhiru. Three days later Dhiru died.

A month later Bhajnu's mother told my mother that her husband was surrounded by spirits. I knew that Bhajnu's parents were shamans besides being tailors and drummers. Their belief in spirits was professional. I asked Bhajnu why his mother thought so.

Bhajnu told me that it was a hospital practice to bury dead infants in the slope below the hospital building. "My mother saw the spirits of those babies. They came screaming up to my father's bed, the first night. My father was sedated. So he didn't know anything about those spirits."

"How about you? You were with her," I inquired with curiosity.

"I didn't know either. I, too, was sleeping on my dari, beside my father's cot."

"Where was she sleeping?"

"On the same dari."

"You say, you both were sleeping on the same dari. Then you must have heard their screaming?"

"You know we are ghadyala people. We believe in such things."

"But you didn't hear them coming up?"

"No. I was in deep sleep."

"How about others in that ward?"

"You mean the other patients?"

"That's right."

"I don't know."

"Did anyone tell you about those spirits?"

"I didn't ask."

Bhajnu seemed quite careful with regards to his ghadyala or shaman's profession. He was now a part-time drummer with his uncle, Gyaru. The uncle, being the senior drummer, played the dhol, the big bass drum. Bhajnu joined him as the damau player, the small high-pitch timpani-shaped drum. He was planning to drop out of school in July. Uncle Ishan kept encouraging him, "Bhajnu beta, at least finish high school. I promise, I will get you a babu's job."

Uncle Ishan had a new post office job. With his help many local high school graduates had gotten the job of 'babu' or clerk. He lived in Puri as his new job required night time telegraph service. I thought it was due to the War. But on Sundays or other holidays he came back to our village.

After Bhajnu's father fell in the gorge, many wanted to destroy it altogether. But it was quite useful in other ways. There was a big *malu* web all around it. The malu creeper virtually made a thatch with its dense and strong expansion. Expert climbers like Gambhir, Dhan, Harit etc. would climb over the thatch and pick up a hundred of big flat malu leaves for food plates during big feasts. The other advantage the gorge offered was as a place for toilet at its foot beside the creek. People from above could not see who was doing what down there, especially in the early morning or evening hours when it was dark. But it was, nevertheless, a risky area. Occasional sightings of a bear or tiger would alert the villagers quickly. For days nobody would have the courage to go there for toilet, etc.

On the last Sunday evening of March, I saw from the rim of the gorge a black bear moving slowly toward the creek. It was not quite dark yet. But it was cloudy. I ran to tell Uncle Sundar to shoot the animal. He ran with his gun toward the gorge area. I ran to tell my mother. But on my way I met Gambhir and told him. He was excited. We both went to the rim. Where was Uncle Sundar hiding? He must have already found a hiding place at close range from which to shoot the damn animal. Gambhir asked me, "Where is the bear?"

I led him a few yards down, but he couldn't see any animal. He still believed me. For a better view, he climbed the malu thatch. Gam shouted at me, "You ass, that's Uncle Gobind. I can see his black blanket and bare butts." I quickly contemplated, he was now seated in squat posture and seemed to be exhaling for excretion.

Gam came back and said, "Now what do you think you did! Tomorrow everybody will know. A son shot his father." I didn't think that Gambhir would be angry rather, I thought he might feel good that the man who deprived him and his mother of his father's land would be shot by his own son. "Don't tell anybody," he warned me.

We both ran to our houses. Neither of us had the courage or common sense to go down and warn Uncle Sundar. He would have heard our warning calls. But how would we tell him that it was his own father! So embarrassing.

In spite of my attempts, I couldn't sleep that whole night. I was seeing my own hunting story with closed eyes in bed. Never getting any honor from it, for it contained scenes of, for example, cremation, arrest, beating, crying, screaming, cussing, running away, ridiculing, suicide, and not being on speaking terms. No comic scene, not even for a moment. A few minutes of intermittent sleep was like intermittent dropping of the curtain to view the next horrible scene.

The next morning I went to see Gambhir. He was working in the orchard with his mother, Lathi dadi. She looked at me and smiled, with a pick in her hand. All right, she was smiling! So I thought Gambhir didn't tell her about my heinous act. "Sorry son! That old bear is still alive," she patted me on my shoulder, "Why didn't you hit him with a big rock right then?" We all laughed and laughed and laughed.

The next Sunday afternoon I saw a young girl, about thirteen or fourteen, working with Gambhir in the same orchard. Then Lathi dadi came out and said loudly, "Gundi, your room smells awful. Come and clean it up." The girl went up. I became curious and went to talk to Gam, "Who is this Gundi?"

Lathi dadi had met Gundi earlier at the Kamaleshwar Temple of Srinagar. She was barely 5 feet and looked smaller than her age. She was sixteen and married and abandoned by her husband and in-laws for whatever reasons. It was not that she wasn't attractive, or didn't bring enough dowry. In work, she was a little slow and less organized than an average Pahari girl of her age. Her in-laws began to look for another girl. They forced her out. So Gundi became a jogini or nun at the temple.

The reason Lathi dadi became interested in Gundi was that their parental villages were adjacent to each other. Dadi's offer of domestic work seemed a sort of salvation for her.

In less than a month she was there working like a family member. Gambhir told me that she was a rajput by caste and that his mother had already made a compromise that she could also cook for them. Brahmins wouldn't eat with rajputs in their kitchen. So it sounded like a temporary treaty of the centuries-long kitchen war of higher and lower castes.

The next month Lathi dadi and Dhan's mother, Aunt Rebti, unexpectedly engaged in a battle that had nothing to do with "higher" and "lower," as both ladies were equal in caste and age. Gambhir's water buffalo was found in Dhan's wheat field. Obviously the milking beast had been in the field for hours enjoying the tender wheat plants.

When Aunt Rebti saw the damage, she couldn't control her anger and frustration. Right from the field, while driving the she-buffalo out of it, she began to yell all the Garhwali insults she knew in the Garhwali style. "You bitch, Gambhir's mother! Your bitch buffalo ate my wheat crop. Do you hear me, you damn dirty woman?...Hey Gambhir's ma!...Hey Gambhir!—"

Our two villages, being at shouting distance, allowed the audiences on both sides to observe or hear inter-village verbal battles. The only physical barrier for the physical broil among these female warriors was Pan Gadnu Creek which divided our villages.

Lathi dadi heard the battle cry of Aunt Rebti. "Hey you Dhan's ma, you Rebti! What makes you so mad?"

"What makes me mad? Come here and see what your fat buffalo has done! You widow bitches don't know how to control your animals!"

"I didn't leave that stupid buffalo there. And don't call me a widow bitch! God forbid, you may be a widow soon, too."

"You whore dare curse me like that! No regret for my loss? You wife of your father!"

"You wife of your father-in-law, you wife of your brother-in-law, you whore of the whole village! Shut up or I will come break your mouth!"

"I will pee in your mouth! Your mouth feels no pain for this damage. You daughter of a whore!..."

"May your dead die. May your cattle be eaten up by the tigers..."

This battle would have continued if it were not for the approaching darkness. Some cuss sentences defied common sense. For example, how does a dead person die? A dead person is a dead person, is a dead person, is a dead person. But it was a very common curse in Garhwali.

The next morning Lathi dadi and Gambhir came to our house to find out if Gundi was with us. Finally everyone knew that Gundi had been missing since the previous evening. She seemed to be the real casualty of the battle between Lathi dadi and Aunt Rebti.

It was Gundi who, as part of her errands, took the she-buffalo without her calf to the creek for a wash. Daily washing made the buffalo clean (and apparently glad to release more milk in the evening). While the buffalo was still in the water, Gundi went inside the nearby watermill to have a nap. By the time she woke up, the beast had already gone elsewhere! Gundi felt so bad that she confessed to a village girl when she heard the battle.

Lathi dadi never blamed Gundi and still wanted her back. Later she even traveled to the temple where Gundi had lived as a nun. But Gundi left no clue.

The month of May would remain unforgettable in my life. Very unexpected news shocked our area like a strike of lightning. Germany surrendered on May 7. Mother had already predicted Germany's surrender without even knowing about Hitler's mysterious end. When I told Ma about this, she reacted quickly, "If Italy and Germany are out, what is Japan waiting for? Japan will forever regret." But we doubted that the Japanese would ever do with their leaders what the Italians did with Mussolini and his mistress recently in Milan Square.

Again the monsoons came and with it my report card with my success in the fourth grade. But for Karun the new rains brought no tears of joy. He had failed.

Now how would he give the news of this loss to his father, Granduncle Bisal? Much more problematic was Karun's mother, Tari. She didn't know how to read a report card, totally illiterate. But she had been very much interested in her son's English literacy. And Granduncle Bisal had only a middle school education, more than enough for a World War soldier like him. So Bisal would tell her about anything written in Hindi or English (or numbers). Both were very hot-tempered and would frequently holler at each other as well as at their children.

I had several opportunities to hear their cacophony…"Wish you were shot dead in the war!" was one of her several wishes…"Hope a tiger gobbles your head!" would be his matching wish. The chances of her wish coming true were very high because humans did very frequently shoot humans. But he was safe now as the war was over long ago. Tigers, on the other hand rarely hurt humans.

The joke in the village, nevertheless, was that they were meant for each other. They had raised nine children together. For them beating the children was as easy as eating bread. Eating united them. All of them ate a lot. We observed them eating together at the occasional festive feasts in our village. It was like gang hunting and scavenging.

I understood poor Karun's problem when he saw my report card. He proposed his plan to me. But I told him politely that I wasn't the right person for his plan because we were totally two different people. So he found Gambhir with whom the plan worked out very well. The two cousins were literally very close to each other as they were from the same family and also went to school together.

Then in the first week of July when our new school year was to start, unusually heavy rains washed away many trails with slides. The school remained closed for a few days. When the rains finally slowed, school started. I had mixed feelings seeing Karun in my class.

A few days later, one early afternoon, Granduncle Bisal, Karun's father, entered our classroom and asked our teacher's permission to have a talk with Karun outside. The whole class laughed when Granduncle Bisal left the class with Karun. Everybody could see that Granduncle Bisal had encountered heavy rains on his way there. He was in his battle khakis. His long army boots were in his hands and his trousers were pulled up to his knees. Other students had no clear idea why his boots were not where they belonged. But as a member of his village, I knew very well that in order to prolong the life of his shoes he carried them in his hands (to protect them from rainwater!).

Karun didn't return to class. But in the evening, Gambhir told me the whole story. The month before Karun had borrowed Gambhir's report card and showed it to his father. While showing it, he held the card very carefully by placing his thumb over the name "Gambhir" and the rest was no problem! After all, both were Bhatras—natural buddies. Then somebody told Granduncle Bisal that Karun and I were in the same class. Finally he himself verified it and beat the hell out of Karun. Perhaps he would not have been beaten so badly if he hadn't given his father the fantastic excuse that there weren't enough chairs and desks yet in the other class.

Then came the most horrible news. An atomic bomb was dropped by an American plane over Hiroshima on August 6. As if this instant mass burning of humanity was not enough, another was dropped on Nagasaki on August 9. Why the stupid Japanese government waited for surrender until after the Nagasaki bombing was another question some of my teachers had. For several others, there was no such question because America rightfully wanted Japan to have a taste of the December 7, 1941 bombing of Pearl Harbor. Some even wondered why a Buddhist country such as Japan didn't understand the Law of Karma, action-reaction.

We were in a Christian school. Very difficult not to mix religion with war. What happened to America's Christian values? How did they go to church and pray to God? Or for God? Was He missing in action?

Or was He the biggest casualty of this war? If God was there, why would we have such wars in the first place?

Some occasionally mentioned "economics" (and of course, "politics"). Anti-Semitism and religious hatred were denounced. Hitler was denounced. He burned not only Jews and Gypsies (who were of Indian origin), but also Aryans (in unprecedented numbers).

Then came the war crime trials. Cries to try Tojo, Hirohito, Truman, Stalin, Churchill, and the Nazis. Some didn't want Churchill, Stalin, and Truman to be tried. Indians knew that Hitler occupied Poland for a short time and he was considered a criminal. But what about Chrchill? India continued to be occupied by Britain and Churchill. Hitler burned Jews, Truman burned Japanese. And what the Japanese forces did was a disgrace in human history. Many wanted not to leave Hirohito unpunished for crimes against humanity.

People were hotly debating the victors' justice.

I was too young to participate in such opinions. I don't think I really understood the war. But the fact remained that this was the highest inhuman war. And my father was part of it. We continued to read the Bible in our school and believed in God's grace. All I (and my mother) wanted was the safe return of my father.

Yes, my father and all the other participants in the war from our village, except one, returned home safely. Granduncle Madan's two sons (both too young and unmarried) were in the war. The older son, Birendra, was missing in action. A young girl had already been arranged for him. She was the daughter of distant relatives of Grandaunt Puna, Birendra's mother. The younger son, Brijendra, looked depressed when he came home alone. In fact, there was no rejoicing or celebration in our village because one of our soldiers was missing.

The leader of the Indian National Army (I.N.A.), Subhas Chandra Bose, was also considered missing by many Indians. But our teachers told us that he had died in a plane crash. We began to believe that Birendra, too, was already dead. Some guessed that like Bhawani Singh of Malli, he might have joined the I. N. A. Bhawani told us that there were thousands of Garhwali soldiers in the I.N.A., but that he had never heard the name like Birendra Bhatra. Most people in our area had only praise for Bhawani and Bose.

I was not sure who should be praised or denounced. I thought my best informant would be my father. He told me very little about the war. But he had his opinions. "Papa, there are so many views about war criminals. What do you say?"

"You mean who should be tried?"

"Yes."

"The real haramzada is dead. He should have been tried."

It wasn't only my father who called Hitler a haramzada, a bastard. Every soldier I met called him names. When I asked Uncle Nawal, he called him a man eater. "Chander, he hunted millions of innocent women and children, like some tigers do here. He is lucky he died. Otherwise, he should have been put in a zoo. Young people like you could have seen this animal. Feed him cucumbers."

"Oh yes, he was a vegetarian!" I laughed.

"A sick animal."

Uncle Nawal, too, was lucky that he was alive. "Uncle, do you feel any pain from your bullet holes?" He had two bullet holes, one on his shoulder and another in his leg.

"Bullet holes? You should some day meet Musaddi Lal Kala of Sumari. His body is full of bullet holes!"

My father also spoke very high of Kala ji. "But son, not very many would remember the sacrifices of our soldiers. This war was not needed, this sacrifice was not needed. All you need is a couple of demons. And then you hope for an avatar. How many monkeys and bears do you remember from the Rama Lila?"

"Hanuman...Angad and his father Vali...and his uncle Sugriw. And also their wives, Angad's mother and aunt."

"The poet didn't list others. It's really a story of few persons. Include a few more monkeys here and there. About a hundred, and you wouldn't read the story. Rama had no way to win the war. Those countless monkeys won the war for him. You will never know how many there were. Real stories have many beings. The ones you read give you a few hours of fun. They are made for fun. There's an art to creating them, for the market. And you buy them for a few hours' fun. You praise them if they fit your views."

He promised me that he would go with me to see the entire Rama Lila, all ten nights, including the final day of Bharat Milap.

Footnote:

Nand Singh of the Sikh Regiment was given the Victoria Cross for his bravery in Burma, March 11-12, 1944.

Abdul Hafiz of the Jat Regiment was posthumously given the Victoria Cross for his bravery in Imphal, India, April 6, 1944.

Kamal Ram of the Punjab Regiment was given the Victoria Cross for his bravery in Italy, May 12, 1944.

Ganju Lama of the Gurkha Rifles was given the Victoria Cross for his bravery in Imphal, India, June 12, 1944.

Tul Bahadur Pun of the Gurkha Rifles was given the Victoria Cross for his bravery in Burma, June 23, 1944.

Agan Singh Rai of the Royal Gurkha Rifles was given the Victoria Cross for his bravery in Imphal , India, June 26, 1944.

Netra Bahadur Thapa of the Royal Gurkha Rifles was posthumously given the Victoria Cross for his bravery in Imphal, India, June 25-26, 1944.

Yashwant Ghadge of the Maratha Light Infantry was posthumously given the Victoria Cross for his bravery in Italy, July 10, 1944.

Sher Bahadur Thapa of the Gurkha Rifles was posthumously given the Victoria Cross for his bravery in Italy, September 18, 1944.

Chapter 6

1945–46

This year's Rama Lila did become very special. My parents accompanied me. Uncle Nawal and Aunt Kanti also joined us on some days. This was a pattern. Not everybody came every night. The biggest crowds came on the nights when the scenes were about Rama and Lakshmana protecting worship, the bow-breaking, Hanuman's visit to Lanka, and the Rama-Ravana fight.

In importance, the role of Hanuman was superseded only by the roles of Rama, Lakshmana, and Sita. Not because they were the most sacred, but because they tested the skills of these actors in terms of length of time and body strength. Hanuman had to be the strongest.

He proposed a meeting to Rama and Lakshmana with his monkey boss Sugriva. He carried both of them together on his shoulders all the way to Sugriva's residence. This was considered a very emotional moment for those who believed that Hanuman was the greatest symbol of true service to God and for those who believed in sheer human physical strength. Fun lovers were interested in the second aspect. Their fun was not derived from the fact that a human was dressed up as a monkey and spoke human language. I had never seen a Hanuman actor looking shaky when he carried the two brothers.

Two men competed for the role of Hanuman that year. The news from an insider, whose father was a member of the Rama Lila Committee, was that these two literally had a friendly wrestling match to prove their physical strength. The match was a draw. They agreed that they would alternate the role at least for a couple of years. The previous year it was Hameed. He did marvelous job. No one ever questioned why a Muslim was given such a sacred role. After all, this was God's play. All were equal in God's world (the whole cosmos is Lord's Lila).

As agreed, Hanuman for 1945 would be Jagat Singh, which meant the "world's lion." Many in the audience recognized Jagat as they shouted, 'Make Hameed Hanuman again.' However, Jagat carried Rama and Lakshmana on his shoulders so bravely and neatly that nobody seemed to doubt his strength. That is, nobody shouted again for Hameed.

Then the night arrived when Hanuman leapt to Lanka and located Sita there in a place called Ashoka Vatika, the sorrowless garden. This is the garden where Ravana kept her surrounded by demonesses. The garden in the yard (in front of the stage) was decorated with fruits and flowers.

Hanuman hid himself in a corner and watched the demons' activities. Ravana came and proposed again to Sita. She refused. He threatened to punish her and even make a meal out of her. She didn't yield to his threats. Then he asked the demons to torture her after he left. He left and a demoness started to talk to her.

Then Hanuman came out and jumped on the demon guards (who were all young boys). They all ran away. Then he broke the ropes on which fruits such as cucumbers, maze (corn), guavas etc. were hanging. Nobody said a word against the destruction of the garden (not even against the display of maze and guava which did not exist in the time of the Ramayana). All that looked very realistic until he ran toward the musicians, the harmonium master and the two drummers. He picked up the harmonium and thrashed it. The two drummers picked up their drums and ran behind the stage. Hanuman ran up to the stage where they were preparing Ravana's court for the next scene. He broke the throne, the stools, and other decorative objects. Fortunately he didn't hit any petromax lamps.

The stage managers understood the problem. Hanuman was drunk. Two big men came out and dragged him out. He was yelling, 'I will save Mother. I will kill those demons…'

That's when many from the audience shouted, 'Where is Hameed? Make him Hanuman.' God granted their wish, as it were. In a few minutes Hameed came out and presented himself as Hanuman to Sita with folded palms, "Mother, I am the real Hanuman…. The other who looked like me was a demon…. I am Lord Rama's real messenger…. Here is Rama's real ring."

There was laughter and applause at every pause he gave. "This Hanuman was real last year, too." "He is a clean man." "He is a true Muslim. He wouldn't touch a drop of alcohol!" Comments like these from individuals in the audience also meant the appreciation of the decision taken by the Rama Lila director and his associates.

The harmonium master with another harmonium, and the two drummers also received applause as they appeared in their corner.

At the national front, just before winter, India's independence movement also began to take an ugly turn. I had rarely heard the name Jinnah earlier. But it was appearing more and more in the news. He wanted a separate country for Muslims. I couldn't imagine Hameed leaving us for a separate country. But no local Muslim seemed to be excited by the idea of a separate country. Could really Jinnah fully speak for all the Muslims? That was the question some of our teachers were raising because Mahatma Gandhi and Jawahar Lal Nehru were also talking about it.

On the local front, the marriage of our principal's daughter became a celebration during the Diwali holidays. One day before the school closed, sweets were distributed in every class. This was a very unusual treat for students. The most unusual treat was the dinner invitation for the entire faculty of the school. The funniest thing at the dinner was a separate tent and kitchen for the brahmin faculty. The principal had made arrangements as the Sarola brahmin had instructed him.

The convention of separate tents meant that if a Sarola male brahmin cooked food in a secluded area then all high caste Hindus, especially brahmins, would eat food there. No Christian or Muslim faculty members, not even any low caste Hindus, would eat in the Hindu tent; they would eat in the general tent with everybody else. Within the tent, the kitchen area would be further restricted to the Sarola brahmin cook or other adult male brahmins who had the sacred thread or *janeu* (Sanskrit *yajnopavita*) on their body.

My father and Uncle Nawal were also invited. But they ate in the general tent, not in the "Hindu" tent. They told the principal that they had been eating with their English officers. All such arrangements were managed, apparently with no problems.

The new year began with bad news: Birendra was confirmed dead. It didn't come as a big shock to others because missing in action generally meant "dead." The winter was not harsh that year. The war's horror was gone, but the issue of India's independence was becoming more and more horrible.

Then in the month of March came *Rama Navami*, the birthday of Rama. A big procession from Puri's Vishnu temple started. The priest came out uttering sacred verses from the *Ramayana* and the *Ramacharitamanasa*, sprinkling water over the temple steps. Then a big decorated palanquin with idols of Rama and his brothers was carried out from the temple. The bearers of the palanquin were all high-caste Hindus. Some untouchables were there, too, but only as bystanders; they were not allowed to enter the temple, nor touch the palanquin. The Rama Lila, surprisingly, discriminated against no one.

March was the month when the inspector of school was expected. That year, our Hindi class was scheduled for inspection. The Hindi teacher was from the plains. It was the first year that a few teachers from the plains joined our school. This unusual move was taken for the sake of unity in diversity. No discrimination against the plains people.

We called the Hindi teacher Shastri ji as he had the prestigious Sanskrit diploma known as "shastri." He, unlike many other Pahari teachers, didn't coach us in advance for the inspection. A teacher's raise in salary usually depended on this inspection.

Finally the day of inspection arrived with excitement. We were excited to see how the tall Englishman would do this year. But the inspector that came to our class was a different Englishman, of medium height, still tall for the Paharis. He entered the class with a smile and said "namaste" facing us with folded palms, standing beside Shastri ji. We all said "namaste' in return. The whole class looked relaxed. Shastri ji also looked surprised. Then the inspector sat in a corner. The chair seemed to be fine for his weight, no accident like last time.

Then Shastri ji asked a student in Hindi, "How many adhyayas Tulsidas wrote in the Ramayana?" The student couldn't answer and said, "I don't know, Sir."

Then he asked another student the same question. This student said, "I am not sure, but four to eight." Everybody laughed, but not Shastri ji. He rather looked upset.

Shastri ji knew that these two boys were local Pahari brahmins as he said, "What kinds of brahmins are you? You don't know how many adhyayas Tulsidas wrote in the Ramayana?" The boys looked quite embarrassed.

Totally unexpected, the inspector came beside Shastri ji and asked his permission to speak to the students. Shastri ji said "Yes" very politely.

The inspector said in Hindi, "Did you understand how your teacher was testing your knowledge? The answer was supposed to be like this: Tulsidas did not write the *Ramayana*, Valmiki did, in ancient Sanskrit. Tulsidas wrote the *Ramacharitamanasa* in modern Avadhi. Both books are about Rama's life. Their chapters are called 'kanda,' not 'adhyaya.' There are seven kandas in each. Scholars may have different opinions. But it's a fact that the Ramayana in Sanskrit is the second or third longest story of the world. English literature has nothing like it. But nobody owns this story, brahmin or not brahmin. It is a world story, a story of humanity. It's about the victory of good over evil. That's the hope we get when we read it."

That was the day when I learned that there were Englishmen, and then there were Englishmen. We must learn about our own history from them.

After a month our school closed for summer vacation. One day later my mother and I went to Kotdwar with my father by bus. This was the first time I saw trains. The town of Kotdwar divided the plains and the mountains, an interesting scene for me. Then we took a train trip to the next station of Najibabad. This small flat town was too hot for me. So we quickly went to Hardwar which was cooler, being situated at the foot of the Garhwal Himalayas. From there we took a bus and returned home via Rishikesh, Dev Prayag, and Srinagar.

When we came home, Bhajnu gave me three pieces of news: Brijendra had agreed to marry the girl who had been arranged for his brother; there would be a ghadyalu for inviting the dead mother of Uncle Prem Lal; and Molu, our baddi, would climb the tallest bamboo and dance at the top of it. "Why is it that you know these future events I don't know?" I asked him.

"My uncle, and maybe I, will be part of them," he said with a tone of pride.

Bhajnu was right. The next week we heard ghadyalu music in Uncle Gobind's house. I went there as I was excited to see how they were going to invite a dead woman and make her talk.

Quite a good number of Bhatras were assembled in the music room. But Granduncle Gobind was smoking his hukka in a corner of the front yard, a few yards away. He looked lost in his thoughts as if he had no concern for this trance music.

The musicians were two shamans—Bhajnu and his uncle, Gyaru. The main musician was Gyaru, who played a drum called daunr. Bhajnu's role was secondary as he played a metal plate. Gyaru was singing spiritual songs in Garhwali while hitting the drum in his lap with one stick. Bhajnu simply repeated every fourth or fifth line of the song while hitting the plate in his hand with a stick in the other.

After about fifteen to twenty minutes Grandaunt Ramni began to shake her head. She was trembling. Her hair was now disheveled as the sari from her head slipped down. Then she began to cry. The shamans stopped the music. Gyaru asked her, "Who are you?"

She was still crying. Gyaru hit the drum with a roll and repeated his question, "Who are you?" This time his voice was tough.

Then she answered in trance, "You called me…I am here." She said in some mumbled sentences like these.

"What do you want?" asked Gyaru in a deep and mellow voice

"I want to meet my children," she responded in a slippery voice.

Then she slowly scooted over to Sundar uncle, who was sitting in front of her. She hugged him and cried, "How are you, beta!" Uncle Sundar, her beta or son, had tears in his eyes. Then she left him and scooted over to Uncle Keshab, who was sitting next to his brother Sundar. She hugged him, too. She cried more as she kissed his head which she was holding between her breasts. She caressed him with her hands and said, "I love you, my beta!" Then she raised her head and rolled her eyes. I thought she was looking for her other "beta" or son as she said, "I am sorry for Prem!…He is lonely!…Tell him I will meet him!"

Why Uncle Prem Lal was not in this meeting was not clear to me. Maybe because she was his stepmother (I never saw them talking to each other). But the trance session made it clear that it was his deceased mother who had possessed his stepmother. I heard sentences such as "Only a mother can show such love" or "Poor Prem Lal missed his mother" or "We should have another meeting for them" and "That's what she wants" and "Yes, she said so" and on and on from the audience. Surprisingly, she didn't ask a word about her husband Gobind, who was not too far from this room. I was sure that she would ask "Where is Prem's father. I miss him very much" or something like that.

Maybe, she hated her husband because he got remarried or married a young woman who was good enough to be his daughter-in-law. Maybe Granduncle Gobind felt like that and so he decided to sit outside. What if she had kissed him in the presence of this audience! Public kissing between husband and wife or between lovers was not done in our society. And never with such an age gap! Only parents hugged and kissed their children openly anywhere anytime at any age. I never saw Granduncle Gobind and his son Prem Lal on speaking terms. The reason for that, as I heard from several adults, was that the son never wanted his father to remarry.

After the trance session was over, I asked Bhajnu why only she was possessed, and not someone else. Bhajnu told me that the trance session was held because she often saw in her dreams a woman looking like the deceased woman. Now I understood that all this was done on purpose. Spirits must suggest such meetings.

Brijendra's agreeing to marry the girl who was already declared to be his sister-in-law wasn't that unusual. In some Hindu communities the unmarried brother's marriage to the widow of his older brother was considered a proper thing to do. But not in our community, absolutely no way. In this case, however, there was no reason for any social hitch. The girl, Trishna, never became Brijendra's sister-in-law in the first place.

Nevertheless, the rumor was that he was pressured by the relatives on both sides. The parents might have thought that before he changed his mind they should quickly and quietly perform a simple marriage ceremony. That was what happened. It was justified for another reason, a very genuine reason. After all, Birendra was declared dead only a few months before.

Why Brijendra was so cold to the agreement didn't make sense to me. The general opinion in our village was that Trishna was an exceptionally attractive girl. And he deserved her. Like his brother, he was handsome.

During the nights, I would often hear the dholki-dance sounds emanating from Molu and Chandni's house. This baddi couple of our village was preparing for the bamboo dance, called *lang* 'bamboo', due next month. This sacred dance was considered a powerful means of preventing a bad harvest. The dance was to be held by the big water pool of kund. It would be my first experience of this dance. But I was given a simple picture of it beforehand.

In this dance there is a sort of role reversal. In the baddi dances the dancer is always female. But for the lang dance the dancer is male. The dancer climbs a very tall bamboo pole to its end and there he places his belly on its padded tip. Then balancing himself on the tip with his navel only, he moves his body around. Each round, called *khand*, is done according to the instructions of the dhol-damau drummers from the ground. The rounds honor not only local gods and goddesses, but also human communities, that is, castes of the region. These rounds are not really a dance, but a ritual.

What I didn't know was that another dance of the baddi couple had been arranged at the village of Kandy the night before. The first part was open to everyone and the second part was restricted to adult males only under a large tent completely covered from all sides.

I went to see the first part, obviously with a good crowd. Uncle Keshab was sitting in the front. When Gambhir, Karun, and I joined him, he did not appear to be very comfortable.

Then the dance began. Molu started playing his dholki drum, singing an invitation to his female dancer Chandni. At the last line of the song we saw the beautiful Chandni at the entrance. She was dressed in a soft, pink, and delicate skirt whose corners she had lifted up slightly with her hands. Then gently freeing her hands to greet the audience, she moved toward the center of the tent, the empty space, with rhythmic steps accompanied by her ankle bells that matched the drum beats. Then she moved in a circle, again holding the corners of her skirt in her hands and jumping high every now and then. At every jump Uncle Keshab shouted a praise by repeating the Garhwali sentence *sarkau,* rhythmically three or four times in quick succession. The sentence meant "Slip off!" There was applause at her response.

We three boys had to leave when the second half of the dance was moved to the tent. Any way, I was sleepy by this time and my parents were waiting for me at home for a late dinner. The big excitement would come the next afternoon, at the lang dance.

The next afternoon, there was a huge crowd beside the kund. People from distant villages came to see this dance. There were enough sacred food items and drinks for everybody, courtesy of the contributions made through the village chiefs called "padhan" (or "pradhan").

Then the ceremony or ritual started. First Molu, the baddi, was given a sacred bath and dressed up for the dance. Outside in the middle of the ground area, reserved for regular dances, was a very long and strong bamboo pole. It was stabilized in two ways. First, it had been dug into a very deep hole. Then several big strong ropes had been tied around it (one end of each rope attached to a stake on the ground and the other end to the top of the bamboo). The dhol-damau drums began the auspicious ceremony.

Molu was escorted to the pole by the priest and a couple of village chiefs. There was big applause when Molu began to climb the very long pole so fast. He had obviously impressed the audience. In seconds he was atop the pole. The dhol-damau drumming stopped. With his hands Molu held the ropes for support as he went around and tilted his body in a prone position on the cushioned pad atop the pole. Then the priest from the ground instructed him in a singsong manner "Take a round for Mother Goddess." Molu responded, "Yes, the good round, Sir!" (*Khand bhale ji*) and he took a round to the right in the same prone position while moving his hands from rope to rope for support. There was big applause from the audience. Then a few more rounds for several other gods and goddesses. The dhol-damau drumming again ended this preliminary divine honoring.

Then came the honoring of castes. First the ruling castes or top rajput castes of the Garhwal Himalayas. The drumming stopped. The priest began to call off in the same manner "Take a round for the Rana rajputs." Molu responded loudly "A round for the Ranas" and he did a round (*khand*). The Rana name meant Raja or the royal family.

After six or seven rounds in this manner, a big burly man in a modern shirt and pants ran toward the pole shouting "Our family's name should have been after the Parmars. We are dishonored. The Parmars are not equal to us. I am going to throw down the baddi." He was stopped by the two village chiefs. He threw them down and moved to the pole and began to shake it. Chandni began to cry loudly, "Please save my man!" Obviously we all were watching Molu up there clinging to the swinging pole. Then I saw Sanman Singh, a young police officer from Kandy, running toward the pole. His moustache matched his strength as he kicked the burly man in the butt. The man fell down but quickly got up and began to wrestle with him.

Then I saw a few more men coming toward the pole shouting "Why did he kick our man?" The men began to hit Sanman with their fists. Sanman's two younger brothers and three cousins ran to defend him. There was a big brawl. Every so often one opponent tried to shake the pole and I thought Molu would drop dead anytime now. Chandni's cries made me increasingly nervous. But Sanman and his party beat the hell out of the opponents. Chandni stopped screaming when all the culprits were dragged out of the area.

I have never been able to understand (like many others) why that burly man didn't consider his community to be more important since it was called before the Parmars. In Garhwal's history the Parmars have been considered the rulers. Later I asked one of my Parmar classmates, not really a royal fellow anymore. He just laughed it out while saying, "That idiot must have been drunk. I don't care whether you put the Parmars before the Pars or after the Mars."

The next week my father left home. He had been promoted to captain. Fortunately the rains had not yet started. The bus route (called 'motor road') from Puri to Kotdwar was clear. Many from our village assembled at the Puri bus stop to give him a special farewell as he was a

"Kaptan Sahab"(Mr. Captain) or Captain Fateh Singh. I had mixed feelings about his departure. Most likely my mother and I would go to live with him in New Delhi. That was what Father was planning for the next year. But for the time being, he had a temporary assignment at Rangoon (Yangoon), badly damaged by the Japanese during the war.

A few days later my report card or result card came. I was surprised to see that my marks in Hindi were "first class." I thought that Shastri ji was disgusted with our Pahari Hindi, not to mention our knowledge of the Ramayana. This time Karun passed and didn't need any tricks to convince his parents.

The month of July came and there was a shortage of kerosene oil. As soon as our school started, we desperately needed the oil for lanterns to do our homework at night. The rationing officer had allowed each student to get an extra kerosene bottle of eight fluid ounces. Karun and I ran to the shop at Puri. There was a big line. We waited about two hours in line to get our 8-ounce bottle filled with this very precious commodity. It was already sunset when we returned home.

As soon as we were over the ridge of the village of Thaula we heard a familiar voice. It was the famous Bisram, famous for his erratic nocturnal musical ecstasies. He was singing a song. Then we came face to face. He was in very old military clothes, with holes here and there. He also donned a military hat. "How are you young fellows from Rajkhet?" he asked us before we even greeted him. I folded my palms and said "pranam" (the customary honor word to greet elders). Karun did the same, but he was laughing.

"Why are you laughing? What's in your hand?" Bisram asked Karun.

Obviously Karun wanted to play a trick on him as he said, "It's something you like." Our kerosene bottles were actually used *desi* (country) liquor bottles. Any local Pahari could recognize them. Karun wanted to have fun with such familiar bottles and Bisram.

"What are you young fellows doing? You are not old enough for that. You shouldn't have that stuff. Give me that bottle." Karun was apparently very much delighted to give it to him as he handed it over as soon as Bisram asked.

Bisram opened the corked bottle and drank all the kerosene oil, as if in one breath.

The same Karun who a few seconds before had been laughing while handing over the bottle, now stood motionless. Bisram returned the bottle. Karun's mouth was as empty as the bottle. Not a word did he speak. It was not just the loss of money, not just the loss of the oil or time spent in the long line, but also the loss of his immediate security.

It was already dark when we reached our houses. In less than a half hour, Karun and his parents came to our house. His father asked me, "Tell me, how in the world could any man drink kerosene oil! If you taste one drop of it by mistake, you spit it out, you don't drink it. But this liar says that Bisram drank the whole bottle. Didn't you both eat pakora and jalebi with that money?"

"No, no, Dada ji. Karun told you the truth—"

"So you ate those snacks and sweets. Liars!" He just slapped and slapped and slapped Karun. When he began to scream, my mother came out from the kitchen. She saw the beating in progress, but couldn't say a word because the beater was an uncle-in-law by the courtesy kinship rules of the village. So she took Karun's mother inside and pacified her.

I felt even more sorry for Karun when he apologized the next day because his father had called me a liar. I just laughed and said, "Maybe some day, dada ji will meet Granduncle Bisram and offer him a bottle of kerosene."

"Hey, that's a very good idea. We can prove that we are not liars."

"Look, I was just joking. Don't try any costly tricks like that, anymore!"

The news of the story of the kerosene oil as a substitute for hard liquor spread fast in our village. Bhajnu made fun of Karun. "Karun! You really made up that story…So how were the pakoras?…Hot, spicy. Right?"

"Come on Bhajnu! It happened. It's real. It's not like your ghadyalu trance. Do you really believe that a dead mother would come back to meet her sons?" I retaliated.

"Well, I saw her coming back without my ghadyalu."

"What do you mean?" I asked jokingly.

"Last week in the evening she met Prem Lal ji...Remember? She had promised that in the ghadyalu. But this time in a lonely dark room. Karun was with me. He, too, saw."

"What did you see?"

"The same thing you saw in the ghadyalu. Except that this time it was Prem Lal ji alone with her. And they were—"

"Shut up Bhajnu!" Karun said as if he was going to beat him. I couldn't understand why Karun wouldn't let Bhajnu complete his simple sentence "And they were dancing in a trance" or something like that. Bhajnu had already made it clear that he believed in trances with or without music. But I decided not to go further with the story of the stepmother who became a substitute for the dead mother.

The Japanese had surrendered on August 14 the year before. Granduncle Madan and Grandaunt Puna believed that their son could not have been killed in the war on or after the 13th of August, 1945. This was why they left for Hardwar to perform a *shraddha* or first annual funerary rite.

July and August are usually the worst rainy months in the hills. We had been hearing news of bus accidents. Every year the bus route is washed away in several places. The hill slides, there are falling rocks and trees, water streams, fog and other road hazards. From Srinagar to Dev Prayag the bus route is parallel with the Alakananda river. Dev Prayag literally means "divine confluence" as the two sacred rivers, the Alakananda and the Bhagirathi or Ganga (the Ganges) meet there. From there the bus route runs alongside the Ganges all the way to Rishikesh, which is a higher suburb of Hardwar. From Hardwar, at a lower elevation, one can see the rise of the Himalayas as well as the small Sivalik mountain range. The plains people believe that a shraddha there leads dead souls to heaven through the gradual rise of the Himalayas. The Ganges is the upward route which takes the soul to heaven from where the river descended down at Bhagirath Shikhar, one of the spectacular Himalayan peaks. The shraddha is performed on the banks of the Ganges. At this time of the year the water of the Ganges is all muddy and flooded.

Some in Puri did advise the couple (Granduncle Madan and Grandaunt Puna) not to believe all that heaven mythology, originally created by the plains people in their ancient Sanskrit scriptures. But they did go to Hardwar to perform the rite on August 13. It was not clear to us why after the rite they decided to visit the holiest temple in the Himalayas, the Badrinath temple of Vishnu. The news came to us that their bus had been pushed down the river by a big mountain slide. Only a few passengers had survived. Granduncle Madan and Grandaunt Puna were not among the survivors. The Ganges must have swept away their bodies. Enough for the mythical liberating way of the Ganges. The villagers felt sorry for Brijendra for whom the actions of the war were still alive in their reactions.

The same day, August 16, we heard about "Direct Action Day." I was not aware of the violent political stage of Indians because in front of me there was a curtain of immaturity. One of the actors frequently mentioned in the news was Muhammad Ali Jinnah, the leader of the Muslim League. He was bent upon dividing India into two nations, one for Muslims and another for non-Muslims. Since the majority non-Muslim population was labeled as "Hindu," that day of August 16, 1946 was chosen by Jinnah to show that Muslims would not live with Hindus.

It was a day of death. The killing started with a call from Jinnah to take direct action against Hindus wherever possible. What Jinnah failed to understand was that the action would have its reaction. Hindus killed as many Muslims. Calcutta suffered the highest losses. The Muslim League government of Mr. Shahid Suhrawardy in Bengal was responsible for the unprecedented four-day slaughter.

Since it was a slaughter of Indians by Indians, it was not labeled as a crime against humanity! Some Indian leaders who, like Hitler, considered Indians dispensable, championed the cause of freedom for Indians! Some of my teachers talked like this.

Who needs freedom from the British, freedom to end the lives of our own people? This was a question many asked in Puri. A famous Pahari Rai Bahadur and leading lawyer (mentor of the famous Pahari politician Govind Ballabh Pant) insisted again that India should remain a dominion within a British Commonwealth, at least for some years. Mr. Cripps, who had earlier been an English negotiator of India's freedom, also offered something similar. But any such suggestion, especially from a Rai Bahadur, to save India and Indians was suspect by the nationalists (including Mr. Pant). As one admirer of the Rai Bahadur wrote later, "The glittering crown of Rai Bahadur from the British government to Brij Mohan ji was viewed as an eclipse on his fully matured political enlightenment."

On the first Monday morning of September, at our school prayer meeting, the principal said, "We pray so that we love each other and won't hurt each other. The principle of love and nonviolence applies to all, everywhere, all the time. We already know how the worst war took place recently among the nations of the world. But this could happen among family members, too." He smiled and then read a letter:

> *"Dear Principal:*
>
> *I request you to permit the absence today of my sons Amar Bhatra and Anjan Bhatra. The reason for their absence is that my older sons severely beat me and my younger sons."*

The whole student crowd laughed at these sentences.

When I got home, I found the story was true. My mother and Aunt Kanti just smiled and gave me the same opinion in different words.

They wouldn't give me the reason because it was a private matter. But later Dhan and Harit gave me some description.

Granduncle Gobind had accused his son Prem Lal of bad behavior and had hit him with a stick. The son hit him back. Then there was more hitting. Amar came to help, but Prem Lal. slapped him. Then Anjan came to help. That is, they beat Prem Lal pretty badly. Then Keshab and Sundar came to help Prem Lal. They beat their father as well as Amar and Anjan.

This description sounded childish to me. But in the late afternoon, I did see Amar and Anjan in bandages. So that day we couldn't play soccer, our usual after-school game. These two players were really limping. They didn't say a word about why or how the fight broke out. Thanks to Dhan and Harit. They were not from our village, but willing to share whatever information they could. Last month they showed their sense of sharing in another case.

Gambhir had gone home early from school. By the time he had slowly gotten over the Thaula ridge, he decided to take some rest. When school was over, the other boys from our village saw Gambhir lying on a rock. Everyone asked Gam why he was lying there. Gam replied the same way to everyone, "Just taking a rest." When Gam was about two hours late, Lathi dadi became concerned. So she and I headed toward the school. But after a few minutes walking, we saw that Dhan and Harit were coming down with Gam on their shoulders.

Gam was in a sort of half-conscious state. When we asked him for the reason, he said, "Just feeling thirsty." Obviously, Harit and Dhan didn't take his words "Just taking a rest" for granted. They stayed with him and when they found that he was unable to stand up and walk, they decided to carry him on their shoulders all the way to our village.

Harit and Dhan's mothers came from their village later in the evening to inquire how Gam was feeling. Lathi dadi and Dhan's mother had a very emotional meeting. First they cried and then both began to laugh like children. I guessed they must have been thinking about their stupid verbal war over the buffalo. But now they ate their words with *arsa* cookies and tea.

On the last class day of September, just before the Dashhara vacation, a school convention was completed. It was a sort of one-hour ritual in which every student had to write about his or her class, mainly about classmates. The best writing from every class was published in the school magazine, a great honor. In my class I was the slowest. Everybody had already left. The class teacher, Mr. Dimry, had also left. He told me that I could take my time and give him my writing in his office.

When I entered his office, I did not see him there. I was afraid now that he waited and waited for me and then left for home in disgust. As soon as I approached the main gate, he shouted my name "Chander" in a way that made me more nervous. He took me in his office and had a chat with me. He emphasized that I should be punctual. "Chander, the rule to be outstanding is to study for twelve hours, at least, every day. Read, read, read and write, write, write." He said and walked out.

If he were not my class teacher, I would have felt humiliated. But instead I felt embarrassed. He sounded upset. Obviously, I had taken too much time and ended up with only one handwritten page, and had made him wait for me. There was not a soul to be seen in the school.

Chapter 7

1946–47

"I am not going!" I said half-heartedly.

"You must go. I have seen the Lila a lot. Come next year, you may be in New Delhi." Mother insisted. For me and my buddies the Rama Lila was an adventure lasting until and later midnight. But Ma and I were missing Papa again. This could be my last year of the Pahari Rama Lila. Where would I have friends like Gam, Bhajnu, Anrit, Dhan, Karun, and Harit! Anrit had moved to Puri with his parents and sisters. He and I would meet at school, but others I would see at the Rama Lila. The married girls of our village would cry whenever they saw us there.

Besides the social interaction with relatives and friends, the repeaters knew that the story would never be the same. The chorus prayers would be different. There would be a singer or team of singers who would sing cheap songs, mostly from Hindi films. They would be sung between every three or four scenes usually with comic skits, totally unrelated to the story. Sometimes someone from the audience would say some funny thing and there would be big boisterous laughing.

Some funny things were not considered funny at all. Dasharatha in Muslim style pajamas and *sherwani* (topcoat), singing Muslim style Arabic *ghazals* (lyrics) in Persian style *shers* (couplets) to please his adamant Indian Hindu wife Kaikeyi.

But this time it changed. Vincent Nathan was Dasharatha and Kishan Singh was Kaikeyi. Nobody questioned why a Christian was playing the role of Rama's father. Vincent had a medical store and Kishan Singh had a small grocery store. Their stores were across from each other in Puri.

The scene opened on the stage with Dasharatha lying on the bed and Kakeyi sitting near his feet. A very familiar scene. Dasharatha sang a *ghazal* to dissuade Kaikeyi from her two wishes, namely fourteen years of exile for Rama and the kingdom for her son Bharata. In return, Kaikeyi sang a song that she would not budge a bit. Dasharatha sang another song. She sang another song. No compromise in sight.

Then Dasharatha said in prose, "Kaikeyi! I wish I had only one wife. Just Kausalya and a son. I tell my sons 'Never have more than one wife and one child. It's good for the family, good for the country, good for the world.' Kaikeyi! Do you know who is the stupidest man here? One who has two or three wives. Tell me—"

Kaikeyi jumped over Dasharatha, up on top of him, and began to choke him. Somehow Vincent managed to throw Kishan down. Vincent was much taller but Kishan was a rajput, a community renowned for valor. Kishan Singh got up and said loudly, "*Sale! Tere bap ka kya jata hai agar meri do bibiyan hain! Zara puchho unse ki mujh se khush hain ya nahin!*"

Now when the audience heard these Hindi sentences 'Stupid! What does your dad have to lose if I have two wives! Just ask them if they are happy or not with me!,' there was so much laughter! What Vincent said was not in the story text. We understood that he made up his own sentences for Kaikeyi, that is, Kishan. Those sentences became too personal because Kishan did have two wives! Not to mention several children from each wife.

Then I heard a lot from the audience. Kishan proved his name 'Krishna.' They say, Lord Krishna had a lot of *gopi* girl friends. Remember his famous dancing partner, Radha! And then later he had several wives, but only two wives, Rukmini and Satyabhama, were famous. They all were happy with him! Krishna had over sixteen thousand girl friends. That's just a joke! Mathura city is hot, hot, hot. Our Yamuna waters of Garhwal made the forest of Vrindavan down there a cool place for Lord Krishna! Very interesting! Now Kaikeyi has two wives! She fathered so many children! Who could have thought of that? Why only in Garhwal! Absolutely no problem! Ours is a cold climate. We need whisky and meat, too. Isn't mythology fun!

Many such remarks from the actors and the audience would break the monotony of the same story every other year. Very independent and interactive actors and audiences.

Anrit and his parents and sisters met me on the day of Bharat Milap. They told me that there would be a simple marriage ceremony for Brijendra, the following month at their house. I understood the need for his marriage and a simple ceremony. Nobody from the village was invited. Otherwise, it would have looked like a celebration. Uncle Ishan had arranged a clerical job for Brijendra in his own department. After the war was over, emergency recruits with a few years of service were discharged from the military. Brijendra therefore had to take up a civilian job.

Brijendra's wife was really beautiful. I saw her when she came with him to the village to occupy her new home. Anrit's parents guided the couple in household and property matters. The village property turned out to be a problem for Brijendra. Some of his fields were now occupied by his own uncle, Bisal. Almost everyone in the village knew this. Anrit told me that his father wanted to intervene, but decided to wait until after the marriage of Shankh, Bisal's second son. Shankh, like Brijendra, was also discharged from the military and had become a low-ranked police officer in Puri.

The whole village was invited for Shankh's marriage in the following month. About fifty males made his barat or bridegroom party. I, too, was a member of this party. Anrit, his father, and Brijendra were not. Karun and his other brothers, except Udai, stayed behind to take care of other things upon the return of the barat. Bhajnu and his uncle Gyaru were the drummers for our party.

The bride's village, Dob, was about ten miles from our village. All of us walked there except the bridegroom. He rode a horse, which was customary. When we reached the ridge overlooking the village of Dob, we heard the drums, dhol and damau, of the bride's side. Bhajnu and his uncle responded with their corresponding drums. What this exchange of drumming meant was that the priest hadn't completed all the rituals of the Vedi (altar) yet. So we had to wait at the ridge for the next drumming signal from Dob. The belief was that the barat must enter the bride's home only after the Vedi was ritualistically ready.

This delay was not considered irksome by the elders of our party. They had brought some whisky, enough for the adults. We young ones and a few adults drank instead the fresh water that was gushing out from the nearby spring. Everywhere was plush green vegetation, but no wild fruits were available around this time. We all ate some *arsa* cookies.

After about a half-hour wait, we heard the drumming from Dob. We all got up while Bhajnu and his uncle responded to their drumming. Some were already drunk. It was customary to carry a couple of guns, not only for fun but also for protection (from wild animals). There were two guns. Shankh fired his gun in the air a couple of times to indicate that we were proceeding. Shankh was not supposed to do it, but somebody else was. "Shankh is a big show-off," remarked a man who didn't sound drunk at all.

Shankh's show-off behavior was witnessed when he and his bride completed six out of seven steps. This was the *sapta-padi* (seven-step) ceremony, or the final seven vows. Here in the hills, the bridegroom could refuse to go with the bride on her sixth step. The bride had the same right. But in reality, only the bridegrooms exercised this right. That meant Shankh needed more dowry as he stopped at the sixth step. The marriage could not be declared legal if he didn't walk with her for the last and seventh step.

The bride's father had to grant Shankh's wishes as much as possible. He was ready to take the seventh step, but his father stopped him for more dowry. Shankh stopped. The bride's father yielded further. Then Shankh was stopped again, this time by the priest. Shankh stopped again. His wish was fulfilled again, very reluctantly. So he was ready to move with her, but the priest stopped him again and said, "Don't move until I say 'Move!'"

"Who the hell are you to tell me like that? I will stop if I want to. I won't if I don't want to."

"You cannot move until the priest says so!" The priest was as firm in his tone.

Shankh grabbed the priest by his neck, "*Ullu ke patthe! Tu mujh ko hukum deta hai?*" (An owl's son! You dare give me order?). "Owl" always stood for "stupid" in this situation. To say *tu* (thou) instead of *ap*, the honorific "you" was already a big insult for the priest.

Others intervened, otherwise his next brother, Udai (who was also discharged from the military) had threatened to shoot the priest with his gun. Somehow, the seventh step was completed. A man from the bride's side was quoted later, "Shankh should have married his mother instead." Actually, when the bridal party was leaving, I overheard some women using even worse words for the groom. These words were supposed to be used only by men. When I told the priest how some women were outraged by the groom's behavior, he laughed and said, "Outrage hates norms."

During the winter there was peace all around the village and school. The school remained closed from Christmas to the middle of February. When the school reopened, each student was given a copy of the school magazine, as customary. Some eight students surrounded me during recess. They were my classmates, all mad at me. Each of them complained that I had insulted them. "What insults are you fellows talking about?" I asked.

"The insults in the magazine!" one of them said loudly.

"What magazine?" I asked in confusion.

Another boy opened the school magazine and showed me, "This stupid class history you wrote. Read here 'If Dinesh had come on time, the English would have left India a long time ago.' How could you write this about me?"

The boy next to Dinesh put his finger on another line, "Look at this nonsense about me 'Matbar believes in fast action. If he ever got married and then his wife got lost in a forest, he would send vultures, not volunteers, to look for her.'"

Then Gyan turned the page with his finger wet from his saliva and showed his lines "Gyan hopes to be a researcher. He misplaces and loses things. But some things he finds under his mother's pillow." Nitya read another line "When (or if) Nitya's head grows big, does the whole world have to tell him that a Ph.D. is not needed to catch small lies?" Dan placed his finger on his lines "Dan is like a freeloader or preacher who says 'Thou shalt not work, for the property of thy Father in heaven is thine'" Thank God, Sam wasn't present yet as I saw the next lines "Sam better take karma and rebirth seriously. Here is a simple sample: One who sneaks into others' bags in class will be born again as a classy sniffer dog for our town's police officers (the bag owners)." Bikram would definitely make more noise: "Bikram! Make noise in a room only if you can make a room; a room and the things in it cost; we will call you a builder of a Taj if you ever make even a toilet." And this about another absent fellow: "Don't ask Kripal for any favors. He will keep reminding you about that. His parents might plan to disown him." I knew right then, I was finished.

When each of them was finished, I said, "Believe me, I swear, I didn't write this at all. I have the magazine. I had no idea, not even in my dreams that I could be in it. Which is why I didn't even open it. Ask Dimry ji if I am the writer of—"

"Liar! Big liar! Making up—"

The bell rang otherwise they would have continued their threats, which I didn't take seriously, any way. When I entered the class there was a big welcome for me. I heard "Chander! Hip hip hurray!" three times. So I was a celebrity. But when school was over, I saw Balam Singh waiting outside. He was waiting for me as he said, "I want to have a talk with you."

I knew instantly, if Balam, whose name meant 'Darling,' wanted to have a talk with me then I would not be able to talk at all. He was the big bully of our class and had beaten some boys. Nobody would dare report him. I was lucky that he never touched me. But I had written about him: "Balam is our Hitler. When he grows up, you will see his half-and-half moustache over his eyes and twisted swastika in his butt." In contrast, I'd written about myself at the end: "I am a nice boy. Ask the biggest bully of the class."

I, like many others, regarded Dimry ji (full name 'Badri Prasad Dimry') as a man fit to be a priest. He came from a family of men who served as temple priests at Badrinath. But here he was teaching us English in a Christian school. Without influence of the Hindu priestly family, without influence of Christian values. How could he have such a biting tongue! Couldn't he have written 'arm' instead of 'butt'! Anyway, Balam Singh, the darling lion, looked determined to devour an innocent lamb. I replied to him, "First, let me go pee. You wait for me here."

I could have peed in my pants. I ran for my life straight home. He must have realized that I really fooled him.

When I went to play soccer, everyone greeted me as if I were somebody. It was due to the magazine article. Then Karun began to box me. After a couple of punches, I asked him what those punches were for. He said, "You are right about me."

"Right about what?"

"That for Karun, the world war is still on in his village."

"Don't tell me it's in the magazine?"

"Come on! You know you wrote that…" He must have looked into my blank eyes, "But that's true of our village. You did so well in writing our history, Chander!" Karun said with one more punch. Of course, those were friendly punches.

After playing, I went in my room and read the magazine again. Sure, there was that sentence. But I wondered what if the magazine statement about Karun had the word 'family' instead of 'village'! Gunshots instead of punches, maybe. And I wondered if there were any funny statements about the two girls in our class! One of them was as pretty as Jagriti. Some boys in the class would look at her more than at their books. I myself wanted to find a way to say at least one word to her.

But there was tomorrow. I began to think of a way to escape my sacrifice. Should I ditch school or should I report Balam. Or should I…

The next day at the prayer meeting I crossed my class line and joined Anrit's class line. "Hey, what are you doing? You are now in a senior class!" Anrit said with a smile. I whispered about my problem with Balam in his ear.

"Don't think of reporting him. Instead, let us make him our friend. Handshake, not handslap. The Gandhian way. The way of Christ. Now let's pray!"

Luckily, I didn't see Balam in class that day. Maybe he was ashamed due to my writing. "He is not ashamed of what you said about him. Don't you know that he often misses classes!" said Gambhir, "He will come after you. Unless, unless…unless Anrit really has a handshake with him! Or you tell Dimry ji."

The next day I saw him in our first class, Mr. Dimry's class. We all were required to note what Mr. Dimry was talking about. All of us, except Balam, were writing. Mr. Dimry asked him from where he was standing, "Balam! I will throw you out if you don't take notes." There was pin-drop silence. "Did you hear me, Balam?"

"Sir! I can't write. My fingers are hurting. I can show you my fingers!"

"I believe you. Take notes from Chander later…. Did you hear me?"

"Yes Sir!"

Oh, Dimry ji, as if that writing of yours was not enough to put me in harms way! Why do I have to face this monster when I was trying to avoid him!

Balam did come to me during recess. "Chander! Don't worry about your notes. Matbar has already given me his." And he disappeared. No harsh tone, no puffed up nostrils, no angry eyebrow, no spitting, no floor kicking, no mean smile, no nothing!

When school was over, some of the boys who were mad at my writing were coming from behind me. I walked faster to the main gate. There I saw Mr. Dimry signaling to me with his hand. I was already nervous, but now became even more. I remembered my last visit in his office.

But to my surprise, this time he walked with me in my direction and that gesture relaxed me (and the boys went somewhere else). His sentences reverbated in my head:

"Chander! Ignore those bullies. They are unhappy. They were exposed by the magazine. Maybe later some of them will brag to their wives and children 'Oh, I was so good in my school work,' 'Oh, I used to work so hard,' 'Oh, the teachers praised me so much for my top reading and writing skills.' If they were top then they would have been in some top colleges, in some top jobs, in some top places. A bully's wife and children may wonder so.... This magazine record speaks of the ability of some classmates to achieve..."

But the more memorable part came to me in my sleep that night. This part I called secretly the "Dimry Dream." He was standing in our morning school prayer in place of the principal, who used to give inspirational talks for about five minutes with occasional quotes from the Bible. I never saw Mr.Dimry dressed up like Rama ready to fight Ravana as shown in the Rama Lila. For clothing, he had only a long dhoti on his barefooted body. Other features included a "V" shaped tilak mark on his forehead, the right swastika on his arm, long ascetic hair on his head, clean shaven, a bow with an arrow in his hands, ready to shoot the bully. Mr. Dimry said more or less what our principal had already said before:

"Chander! Learn to hit the right target. Keep improving your record of hits. Persons of achievement must speak by records, not by words. For achievement, work hard and harder, and on or before time. Delay and despair are cross-cousins. They act quickly when you act slow. Finish your job yourself. Don't say 'Let somebody else finish it.' Maybe somebody else will finish it first and you next. Honor time and time will honor you…and you will be far from the crowds and the crowds will be near you…Some of your class bullies will be begging you for a stroke of your pen. Then you can give them good advice. But don't if they have achieved more than you. If you have to, talk reasonably, not rashly. Remain awake while they sleep. Look for big and beyond…Chander! You need more and more friends or you will whine, fear, and fail. You have only to blame yourself if you can't make many friends. If you don't have friends, then borrow some from others and retain them. Share your gains with them. Larger and longer friendship is an investment for greater and longer happiness. Remember, Rama won because he made so many friends."

He spoke these sermons and began to retreat toward the mountain, into the oaks and then to the pines. Then he turned his face back to me and raised his bow, "Chander! Don't be afraid. Avatars do come to punish demons." I was simply speechless for this booster (I already had my morale raised by the publication of the magazine article), but I did raise my folded hands for the guru (and a descendant of the Badrinath temple priests) to say *namaste*, 'I salute you.'

I kept looking at him until he disappeared behind the majestic deodar trees of the mountain. The rays of the sun softly brushed my body through thousands of conifer leaves of the deodars. The only thing I could see above and behind those deodars were the plush green peaks which looked so far, yet so near.

When I woke up, I felt very good about myself.

The next month another English school inspector came. He skipped our class. I met Anrit and told him about the inspector. "You are lucky that he didn't visit your class!"

"Why?" I was curious.

"He asked us 'Who in India won the Nobel Prize for literature?' Everybody shouted 'Rabindranath Tagore.' But I was stupid to raise my hand—"

"You gave him a wrong answer. Right?"

"No. His question was wrong."

I was puzzled for a moment because I also knew that Tagore was the right answer. "Look, the inspector can't be wrong if he simply asks you 'Who is the Nobel Prize winner of India in literature?'!"

"I told him 'Sir, it's not the winner, but the winners.'"

"You mean there are more Indians in literature?" I asked with a laugh.

"Sir, Rudyard Kipling had already received the Nobel Prize before Tagore. Kipling is Indian, too."

I laughed. But Anrit sighed and looked way out toward the horizon as if his eyes were seeing something over and beyond those mountains in the front. I said, "I am sorry, I didn't mean to laugh at you. It was just your answer."

"I know. The whole class laughed. The teacher and the inspector didn't laugh, but they did smile."

I clung to Anrit and cried. My real "big" brother was deeply hurt inside. "Never mind, Chander! It's all right. We are what we are told we are. We rarely question that."

I felt that Anrit might have started showing the signs of his father's behavior, the behavior of Yogis, the people who see themselves "united" above and beyond the ordinary. His father, Uncle Ishan, had told me this definition of a Yogi when I asked him once why he became a jogi. He corrected me. His interest was yog (yoga), yoking people to people. "Yogi and jogi are one and the same words. So are 'yoga' and English 'yoke.' I am interested in its English meaning, too. But a jogi meant a mendicant." This was how he explained it.

More interesting was his further elaboration, "Son! For a yogi, there are no nations, no boundaries of countries, race, religion, gender, caste. To be a soldier in the British army or any national militia against the British was not for me. I believe in yoga's first vow of not killing others. In the big war, the others were the Germans, the Italians, and the Japanese. I couldn't have killed any of them. All of them deserved to live." Then he breathed a long sigh, "Yoga and yoke are the same words in origin. Yoking the enemies was and will be the way to live. Enmity must end before death. I wish Hitler had adopted yoga. He would have lived longer. So would have his innocent victims." Uncle Ishan's eyes were wet. I now understand the message of yoga. It was kindness. It was a joining.

The month of June, our summer vacation month, brought uncomfortable news. After Wavell left India, Mountbatten became the viceroy. Prime Minister Attlee was determined to grant India her independence. But there was gloom in Puri. India would be divided into India and Pakistan. Jinnah was being discussed more than any other leader.

The elder Muslims of Puri didn't consider Jinnah an authentic Muslim. They often told us that a 'pak' or pure Muslim wouldn't touch alcohol and pork. "A sincere Muslim believes in universal humanity," said my Muslim barber in Puri (his word for 'humanity' was the Arabic *insaniyyat*). We wondered, if a barber could understand Islam as it should be, what was wrong with Jinnah? Such a brilliant lawyer, educated in England.

Uncle Ishan didn't consider Jinnah a Yogi. A yogi yokes people, unites them. Jinnah saw humanity divided, or he wanted to see it that way. Many believed in what he told them to. That made both Hindus and Muslims very sensitive. These sensitivities could be bloody. He had already shown that how many fanatics believed in his plan of "Direct Action," the action of killing, the action of religious terror. He could do it again to divide the people. He wouldn't care how many innocent Muslims would be killed by Hindu fanatics.

And what about mixed marriages, a Muslim to a Hindu? Jinnah should have saluted them because it 'united' the people. In fact, Jinnah's second wife was not a Muslim. So what went wrong with this Muslim man, a husband of a Parsi woman?

My report card came and, as usual, I passed (actually, I was first in the class).

Papa was transferred to Andaman and Nicobar Islands. The Japanese had inflicted a lot of damage to these islands during the war. So Ma and I could not move to New Delhi that year. All my excitement died.

Brijendra and his wife Trishna came home in the first week of July. He decided to claim some of his father's property, especially a couple of fields that had mango and walnut trees along the Pan Gadnu creek. Gambhir and another man were with him to carry mangos for sale in Puri. Gambhir was just like a monkey. He went all the way to the top of the mango trees and picked up the more mature fruits. Bisal, his uncle, saw him picking mangos. There was some argument between them. Gambhir stopped picking, but Brijendra and the porter continued. By noon they had collected sacks of them.

The next day was Sunday. Bisal and his two sons, Shankh and Udai, were home. They were waiting for Brijendra. They inquired of Gambhir. He obeyed them and found Brijendra beside the gorge. Shankh and Udai came with their guns and followed Gambhir. Gam must have thought that Udai and Shankh were using a simple scare tactic. He brought Brijendra.

In the meantime, Granduncle Bisal arrived there with a big sickle in his hand. The father and sons jumped over Brijendra and began to drag him toward the gorge, as if to throw him down the creek.

That was when Gambhir ran to my house and told me what was happening down there near the gorge.

We both ran down with Karun and Uncle Keshab. Somehow we managed to stop the further beating of Brijendra. Gambhir and I were surprised that Uncle Keshab didn't bring his gun nor did he threaten the perpetrators. "This time he acted like a lawyer. Usually, that was not his way. He now thinks, it's just a family matter," Gam said. But both Gambhir and I feared there would be further beatings of Brijendra. Sure, all the parties were Bhatras, a family matter. But this wouldn't be the last violent family action. Granduncle Bisal and his two sons warned Brijendra of this. They told him that they would kill him if he ever touched those mango trees again. In fact, they warned Gambhir, too. We felt sorry for Karun when he apologized to Gambhir for the whole mess created by his father and brothers.

School opened the following week. Gambhir and I met Anrit and told him about the mess he had missed in his village. "Uncle Keshab is right. It's a family matter. All of us should remain united," he reacted. I wasn't impressed with his reaction.

There were some changes in my class. Balam Singh was not there. He failed and now was one year behind me. I was relieved because the very sight of him scared me after my article had been published. We now had a new class teacher, Mr. Akbar, from the plains. The school was excited because of the news that there would be some preparation to celebrate India's Independence.

The first Sunday of the school year was always considered a big relief. But it didn't turn out to be so. I saw Gambhir in the morning while we both were out washing our clothes at Pan Gadnu. He told me that Brijendra wanted his help in picking more mangos in the afternoon. I reacted quickly, "Hey, don't say 'yes' or Shankh and Udai are going to shoot you. You will fall from the tree like a bird-eaten rotten mango."

"No, I have to help him. He is like me. No brother to help him, no father to guide him." Gambhir said in a cool manner.

"I tell you Gam, you are in real trouble. Don't go!"

"I've already said 'yes' to Brijendra bhai. I can't back off."

"Can I come with you?...In case you are in trouble I—"

"Yes, you can come, but stay away. Don't come near my tree." I know he allowed me to come very reluctantly. Maybe he thought that it was their family matter. I was not a Bhatra, just a fellow villager.

I still thought that Gambhir wasn't serious. I was wrong. Out of curiosity, I took a walk to Pan Gadnu. It was a clear sunshiny day. Down there I saw Brijendra under a huge mango tree. On its top, Gambhir was singing a Hindi marching song written by Jay Shankar 'Prasad':

From the high Himalayan top
the pure reasoned voice,
the self-shining illuminating
freedom calls—
You are the immortal brave son. Think well. You are firm on your promise.
The path is praiseworthy and pious. Keep marching, keep marching.

Whatever Gambhir's reasons were, the song didn't have to be so high and loud. Those three dangerous fellows were home. What if they found out?

Then I saw the same porter again coming down toward us. Brijendra asked him, "Everything is in order?"

"Yes Sir." He answered with a smile.

"Did those three soldiers see you?" I asked him nervously.

"Oh yes. I passed by their house." He smiled again.

What a stupid man! The man on the top was singing a loud marching song and this man passed by those soldiers. They would definitely march down and kill these stupid mortals! Before I had the chance to ask the porter why he was smiling, Udai fired a shot from above and yelled, "Get down, you stupid Gambhir or I will kill Brijendra!"

Gambhir stopped singing and shouted back, "Come down! We have mangos for you."

The three came down. Bisal had a big stick in his hand. Shankh and Udai had guns.

Bisal hit Brijendra with his stick. Brijendra grabbed his hand and threw him down. Then Shankh and Udai dropped their guns and jumped on top of Brijendra. Gambhir shouted from the tree "Help, help!" Before I was able to shout, "I can't," two men leaped out like bullets from behind the bush. They were in khakis with gloves in their hands, military boots on their feet, and masks on their faces. They jumped on Shankh and Udai. One began to beat Shankh and the other Udai. Brijendra went after his uncle, Bisal, and began to beat him with the same stick. The broil continued until all three fell to the ground, almost unconscious. Then Brijendra asked me, Gambhir, and the porter to run away. The mystery men also ran away with Udai and Shankh's guns. We ran toward home, whereas the mystery men went further down along the creek. I was still wondering whether Udai, Shankh, and their old father would survive.

Of course, they survived. Uncle Keshab and Uncle Sundar took care of them when they heard "Help, help!"

Gambhir told me that nobody had any idea who those mystery men were. I couldn't find out any thing. Although the action of the war was over, its reaction was not. Uncle Bisal from World War I and his sons and a nephew from World War II continued the war at home.

As usual, I went to school with the others. The rains came hard that month. The wall behind Bhajnu's house gave way. The rubble made a big hole in the back wall of his two-room house and water gushed inside. He had to miss school for three days. Their neighbor Bhadu, a mason, began to rebuild the wall and repair the hole. In the meantime Bhajnu and his mother began to sleep out on the verandah. Bhajnu resumed school.

But the following week, on August 2, Bhajnu missed everything. I couldn't believe it. Bhajnu had been killed by a tiger the previous night. After hearing the news of his house problems, his mother's sister and her husband came to help. Their village was near Tehri, where people often slept out on the verandah or in their yards during the summer. Bhajnu and his uncle put their cots out in the yard and slept. Around 1 a.m., the tiger attacked the sleeping Bhajnu. The uncle heard Bhajnu scream just once and the next moment the tiger had dragged him by the neck and thrown him down into the next field. Everybody there shouted. The tiger ran away, but Bhajnu's throat was deeply punctured. They brought him back up. He was unable to breathe well enough to remain conscious. Within one hour he passed away. In the morning, they took his body away to be cremated. Almost every villager came there to see him off. We were in tears and were afraid. Bhajnu's mother was totally distraught.

The reason for our fears was that the tiger could become a man-eater since it had tasted human blood. Then the tiger would have absolutely no fear of humans. The news spread quickly. Uncle Keshab took charge of killing the tiger.

For this purpose the most important thing to prepare was a *machan*, a scaffold on a tree or on poles. There were several trees near the yard. That same day, the machan was ready and stood at a height of about twenty-five feet. The tiger couldn't jump that high, but still would be close enough to lure it when shot from the machan.

The tiger was expected to come around the same time. Uncle Keshab and Uncle Sundar sat on the machan. A sleeping human dummy was placed on a cot below. For more bait, two playful calves were tied around the tree. The tiger didn't show up.

On the following day, they tried the same thing. Now Uncle Keshab was alone in the machan. Gambhir and I had also joined him, but only as onlookers from the window of Bhadu's house. Suddenly, we saw a flashlight from the machan. That was a signal that the tiger might have been spotted. But it turned out to be a false warning. There was no tiger. I was feeling sleepy. Gambhir was already fast asleep lying on the dari. I also lied down on the dari and closed my eyes.

Suddenly, we both were awakened by a succession of gunshots. We got up and saw a dead tiger below. Bhajnu's aunt brought his mother,

Jaima, out to show her the tiger. She stood with Uncle Keshab next to the dead tiger. He held her in his arms and said, "We have taken our revenge!"

"Yes, revenge!" and she kicked the big male tiger three or four times and then sat on its dead body beating its head with her fists. Suddenly she screamed and got up in frenzy. Her eyes began to roll and her body began to shake. She placed her hands over her head and shouted "I am Bhajnu...I am Bhajnu! I am his spirit!...He sucked my blood, I am going to suck his blood." She sat over the dead tiger again and bent over its neck. With her teeth she began to bite its throat with heavy grunts. Then Uncle Keshab lifted her up, wiped her face, and took her inside.

It was a big relief that the man-eating tiger problem was over. In school, there was big news about how Uncle Keshab had killed the man-eater. Several friends, even some bullies, asked me and Gambhir how the actual hunt took place. There was also talk that Uncle Keshab was going to be honored in a civic ceremony at Puri's Rama Lila grounds.

Uncle Nawal came home for a short vacation. We decided to take Vijay for his first visit to Puri on Indpendence Day. Uncle brought with him a new radio. On the morning of August 15, the news of Nehru's speech inaugurating a free India was in the air everywhere:

> *"Long years ago we made a tryst with destiny and now the time comes when we shall redeem our pledge, not wholly or in full measure, but very substantially. At the stroke of midnight hour, when the world sleeps, India will awake to life and freedom. A moment comes, which comes but rarely in history, when we step from the old to the new, when an age ends and when the soul of a nation, long supressed, finds utterance. It is fitting that at this solemn moment we take the pledge of dedication to the service of India and her people and to the still larger cause of humanity."*

Our school celebration was separate from the main celebration that took place in Puri. For our celebration, we joined many other villagers on our way to school. They went to Puri and we to our school with a tricolor flag of free India and we sang the marching song of Jay Shankar 'Prasad':

> *Himadri tunga shringa se*
> *prabuddha shuddha bharti—*
> *swayam-prabha samujjwala*
> *swatantrata pukarti—*

(From the high Himalayan top...freedom calls—)

The principal inaugurated Independence Day at 10 a.m. (it was the announced time). Anrit was asked to hoist the flag. He never told me that he was going to get this honor. The senior history teacher, Mr. Davis, gave a brief speech of how India had struggled to come to this historic day.

The most unexpected piece of our own history that he added at the end was, "Yes, Anrit is right. Rudyard Kipling is the first Indian to get the Nobel Prize in literature. Tagore is the second." I heard some laughter.

"I know some of you are wondering about this fact. Kipling was born in India. Who knows, if he were alive, he might have been given the same right to stay here, just like any Indian born here. Kipling is as much an Indian as Lord Rama. Remember, Rama's ancestors were Aryans who came to India to rule. So did Kipling's ancestors—"

Again, there was some laughter.

"But unfortunately, the English rulers lost a great opportunity. They could have paved a path to a new world, a united world. They could have made all their colonies including their own nation as one country, with no royalty. All people could have been given equal rights, with freedom to settle in any part of the united country. This big bloody struggle for freedom would have been unnecessary. There was no need to make new and separate countries on the basis of race or religion or—"

"But we never want to be colonized people." Someone shouted from the audience.

"We will remain as colonized people. We will sacrifice anything for a lazy sport like cricket. We will use English as our national and official language. We will have pants, shirts, jackets, and shorts. In our hills, we will use whisky and bagpipes, whenever possible and—"

Then there was big laughter.

After his speech and a few more announcements from the principal, we went to the auditorium where refreshments were being served. For us, this part was far more interesting—fried potato gutkas, puris, biscuits, laddus, etc. The history teacher was also there and said, "The potatoes and biscuits are our colonial heritage. They will be more and more popular in India!" Two other teachers were talking about Nehru's speech. "It was a good literary piece. Doesn't reflect the reality," said one. "Well, what else could he do at this time, except give a few speeches!" Another commented, "It's a sad day for India. People are divided. While we are enjoying sweets, thousands of people have already lost their lives and homes at this moment, all due to religious terror." "Worse days are ahead! You will see more and more religious terror here and there!" another added.

The Puri celebration was grand. Uncle Nawal and Aunt Kanti were there with Vijay. They were impressed with this historic foundation of the largest democracy, a new hope for the world, bad news for kings, queens, and dictators. Uncle Nawal said, "Mr. Qureshi hoisted the first flag of the new India. Thanks to our leaders! A Muslim became our first Indian district magistrate. He gave Jinnah the answer. We will not remain divided. The world will be united." We were told that Pakistan's flag had been hoisted by Jinnah the day before. How many will know elsewhere what Mr. Qureshi said and did today, in the Himalayas!

But by evening, the news was not good. Gandhi was in West Bengal, which had become a war zone between Hindus and Muslims. Not even the Japanese bombing during the war had killed that many Indians at the eastern front (at the time we didn't know that the western front, Punjab and Sindh, would be even worse).

Uncle Nawal and I were sitting together and listening to all sorts of news on his new radio. We ate dinner together. During dinner I said, "India was divided by Jinnah. Why couldn't our leaders stop him?"

"Son! Gandhi was willing to make him the first prime minister of India or whatever he wanted to be. But let me correct you...." He got up to stop Vijay who threw his new soccer ball at him. He sat down again with me. "Chander! Let me answer your question about the partition. India was divided in the kitchens of Brahmins—" Vijay threw the ball again. "Why don't you finish your roti, Vijay? Then we will play football together." Uncle continued with me again, "Remember the two separate tents at the marriage of your principal's daughter?"

"Yes, I remember. You ate in the general tent."

"But the brahmins didn't. Right?"

"Right."

"So we have two tents now!...Who are these Muslims of Pakistan? They are us. Almost all of them are converts. Why so many converts? Because Brahmins won't eat with them."

"I understand your view."

"It's not my view. It's our history...But many don't learn from history. You know the Shankaracharya of Badrinath. He still defines Hinduism by four divisions: Brahmins, Kshatriyas, Vaishyas, Shudras. You will never be a shankaracharya. Your mother has no chance either. Bhajnu's uncle or mother has no chance either. You discriminate against your own people and then blame Jinnah! Jinnah is a reaction of our actions."

"How did we accept this four-division system?"

"That's an ancient custom. But it has become the reason for the war we fought in Europe."

"You mean Hitler?"

"Yes, Hitler. He knew that Aryans were white people. In India, they discriminated against black people, the Shudras. The whites became the priests, warriors, and merchants. Shudras deserved to remain servants. Hitler had the same agenda. All others should serve the whites or be eliminated. So Jews and Gypsies became his victims." Uncle sighed.

"Uncle, do you believe in the caste system?"

"We have to break it if we don't want a further breakup of India, son!" He went beyond my question as he added, "Religions are like mosquitoes that sing sweetly and suck out humanity or inject mass fatal hate." (Many others had similar opinions. In summary, "Religion is evil.")

Then, as promised, we got up and played soccer with Vijay. He really enjoyed it. We had a hard time stopping the game. Uncle would tell him "You have to go to sleep soon, Vijay," but Vijay would whine "Football! Football!"

Chapter 8

▼

1947–48

The Rama Rule has returned to free India,
the sacred land.
The days of sorrow have passed away;
all is your Maya, Lord!
Lord! Let our wish be fruitful;
you have rained down the juice of immortality.
City dwellers! Celebrate! The Rama Rule has
returned.

This year's Rama Lila was the first in free India. The song *Ram Raj aya* ('The Rama Rule has returned') opened the first night. Then Mr. Dhyani gave his final speech:

"Brothers and sisters! Welcome to the first Rama Lila of Independent India! This is my last year as the chairman of the Rama Lila Committee. It has been a great pleasure to serve the Committee. What did I learn from my work? I will sum up by quoting two verses of Tulsidas. The first is 'The world has all the things. The actionless man does not attain them.' The second is 'I know the whole cosmos as Sita and Rama. I bow to it with both hands folded.'...Unfortunately, our part of the cosmos is divided due to hatred. We failed to see it as one single Lila of the Lord, the sport created by his Maya. To honor this sport we have made sacred places—the temples, the synagogues, the churches, the mosques, the gurudwaras—to name a few. Please do not dishonor any of them. The sage has said 'The whole cosmos is Sita-Rama, the creator and the creator's magical power. That's what this Rama Lila is about...Tonight I want to be very brief. I will end with my thanks to you all and to the people who have worked for the Lila."

There was big applause with standing ovations. When people kept on clapping, Dhyani ji raised his voice. "Thank you, thank you...Thank you so much...This all happened because of the first poet of the Lila. He flew the story of Rama to us from the tree of best wishes. So please join me in honoring him." Then he recited the following Sanskrit *shloka* couplets:

> *I bow to Valmiki the cuckoo,*
> *who climbed the branch of poetry*
> *and cooed sweetly*
> *the sweet word 'Rama Rama.'*
> *May all be happy, may all be disease-free.*
> *May all see the best, let no one have pain.*

Then the chorus started the prayer song, beginning with the word *omkar* "Om, with its dense and denser sound, created existence, space, the sky..."

On the tenth night, Dhyani ji addressed the audience one more time in which he mentioned that his speeches were going to be compiled. He also thanked Uncle Keshab for killing the man-eater and offered best wishes for his daughter's forthcoming marriage.

We knew that the marriage of Uncle Keshab's daughter, Jagriti, was going to take place the following year on January 30. His son, Laksh, told us that they were planning an unprecedented wedding. It was natural for us to get excited, a lawyer's daughter was getting married. Everything else began to look less interesting when some of the wedding preparations began to surface. For example a small stadium was built on our village soccer field.

The only noteworthy thing that happened before January 30 was that Tehri State would no longer be ruled by the Maharaja.

On January 11, two young members of the opposition, Nagendra Saklani and Maulu Singh, became martyrs. They were fatally shot by the S.D.O. and the police superintendent of the Maharaja, near Kirtinagar on the northern bank of the Alakananda, across Srinagar. The two culprits tried to hide in the nearby forest. Some women, who were collecting grass and wood there, saw them. They caught the two murderers.

The bodies of Saklani and Singh were not cremated right away. Instead the leaders of the opposition decided to carry them all the way to Tehri. On the long and tedious on-foot journey from Dev Prayag to Tehri, people saw the martyrs' bodies being carried in a funeral procession. At the front of the procession were Trepan Singh and Devi Datt Tiwari, with headbands red-spotted by the blood of the martyrs, shouting "March to Tehri." The news and emotions spread around quickly.

On January 15, by the time the dead bodies arrived at Tehri, thousands and thousands of people had already gathered. The town was jammed.

At 2 p.m., the funeral procession proceeded toward the confluence of the Ganges and the Bhilangana river. Immediately a funeral pyre was prepared. The famous Chandra Singh Garhwali lit the fire and the two heros were all ashes. Saklani's brother had only arrived in time to see their ashes. The huge crowd was fired-up. The Maharaja and his father knew that this fire was going to engulf them. They disappeared from Tehri.

On the morning of January 16, a public meeting was held at Tehri with over 15,000 people in attendance. This was a huge amount of people for a town at that altitude and time. One of the leaders, Daulat Ram Kuksal, presided over the meeting. From the meeting came the announcement: the Maharaja administration was over. Dev Suman's dream was a reality.

Finally, January 30 came with great excitement for our village as if this day would be remembered forever in the world. The barat or bridegroom's party literally descended upon our village. The line's front end was near Bagh Duln ('Tiger Den') and the end of it was still not visible from our village. There were more than one thousand men, not counting the bridegroom, two horses, and the band musicians. The bridegroom was a recent law graduate and his father Dayal Sundryal was the rich owner of several grocery stores in Puri.

The welcome was done deliberately in front of Bagh Duln to remind the guests that Keshab Bhatra killed a man-eater, even though not at this spot.

From Bagh Duln, all the guests proceeded to the stadium. The musicians led the party. Three bagpipers and four drummers made up the band. About a dozen hot-air balloons were released in the sky so that people from the entire area could see the height of the celebration. People miles away could sense the celebration with the majestic music of the unmistakable bagpipes.

All entered the stadium. It was well covered with a heavy canopy and thick canvas screens. The sky was cloudless with no trace of snow on the ground. Four big bonfires were prepared outside, around the stadium. Inside, there were thick daris covered with rugs from wall to wall. Nobody could have seriously complained about the cold. Most guests were from Puri, located much higher than our village. Several petromax lamps placed all around brightened the whole area.

Among the guests, some were very familiar faces like our teachers Mr. Akbar, Mr. Davis, Mr. Dimry, and the town's well-known personalities like Mr. Dhyani and Rai Bahadur Brij Mohan. Among the tow horses, one was Rai Bahadur's (the other for the bridegroom).

Each guest was honored with a garland and a cup of tea with warm jalebis. The servers and cooks were all hired from Puri's sweetshops and restaurants.

When all were seated, there seemed to be a lull. The band was quiet now. Guests were making jokes about so many things and people. One jalebi joke about the Rai Bahadur and his horse was enjoyed very much by my teachers (the Rai Bahadur was sitting a few yards away). Mr. Davis was the narrator of the following story:

It all happened when the Rai Bahadur was on a tour at Banghat, a small marketplace situated on a small riverbank, between Puri and Kotdwar. Here tourists could have snacks, tea, and meals. It was noontime. The Rai Bahadur dismounted from his horse in front of a jalebi shop. He saw fresh jalebis being taken out from the hot syrup pan. He signaled to the waiter and asked to bring a jalebi to sample. The waiter went inside the shop and came out to tell him that he would have to buy it. He insisted that he would buy a lot if he liked the jalebis, but first he would have to taste one jalebi. The waiter went inside and came back with the owner who told the Rai Bahadur that his jalebis were too costly, there was no free piece. And he quickly went inside. The waiter was still outside. The Rai Bahadur asked him how many jalebis there were. The waiter told him that there was a big *parat*, a giant size plate, full of fresh jalebis. The Rai Bahadur asked its price. The waiter told him the price. The Rai Bahadur gave him money for the whole *parat*. The waiter went inside. In a minute, he and his boss brought the giant plate together and placed it in front of him. They quickly went inside. But in about a couple of minutes, they came out. They heard some sort of noise and laughter in front of their shop. The Rai Bahadur's horse was eating the jalebis from the plate while he was drinking tea in the shop across the way. The horse was surrounded by onlookers who were making fun of the jalebis.

This story of the Rai Bahadur made me curious. I went to sit near him where he was talking to the two musicians, one singer and one tabla player. He requested the singer to sing a *raga, darbari kanra* The singer told him that he was going to start with *kalyan rag* in the sixteen-beat rhythm. "Yes, kalyan or yaman kalyan should be the first raga for this auspicious occasion. And it is an evening raga," the Rai Bahadur said.

Their talk didn't make too much sense to me. The singer asked me to make an announcement. Everybody was talking to everybody.

So, I thought that police officer Uncle Prem Lal should make the announcement. And being the big brother of Uncle Keshab, he was the right man to do it, but I couldn't see him anywhere. I saw his father and other brothers. Then suddenly Uncle Keshab passed by me and I asked him. He made the announcement. And the music started.

After the first raga, the singer sang the next. When that was finished, the Rai Bahadur told the singer that he should have used an A flat microtone instead of a plain A flat. The singer was feeling a little embarrassed, but then the Rai Bahadur said, "Well, your harmonium cannot produce microtones. What can you do about that! Do you have any composition in fifteen and a half beats?"

The singer said, "Yes. My tabla player knows the *tal* very well."

I didn't understand a damn thing about their musical talk, but I saw that only the Rai Bahadur was nodding his head or hand, unlike during the previous compositions when many others in the audience moved their heads and hands and occasionally said "wow, wow."

Then Uncle Keshab came to me and asked me to announce dinner. This made me very happy that he chose me to make the most important announcement (people come together because of food). I asked him, "Why me?"

"You are the first student from our village to be at the top of the class. And you are a great writer. Enough evidence. Now go announce or I will punch you, captain's son!" He laughed. But I told him that Uncle Prem Lal would have been the best man to make announcements. I was sad to hear from him that he was not feeling good. Now I understood the reason for his absence. Surprisingly, all of his children were there.

"Now go announce. Jagriti will be happy to know that you did so," Uncle said as he moved away from me.

I didn't have the courage to make the announcement. I quietly whispered in the ear of the singer when he stopped singing. He made the announcement that dinner was ready and that he would start with *malkauns* after dinner.

Dinner was over. The singer started playing a note on the harmonium while the tabla player was tuning the right-hand drum. Then a man came and whispered into his ear. I thought it might be a request for another raga instead of *malkauns*.

The singer signaled to the drummer who instantly stopped tuning. He stood up and said loudly, "Please, please...Please everybody! We cannot have music...Mahatma Gandhi has been shot dead by a lunatic."

The announcement was heard on the radio.

There was calm for a few moments before a man rushed around wildly shouting, "I don't believe in God. He could not save Christ...I don't believe in Rama. He could not save Gandhi. Damn killer. Coward, coward. He can't be a Hindu. He killed an unarmed man. Coward, coward, coward..." Two men took him away very gently. He was a guest.

Most guests gathered around the Rai Bahadur since he was known for his understanding of Indian politics. He was the mentor of the state's chief minister, Govind Ballabh Pant. He had two master's degrees, one in English and one in Sanskrit, and a law degree from the University of Allahabad, the place from where many Indian leaders came. Nobody could match his stature in the hills.

Mr. Davis requested him to say something about Gandhi. The Rai Bahadur said with a sigh, "The shortest distance between two viewpoints must be a straight talk, not a shotgun. More than two thousand years ago, our Jain saints gave us the philosophy of *anekantavada*. That is the philosophy for all times, everywhere." He asked a young man to bring him a glass of water.

He quickly brought water. The Rai Bahadur took a few sips. Then he asked Mr. Davis, "Where was I?"

"At anekantavada."

The Rai Bahadur continued, "Anekantavada means 'many voices.' Any objective reality is understood in more than one way, in more than one statement, differently by different persons. One statement has more than one interpretation, more than one end. But listen to all voices with reason, not with violence. That's why Jainism preached *ahimsa*, nonviolence. It is the first religion in human history that believed in compassion, not in God, as the savior of all. One voice and one God are folk beliefs, bad for democracy and scholarship."

He paused to drink water. Then he continued again, "Gandhi cared to listen to any voice even when he disagreed with it. He is rightly called Bapu, father. Like a good father he listened to all his children. Bapu stood for love. History will remember that. Isn't that right Mr. Davis?"

"Yes Pandit ji!" Mr. Davis agreed.

"Why don't you say something about Gandhi? You are a history teacher," the Rai Bahadur encouraged him.

"Pandit ji, I cannot match your knowledge. But, as a history teacher, I believe that Christianity is connected with Jainism. Jainism is older than Buddhism. Buddhism received *ahimsa* from Jainism. Buddhism went to the Middle East and gave rise to Christianity—"

"My history professor at Allahabad also held that view. Sorry for interrupting! Continue!" the Rai Bahadur said.

"It is perfectly all right, Pandit ji. I am just an Indian Christian. But Mahatma Gandhi was the greatest Christian of the world. He came full circle, to the compassion of Jainism. How could a man be so cruel to a man who wouldn't even kill a mosquito!" He began to wipe his tears.

I saw others, including his colleagues Mr. Dimry and Mr. Akbar, in tears.

"Do you have any predictions based on your knowledge of history?" The Rai Bahadur asked Mr. Davis.

"Yes Pandit ji, I have. Like Gautama Buddha and Jesus Christ, there will be Mahatma Gandhi statues all over the world. Iconoclasts will try to destroy them. But the world will create more and more. Idolatry of compassion is the way to human salvation."

Mr. Dimry got up and asked me to bring some water.

He took me aside when I gave him water. He drank some and quietly said to me, "Gandhi would have been very sad if he had seen such a big party."

These praises continued, until the *muhurt* "auspicious time" for the wedding came.

The wedding turned out to be lusterless. No dhol-damau was played. No sweets were distributed. It looked like a ceremony between a funeral and a wedding. The father of a nation died and a daughter in that nation was being given away forever!

The father of the bride put her right hand upon the bridegroom's right hand and asked him, "In the matters of duties, earnings, and pleasures of life, you will never bypass her?"

"I will never bypass her."

Then quickly the bride and the bridegroom stood in front of the fire pit that was in the middle of the altar (Vedi).

The priest was our Hindi-Sanskrit teacher. In a choked voice, he asked the couple to go around the fire seven times. Each time the groom lifted the right leg of the bride and asked her to step on a rock there. She stepped seven times like this, very quickly. The priest pronounced every mantra briefly. For example, he said 'now the first step is for pleasures, the second step for energy, the third step for riches, the fourth step for welfare, the fifth step for family, the sixth step for the seasons, the seventh step for friendship.'

In earlier weddings, I noticed that these steps were taken by the bride with longer mantras and vows.

At the end, the bride sat on the left side of the bridegroom. He poured a pinch of red vermilion where her hair parted. The priest sprinkled water drops over them with the Vedic mantras for good health. All attendees showered them with rice and flowers for blossoming. The priest blessed them first in Sanskrit "*Saubhagyam astu*"(Let there be good fortune) and then in Hindi "*Tumhari jori Ram aur Sita ki tarah ho*" (May your pairing be like that of Rama and Sita). He wiped away his tears.

Then Jagriti with her new husband, Sad Dharma, stood beside the altar, touching her parents' feet for their blessings. Uncle Keshab and Aunt Shaila burst into tears. Her brothers Jagjit and Laksh also were in tears. Jagriti looked even more beautiful, barefooted in her tears and *ghagri*, the wedding skirt. Her tears took me back to the time when we were reading the *Rama Drama* together.

I recollected how she explained many things that I didn't understand. For example, she said, "Chander! Sita really never had svayamvara or self-selection in her marriage. Her father decided that only the bow-breaker would marry her. She could have said that she would marry Rama, no matter who broke the bow. But she had no choice." Then she had another complaint, "Chander! Why don't they allow girls to play women's roles in the Rama Lila? I wanted to act as Sita. My parents were upset when I told them so."

I at once gave her the chance of her life, "Didi! You can act as Sita, right now." I never thought that she would like my idea, "Fine. Would you act as Rama?...Hey! Your name is Rama Chandra. But we say Ram Chander."

Then in a few selected scenes she acted as Sita and I as Rama. Three scenes became very emotional.

The first one was when I actually broke a cheap bow and she put a small garland around my neck. Like me, she looked thrilled.

The second one, where Kaikeyi gave mendicants' clothes to Rama and Sita. When Sita failed to wrap her regal body in those clothes, Rama began to help her. Now she looked like a jogini and Rama a jogi. I began to sob. "Chander! Dear Chander! It's only a play." Jagriti consoled me as she caressed me gently with her hands.

Then, later in another scene, Rama questioned Sita's character because she lived in Ravana's Lanka for so many years. I refused to act as Rama. "Why?" Jagriti asked. "You are so beautiful," I said. "I can't allow you to burn. No, no!" Jagriti insisted that I say Rama's lines, "Chander! They have been burning women in this country for ages. Men here have kept several women at once. Some called those women wives. Those men should have been questioned. Instead, many were honored as holy men." Then she whispered into my ear holding my head between her tender hands, "Don't you think some Bhatra men are worse than dogs?" I screamed "No, no" and likewise Jagriti screamed "Yes, yes" so many times that Mother came up from downstairs and asked both of us, "What's going on?" The scene was so embarrassing to both of us. (But I still vividly remember Jagriti's soft touch and penetrating voice.)

One day at sundown after I had finished my first Rama Lila, in front of Bagh Duln (Tiger Den), Jagriti asked me, "Did you like the Rama Lila of Puri?" "Very much, very much. But it's because you prepared me for it. Someday I will give you a sword." She said, "What would I do with a sword? Marry?" and she laughed. I joined her. But she laughed so much that tears began to well up in her eyes. I raised my hand to wipe them. She wrapped me in her arms. And moments later, I felt wetness on my cheeks. Her face was glowing even when the sun had already set. I saw a big flock of Himalayan mynas (*sentula*) descending on the giant *kharik* tree in front of us. It was time to go home.

Tears and tears and tears—they are not one and the same stuff every time. That I could see now at her wedding.

That unusually attractive nymph, standing beside a stranger, was to go away with him forever, at such a tender age. I could not wipe her tears now. They were out of my reach. It was too much for me. I ran away, in tears.

But I slept very soundly. I had a couple of dreams. She was not in them.

When I woke up the next morning, the first thing I did was to sit with Aunt Kanti in front of the radio. Vijay was still sleeping. My mother had already left the house to help Aunt Shaila for the farewell party. The news on the radio was all about Gandhi. The reporters kept talking about how shocked the world leaders were and that they sent condolences and eulogies. Every newspaper in the world seemed to carry headlines about him.

I was not surprised as I witnessed a brief set of eulogies that night in an environment meant for celebration. The guests were not even prepared to say anything like that. Whatever they said came as a quick reaction to the news. But the prepared eulogies were long.

Then I ran to relieve myself toward Pan Gadnu. There I saw hundreds of men sitting all along the two banks in long lines. The scene was beyond my imagination. I never saw so many bare bottoms before. For a while, I tried to recognize some whose faces were familiar to me. But how could the bottoms tell what the faces would look like? Or how could the faces tell what the bottoms would look like? I failed to answer such tricky questions. Even when someone got up, I could not recognize him. Every face was partially covered (the morning was cold). All I wished for was some sort of mysterious water, like a Noah's flood. My own favorite spot smelled so awful.

In about an hour, all the guests were gone from our village. The band disappeared, not a drone, not a drumbeat was heard. Only the bride and the bridegroom and his immediate relatives stayed on until the late afternoon.

The month of February began with Gandhi's life, which had just ended at the end of January. I was moved by the life-song of the child born with the name Mohandas becoming Bapu and Mahatma, sung in the most dramatic voice of Mohammad Rafi:

> Listen, listen, the people of the world!
> to this immortal story of Bapu.
> Such a beautiful clean life,
> like the water of Mother Ganges.

Then Rafi raised the pitch of his voice to the end of his exceptionally long range at the end of the song (when Gandhi was shot):

> Bapu said 'Rama Rama'
> ....
> And he became Rama's beloved.

Rafi's voice must have made millions of people cry in India. And Albert Einstein, the greatest scientist our human history knew so far, wrote this sentence about Mahatma Gandhi:

> *"Generations to come will scarcely believe that such a one as this ever in flesh and blood walked upon this earth."*

It was translated into many languages. Will there really be statues of the Mahatma in many countries? I was wondering about my history teacher's prediction after I heard such a verbal statue of him made by Einstein.

Rama's birthday, *Rama Navami*, came in March. This was his first birthday in a free democratic India. Puri had planned a big celebration. The procession, with Rama and his three brothers in a palanquin, was expected to leave from the Vishnu temple at 10 a.m. and move around the town until noon. People from adjacent villages were encouraged to participate in this big festivity. Most villages were expected to form their own parties and join other parties on their way and then converge at the temple from all directions.

Our village party was very small.

Fortunately, Anrit and his parents and sisters were in the village at this time. The Gwar folks came with about ten people and joined us. Not everybody from our village was with us, but I was happy to see Anrit and his father accompany us. Uncle Ishan told us that a big crowd, bigger than what we saw in all the ten nights of Rama Lila, was likely to come for this occasion. The Puri police would be all around. It was expected that some refugees from Pakistan might become very emotional and show hostility to our local Muslims. Some refugees wanted every Muslim to pack up for Pakistan. There was a rumored reply that Hameed had given, "I cannot live in a country where fanatics deny their clear connection to Hanuman." Still, police protection was needed.

So I asked Anrit, "Then Uncle Prem Lal must be around?"

"No, he is sick," he said.

"What is his sickness?" I felt sad.

But Anrit didn't look sad, "Some unmentionable disease."

We all proceeded to Puri. On our way, we joined the parties from Kandy and Thaula.

When we were near our school church, we heard people shouting such things as "*Mandir me jana chahte hain, sale! Maro in sab ko!* (The bastards want to go inside the temple! Kill all of them!).

When we saw some people running toward us, mostly women and children, we asked them what the brawl was about. They were "doms" or untouchables, running for their lives. One of them begged us, "Please run fast! Save some young men over there or they will be killed!" Uncle Ishan and Anrit ran toward the scene. We boys also ran behind them.

The fighting was horrible.

About a dozen men were beating three young men very badly. Uncle Ishan yelled, "Stop beating them. Please, stop the beating! Let them go!" Nobody stopped.

Then Uncle held a big man with his hands and told him, "Enough is enough! You can't beat them like that!" The man pushed Uncle. Anrit jumped on top of the man and kicked him in the groin. That made him scream in pain. No sooner did two other men see him screaming than they jumped on top of Anrit. Uncle got up and punched their faces so badly that both fell to the ground. He shouted, "All of you go away, now. Or we are going to do the same to you." One man spat on Uncle. He simply wiped his face. Anrit stood by Uncle's side.

Then four other men surrounded Uncle and Anrit. Before they could do anything, they got a terrible beating from Anrit and Uncle.

In the meantime, I saw the big man getting up with a big stone in his hand. Before he could get up, Gam, Karun, and I grabbed him and beat the hell out of him. Gam and I imitated Anrit. He kicked the big man in the groin and I kicked him in the butt. When the big man lifted his face groaning with his hands over his groin, Karun punched his mouth several times, saying "Shut up" with each punch. Some blood oozed from his lips. Gam spat on him and said loudly, "Sir! Now you know how it feels to hurt others. You son of a bitch, sir!" We were ready now for any challenger as we raised our fists. Anrit looked at us and raised his fist to cheer us up.

Dhan and Harit got hold of the three young injured men and took them away.

Then Uncle addressed the fleeing culprits in a loud voice, "We will be there at the temple to see you all!"

I was in total amazement that Anrit and Uncle had hurt all the culprits. A couple of them would be better off going to the Puri hospital instead of the Vishnu temple!

"Thanks boys! That big man would have split open our skulls with that big stone." Anrit patted all three of us. We three were not the real saviors, Anrit and Uncle Ishan were. Harit and Dhan were not there.

"Anrit! How could you and Uncle do what we just saw?" I asked him. Still, stunned.

"Do what?" He responded back with no sign of curiosity, bragging or wonderment on his face or in his voice.

"You beat the hell out of that many bullies!"

"Oh, I received training for that."

"What training?" Gambhir asked.

"I will tell you later when Father isn't around."

We all reached Puri and saw the beautiful *doli* in which Rama, Bharata, Lakshmana, and Shatrughna were seated (as big dolls). There we met Harit and Dhan. Anrit asked them, "Hey, where were you fellows?"

"In the hospital," replied Dhan, "Those three men you saved had bleeding bruises. We had to take them in for quick treatment"

"You really saved those fellows. Thanks." Anrit said.

"But, Anrit! How did you and your father beat all of them?" Harit asked.

"Now my father is over there with Karun. Let me tell you quickly before they join us."

"Why are you scared of your father?" I asked him.

"He just wants to be quiet about his training."

"What training?" Gambhir asked again.

"Gam, you remember when my father left us to become a yogi?"

"Not only I, but also Chander and Bhajnu. We were concerned about your future. Right Chander?" I nodded my head.

"During that time Father met a Tibetan Buddhist monk at Hardwar. Father spent six months in the Shiva temple there. Lama ji also stayed there for five months. He taught Father the art of self-defense. Then I learned it from him. One branch of it is known with its Japanese name 'karate.' But the monk told Father that its roots are in India."

"Can you teach us?" Gambhir asked.

"Yes....That's all I can tell you right now. Father and Karun are coming here!" He was looking in their direction.

In the late afternoon Anrit, his father, and I were passing through the Vishnu temple on our way home.

From the outside entrance, we could see a big crowd in the temple yard. Up on the temple roof, all sorts of birds—from big crows to small sparrows—were waiting for *prasad,* the free sacred food, offered to animals in temples. The rooftop was loaded with bird droppings. Some stray dogs were also looking for the same free food. A few male dogs sounded very impatient from their barking. Some of them were also freely urinating around the area. About half a dozen beggars, all of them disabled, were sitting outside the entrance. A few jogis and joginis were clearly visible inside.

When we entered the yard, we saw that the crowd was divided. Between the two divisions a few police officers were strolling around. The smaller crowd was being addressed by Mr. T (he was known by this name), the new middle-aged leader of the shilpkars (untouchables) of our area.

Anrit and Uncle Ishan went over to a police officer. He told them that the people gathered there after the news broke that three 'doms' were beaten and admitted to the hospital. He warned them not to join Mr. T's side of the crowd. They were all untouchables. The temple yard was their border. None of them were allowed to even sit on the steps connecting the yard to the temple door. Local people recognized each other's castes only by contact. But I had heard some brahmins claiming that untouchables could be recognized not only by face but by smell, too. Not even dogs could differentiate castes by smell! I could not have recognized the untouchables on the other side if the police officer had not told us.

We joined Mr. T's speech in the middle (later I read his complete speech in Hindi in the newspaper):

"The shilpkars built all the temples of India. Why can't you allow them to see God there? Look, God, gods, and goddesses are human creations just like these temples. But the point is to have equal rights for all. You can beat your drums, but not your women and shudras. The untouchables who were beaten today near the church can enter the church. But they can't enter the temple they built themselves. You think that our struggle for freedom is over. No, it's not over until—"

"Shut up!" Someone from our side shouted. I heard some jeers, too. But there were matching applauses from his supporters standing by his side.

Then I saw two police officers moving toward our side. There was silence again. Mr. T resumed his speech:

"The 'high castes' ought to understand the need to help the 'low castes.' This morning, the people of Rajkhet and Gwar, showed their understanding. They saved those three young helpless untouchables from a bunch of man-eaters. These high-caste saviors are like the white people of Europe throwing out the Nazis, the Aryan supremacists—"

"Who are they," someone shouted again. I became apprehensive. Anrit and Uncle didn't show any signs of movement. I stood there quiet as I saw more officers moving around. Mr. T started his speech again:

"If the top classes continue to downgrade us as second class citizens, then we will wage the highest war yet. This is a war for equal access to the highest space and time. And many of you must and shall stand with us. Or what may sound very ordinary right now will be the forecast for forthcoming nightmares here and everywhere." I heard more jeers this time. But he continued:

"We are insulting Rama today on his birthday. Rama was a model of good behavior. He gained the cooperation of non-Aryan people, the monkey people, the bear people, and befriended Guha and Shabari—all shudras, all non-Aryans. Imagine a prince feeling our pain when walking for fourteen years with no shoes, eating the worst food, living in thatched cottages. You can, at least, come down from your temples and touch us, not bully us. Rama was no bully. He comforted the meek and fought the bully with his bow and arrows." Then he paused when he was applauded by the people standing behind him.

He resumed his speech:

"We cannot celebrate Rama's birthday and will not attend the Rama Lila until the doors of the temple welcome all. So I need your pledge. Please raise your hands! Your raised hands will signal the beginning of the end of the war between 'high' and 'low'! Let your hands say 'Yes. Anyone can climb up the Himalayas.'"...He moved his head all around and addressed the audience again:

"I urge you all to raise your hands like the Himalayan peaks. Everybody can see that the Himalayas are open to all."

He waited to see raised hands. On his side of the crowd, most hands went up. On our side, I could see only two people with raised hands: Uncle Ishan and Anrit.

("Make the whole Himalaya a free international park," said Anrit in such a low voice as if it were meant only for me and his father.)

Then Mr. T said loudly, "Your raised hand is your right voice. I need your hands raised up! Don't hesitate to raise your hands." He moved his hands up and down to encourage the audience.

Suddenly a few rocks were thrown at him. One rock hit his hand and he stopped moving his hands. His hand was bleeding. "Please do not make a holy place a bloody place," he cried out loud. But moments later one of the rocks managed to hit his head. He fell down.

I looked at Uncle Ishan and he nodded his head, his right hand still raised. Tears were rolling down from his eyes. He was not even trying to wipe them, simply nodding his head. I raised my hand.

Suddenly I felt a stone tap on my shoulder. I turned around. It was Sad Dharma, Jagriti's husband, standing behind me with a small stone in his hand.

"I promise I will go after those rock throwers in court," the young lawyer said. And he threw that stone up on the temple's roof and all the birds flew away from there. It was a very soothing surprise for me.

"How is Jagriti?" I asked him.

"Over there!" He pointed his finger in her direction.

I ran toward her. In a fraction of a minute, I found Jagriti's arms around my neck. Then she wiped away my tears with her soft fingers.

0-595-22229-3